there is no death, there are no dead

EDITED BY
AARON J. FRENCH & JESS LANDRY

Let the world know:
#IGotMyCLPBook!

Crystal Lake Publishing
www.CrystalLakePub.com

other anthologies from Crystal Lake Publishing:

Arterial Bloom, edited by Mercedes M. Yardley

The Shallow Waters flash fiction series,
edited by Joe Mynhardt and Monique Snyman

Tales from The Lake Vol.5,
edited by Kenneth W. Cain

Lost Highways: Dark Fictions From the Road,
edited by D. Alexander Ward

*Behold! Oddities, Curiosities and Undefinable
Wonders*, edited by Doug Murano

Gutted: Beautiful Horror Stories,
edited by Doug Murano and D. Alexander Ward

WELCOME
TO ANOTHER

CRYSTAL LAKE PUBLISHING
CREATION

Join today at www.crystallakepub.com & www.patreon.com/CLP

table of contents

haunt me

GEMMA FILES

peak to me, I'm ready, I'm open. I'm always open. Can't you see? Just look at me—no, closer. Look deep. You'll never find anyone else as easy to talk to, to talk through. *No one quite like me.*

Ah yes; that's right: Now you understand. Open locks, whoever knocks; fly open, bar and band. So find the door and welcome yourself in, spirit. Ghost. Guest.

An empty house, and all for you.

Assume the time is 1993, Peazant's Folly at least a year in my rearview. I'd woken up feeling flayed, and that never went away. I was fifteen then, thirteen when Gala rented me out to the Freihoeven Institute for Parapsychological Research's cataloguing expedition as well-established professional psychic Glenda Fisk's apprentice, on the promise of $10,000 and a "consulting" job once the house was mapped (or cleared); it was Glenda who made the initial deal, though Drs. Jay and Jay, the Freihoeven's founders, were all too happy to sign off on it. Then the house killed everyone on our team.

Everyone but me, who it simply raped inside and out, before letting me . . . well, not stumble away, exactly. Nothing so easy.

I remember watching them find me, after. Standing in the corner of the room, at the very end of my frayed and twisting silver cord. I was a husk right then, the inside-out ectoplasmic double of my physical self, barely visible except as a shadow and struggling to remember who I'd been—budded off and inversely reflected, pitch-black and shiny like La Brea tar. Fading in and out as I hung there, and all the while wondering: just *who* was that pale girl on the floor, exactly, comatose and covered in moving bruises . . . her glasses skew-shattered, colorless straw hair fanned beneath her like a broken ruff? Was she breathing? Did I know her? Should I care?

Oh, I could have blown away, blown *out*, like a candle. It seemed the right thing to do, in context. The only thing.

Until I looked a little closer, thankfully, and realized the bruises wreathing her skin—my skin—made words.

COME BACK CARRA PLEASE CARRA

CARRACLOUGH DEVIZE THATS YOU THATS ME IM YOU

PLEASE COME BACK COME IN

COME HAUNT ME LIKE A HOUSE YOUR HOUSE OUR HOUSE

OH CARRA PLEASE

I guess it was the "please" that did it in the end. Since so few people ever asked, let alone politely.

But then, we both knew that.

haunt me

So: 1993. I'm awake again, body and soul firmly bonded back together, aside from the occasional astral projection side-trip. Came awake all at once after three months in the Toronto Sick Kids' Hospital's coma ward, shattering every window on my floor with a sudden telekinetic blast. There wasn't a lot to show what'd happened, at least on the outside: A broken hip, a lingering limp. And, of course, a complete inability to shield myself anymore, to keep myself from playing scratch-pad to any passing consciousness without a mouth to talk through.

Sometimes I could fold my sleeves down and ignore it, pass for a too-young weirdo with bad tattoos, albeit ones that tended to re-write themselves at will. Other times I was overwhelmed, caught in the flood, vomiting out ectoplasm like cigarette smoke made from displaced adipose fat, dead skin-cells, body-water, and the occasional squirt of spinal fluid, all held together with static nerve-charge. Talking in other people's voices, bearing their testimony like a brand. Levitating 'til I hit the ceiling so hard, I knocked myself unconscious.

I was a mental medium when I went into the Folly, a physical medium when I came back out—not that big a distinction, really, in context. Fifteen years old, never dated a boy, never kissed a girl. Spent most of my childhood making up for my father being dead and my mother being unable to get over it. Being gifted. Being the breadwinner. Paying for my own food and Gala's booze by reading objects, reading people, reading places. Chatting up the dead. It paid the bills, before and after—electric, water, TV. Hospital.

Though no, I need to be a little clearer, probably: After the Folly, my medical bills went to Dr Guilden Abbott, who paid them out of the Freihoeven's petty cash fund. As an investment.

When the Drs. Jay died, out in the field, they left Dr. Abbott to take over. He became head of the Institute, and as such, he inherited . . . me, along with all the rest. That's how he felt about it, or said he did. Not to mention how it's hard to make friends, when you're this sort of freak; harder still, to keep them. Dr. Abbott banked on that, I'm sure, just like Gala always used to. And me?

I was used to being used. It felt—familiar.

Back then, that was enough.

We dive in with our eyes closed, to save ourselves from blindness. How can we ever know what we'll bring back?

Here's how it starts, almost always. I sit down, open my bag, pick out an instrument at random: Charcoal, chalk, pencil, ballpoint, marker. Paper already spread and waiting on the table. Gala insisted I use cheap rags from the dollar store, glue-bound at the top, mainly because she wanted to be the one who turned the pages. Sometimes she didn't move fast enough, and I ended up scribbling on the table: Long tangled strings of words written up, down, sidelong or widdershins, jumbled together without punctuation, both forwards and backwards, not to mention (on occasion) in scripts even I can't read: Pinyin, Cyrillic, Ogham, hieroglyphics. Crossing the River.

These days I use butcher-paper, like Henry Darger

drew his tiny-penised little girl monsters on, and all whoever's sitting at my right side needs to do is just keep on unrolling. While whoever's on my left does the sadly difficult task of trying to jot down whatever words might appear at the same time—the *very* same time, usually, annoyingly enough—on *me*.

(They like to annotate, the dead. Talk over each other, crowd each other out. They're selfish fuckers, when it comes right down to it.)

It's called automatic writing, Carra, Gala told me, the first time she stuck a pen in my chubby little hand. *All those people you hear speaking, all the time—all those voices talking to you, even when you're asleep. It's how you get them out. You take down what they say and deliver it to the right person, like a letter. Because they just want to be heard, that's all; they'll be so grateful, wait and see. They'll love you for it, baby.*

I'll love you for it, too, being the clear implication, though I already knew better, just like I knew not to argue the point. Let alone never to blurt out, even in my little kid's voice: *But none of that is true, so why even say it?*

So I picked up the pen instead, and waited.

And it did get easier, the more I did it, if not better. Yet sometimes someone would enter me who'd drifted so far they'd moved beyond speech, only able to whirl and scream like a disjointed memory-hurricane, channeling bursts of seemingly unrelated images down my nerve-bundles in harsh electric jolts, an old-school modem's shriek of clumsily-unloaded data: ***I am I was I must I want I need Give Give Give meeeeeee or diiiiiie toooooo YOU LITTLE BITCH—***

For them, I could only offer the chance to print what was left of their perceived injustices onto whatever surface I could reach fast enough. I've never been much of an artist, but few people are, alive *or* dead. I have the pictures drawn self-blinded, eyes clenched 'til I felt my pupils strain against their lids, to prove it.

The first one I remember was of an old man with one eye, while visiting my cousin Hesta, then only recently married. It was in Overdeere, Ontario, where odd things crouch behind every tree; don't ask why. Our family is complicated. It doesn't bear going into.

I was eight, which at least got me my own bed, Gala banished to the adjoining room. I remember walking in and sitting down, leaning back then freezing, current-caught; how everything glitched, spiked, my pulse hammering fast enough to drone. Pins and needles everywhere. How my eyes rolled back as the world faded, became a mist, a line, a dot. Then waking up after who knew how long with my hand already in motion, jerking back and forth, nib of the dried-out pen I didn't even know I'd picked up somewhere digging deep into the wall's plaster, leaving a trail you had to squint at to understand. A line entirely without ink, white on white and *into* white, the image it captured only defined by cast shadow.

I made a copy of it afterwards in my diary, the one with the lock, and never showed it to anyone. Crept downstairs to find a knife and scraped it away, leaving only a slight depression plus a small white pile of shavings underneath the bed.

Hesta called later, once we were back home in Toronto, to complain: *We found a knife in her* pillow, *Geillis. Like she was planning to slit all our throats in*

6

our sleep. To which I remember Gala snapping: *Don't worry yourselves, we won't be coming back anytime soon,* before hanging up and looking around, that *look* sparking in her eyes once more—hazel brown-grey shading to silver, to copper, to bronze, and all of it glinting like money.

You've been holding out on me, she said, without much surprise. *Bad girl. What did we say about lying?*

. . . don't, unless you can get away with it? I asked, finally.

She frowned, and slapped me, hard enough to make my skull ring. Always on the same spot somehow, driving the oldest lingering bruise even deeper, a sting at the fresh pain's tail; that was a trick she learned from Dad, I bet. To make it show less, but hurt more.

What a terrible thing to say to your own mother, she told me. Knowing full well the voices in my blood would chime in with the rest even if she didn't, words come curling around my wrist, fading almost the very moment I read them: EVEN NOT EVEN YES EVEN IF ITS TRUE TRUE TRUE

Yes, it happened back then too, but far less often, less insistently. The dead knew not to test my limits, because I still had some.

The old man was my great-uncle, apparently, I eventually found out. Another Devize, one more in a long, looped line of them. How he lost his eye was uncertain, since everyone who knew was already dead, and I wasn't about to ask them.

I already knew damn well they'd seek me out and tell me, later on.

Some people are simply too long dead to remember who they were, though. Or even if they were people. They need their memory-hurricane jogged, to have the current run backwards. They need to be . . . reimagined.

That's what brings us here.

I was sitting up in bed, sweat plastered all over from my last bout of PT—only one chair per hospital room, so Dr. Abbott got it. He'd come over from the Freihoeven on lunch-break with a grilled cheese and fries from Fran's Diner; he usually did that at least one day a week, to tell me what was going on, read the most recent files to me, as if hoping to talk shop. I'd enjoyed being away from Gala the first few months of my recovery (who wouldn't?), but it was beginning to pall; the TV never stopped switching between channels every time my thoughts shifted, and all the radio ever played was static. I was also looking into how to get myself legally emancipated so I could at least move out rather than having to look after Gala for the rest of my/her life, but it looked like never having gone back to school after fifth grade was an insurmountable obstacle. *I was working,* I could argue, but what would I say when they asked me *At what?*

The only other option I could think of was throwing myself at the mercy of Child Protective Services, trying to get Gala declared either abusive or incompetent, and even if that worked, I'd have been sucked into the foster system for . . . four years, at minimum. Gala, at least, was used enough to what living with me had originally been like to handle the newest stuff without screaming. The one thing being drunk all the time actually helped with.

"I interviewed a man once who could imbed psychic images on film and videotape," Abbott told me, paging idly through his ever-present thick manila folder. "By adding ectoplasm to the emulsion, imbedding extra data through electrical signals. A useful trick to learn, I should think, especially for you. Much less stressful than most forms of mediumship."

"Oh yeah? He still around?"

"Probably not, sadly. This was nearly twenty years ago, and he was old then; he'd be, oh . . . over ninety by now, I suppose . . . Hm." His voice changed, and he closed the folder. "No, I'd better skip this one."

"Too dangerous?"

"Too complicated. Legally, I mean." Abbott tapped the file. "The subject here is still dealing with Workers' Comp and wants very much to keep it under wraps that he's been talking to us, so it doesn't affect their decision. My name can appear on a letter or two without remark, but—the Folly expedition *was* news. So many casualties."

I was there, I didn't reply.

"I'm down with being off the books," I said, instead.

He looked thoughtful. "Actually, it might help if you *were* an employee. You'd be covered by the Institute's existing NDA. Though you'd need your mother's permission . . . " He trailed off as I rolled my eyes, grabbed a piece of paper, and scribbled a back-of-the-cheque-ready facsimile of Gala's signature without even looking. "That also would be complicated, for me to accept."

"Legally?"

"Ethically."

"Give me a fucking break, Doc."

He sighed, re-opened the folder—he'd marked his place with a finger—and handed me a few paper-clipped pages. It didn't take much reading. Two weeks ago, Dr. Justin Lewis (age 30, assistant curator at the Royal Ontario Museum) had taken a tumble down the ROM's main staircase under the faces of the Pole of Sagaween, breaking both legs and putting his back in traction. He'd told the Board he'd slipped on an inexpertly washed floor, but in a phone call to Dr. Abbott (which Abbott had recorded and transcribed), he'd told a story which someone working anywhere else would've probably found . . . unlikely.

A: You say it started months ago. How many, exactly?

L: I'm not sure. Things might have been happening earlier, and I just missed them . . . you know, lights flickering, weird sounds, misplaced items. But three months back, that was when I really started to feel something, for the first time. I'm sure of it.

A: Cold spots? Prickling sensations?

L: No. I was reviewing some recent acquisitions in my office; it was late, after dark. And something touched me. Like a hand on my face. It was very gentle. But then it . . . stroked my lips. I could feel them, fingers I couldn't see. They felt—warm.

haunt me

A: (PAUSE) That's unusual.

L: I thought I'd fallen asleep, dreamed it. Then, two nights later, I was wrapping up to leave when I felt something take my hand. I saw the skin dent where it gripped me. It pulled me back to the desk, and I—I let it. I didn't know what else to do.

A: What happened then?

L: Nothing much, that time. Held my hand with one set of fingers, stroked my mouth with the other. Still invisible. I stood there, not fighting, 'til it let me go.

A: A clear escalation.

L: Obviously, yes. But even then, I never thought . . . didn't expect it would . . . (PAUSE) You have to understand, it wasn't threatening, just—lonely, desperate. Like it would do anything, so long as I wouldn't leave. (LONGER PAUSE) It got worse after that, stronger. Like it would happen during the day as well, for longer and longer periods of time. And it started touching me . . . inappropriately.

A: Violently?

L: No, not really. More frightened than angry; frightened I might shrug it off, reject it. But it kept on happening, during meetings, phone calls; I would feel arms embracing me, a weight on my back. Kisses on the side of my neck. Felt . . . it, pressing into me. Hard. Do you understand what I'm saying? Or do I have to be more—

A: —explicit? No.

L: Thank Christ for that. (PAUSE) My concentration was shot. The more I tried to get away, the more—what's the word—tangible it became. The hands, their fingers were long, flexible, dry. Rings on each, nails long but slightly torn. They had wire wound around their tips. Jewelry rattling as it moved, digging into me; it clicked when it walked. Its mouth was dry, too, tongue cold . . . lips drawn back, like it was snarling. They never seemed to move. And teeth—so many teeth.

By the end, I was terrified to be alone, equally terrified that my colleagues would see me jump or scream in panic and ask why. I didn't have any sick days left to take. That last night, the director ordered me to stay behind and catch up on work I had let slide, so I did. I didn't want to lose my job. (PAUSE) Then, for the first time, it tried to remove my clothes. It fumbled at me like it didn't know what buttons were, or how to work a buckle, but I'd had enough. I fought it off, screaming at it: Stop, I don't want you, you're awful. *Ran from it, like I was on fire. And when I stopped, midway down the main stairs, to catch my breath—nowhere near the edge of the landing, just leaning back against the far wall—it grabbed me from behind and it threw me down the steps, like I was a doll. Like a kid having a tantrum.*

A: You probably shouldn't have insulted it.

L: Oh, you think? (VOICE BREAKS) I'm scared now, all the time. Scared it'll come find me. I don't think it can, but—you understand what I'm saying? I can't eat, can't sleep. And I can't run anymore, either.

haunt me

A: Tell me what you need, doctor.

L: So you believe me?

A: Of course.

L: (LONG PAUSE) Just . . . find out what it wants. Get rid of it, if you can. And make sure . . . make sure it doesn't know . . . it was me who told you.

"Sounds like a mummy."

"The *ghost* of a mummy?" Abbott thought a moment, silent. "Not impossible. But the ROM only has one mummy on site, and it's never bothered anyone before. Besides, Lewis doesn't work in Egyptian Antiquities."

"Where *does* he work?"

Abbott checked. "Sumeria and Ur, usually, in the cylindrical seal collection; neither civilization mummified their dead, as I recall. Though he's been helping to organize a display of proto-Minoan hieroglyphics recently."

"Did the Minoans mummify people?"

"No, they inhumed them in a *larnax*, a chest-sized coffin, or made them house-tombs—literal houses, to keep all their grave goods in. They didn't seem to make a lot of distinction between this world and the next, so long as you could take all your stuff with you."

"It's pretty hot and dry on Crete, though, I'll bet; the bodies might have ended up much the same way. Do you have copies of the stuff he's been working on, anywhere?"

"No. Should I?"

"Maybe." He handed the file back, and I skimmed

through the rest of it, thinking out loud: "If he's afraid of it following him even though it never has before, then we might be looking at some sort of poltergeist effect. And yeah, I get that almost never happens with men, let alone adult men, but . . . did he seem straight to you?"

"I . . . really hadn't thought about it."

"He's male, this thing manifests as male—if he's still closeted, it might be some sort of weird sexual tulpa he's inflicting on himself, without even knowing it. Like he spends all day and night surrounded by sexy naked Ancient Cretan guys with long, oiled hair and their dicks hanging out, leaping over bulls and such—"

"From the way he describes it, it strikes me more as a very *dead* naked Ancient Cretan. Not such an attractive prospect."

I shrugged. "Sometimes things just don't come the way you think they will, even if you're sure you'll want them no matter what . . . not even when you've invited them in. Especially then."

Sliding briskly over what *that* idea immediately called to mind, or trying to. The Folly's very special way of rummaging around in its victims' ids, their most sub-subconscious, looking for honey to bait the trap with: *You could have this, or this, or THIS, if you only stay. You could have whatever you want, if you only stay with me—allay my loneliness, my hole-shaped hunger. Be my future, my immediate future, in an endless maze of such.*

Denys Peazant made himself a hallway full of bronze mirrors back at the 20th century's turn, hoping to conjure up an oracle of his very own, an indestructible sort of phantom Delphic Pythoness, made from the mephitic fumes of the Underworld. And he sure must've sniffed enough of them to kill him, in his time . . . but when he died, he left what he'd called up behind, endlessly craving someone willing to finally ask the same question somebody posed to its living counterpart when she was older than hell, squatting inside a cage over her smoking hole: *Sibyl, what do YOU want?* So that it could answer—

(*I want to die*)

Be asked, and answer, yeah. And kill anybody who couldn't deliver on that answer—kill them, wreck them, turn them inside-out. Leave them like me.

"It wouldn't be the first time buried emotional conflicts have manifested in a psychically destructive manner," Abbott agreed, before realizing exactly what he was agreeing with, in my case, and at least having the good grace to blush.

"Hardly," I replied. "But I take it you'd like a second opinion."

"I can't ask you for that, Carra."

"Can't you? Why'd you come here, then?"

He sighed. "I suppose . . . I was hoping I wouldn't *have* to ask."

"Which is why I volunteered. There you go, easy-peasy. Now say thanks."

" . . . thank you, Miss Devize."

He didn't look at me. And I certainly didn't have to be psychic to read what he was thinking, even though I did: *As we both already knew you would.* Because . . . what the fuck else would anyone who'd met me before expect me to do, under the circumstances?

I only have one trick. It looks like a lot of different tricks, from the outside . . . but really, there's only one.

And without it—without the opportunity to *use* it, let alone make money doing so—

—I have nothing. *Am* nothing.

I was always going to be haunted, I knew that now. Now Peazant's Folly had broken all my locks, knocked down all my doors. Now that I had no skin. Which meant that all I could ever do, from the moment I woke back up on, was pick the guests I played host to. And hope like hell I could persuade them to move on afterwards.

Chains of words circling my wrists like snakes before climbing up and down along those fresh ladders of raised pinky-white tissue, marking the place where my *next* set of failed suicide attempt scars would probably go, one day, when I'd had enough of this newest phase of my life: NOT AGAIN NOT YET NOT THIS SOON CARRA CARRA PLEASE. VERY DANGEROUS FOR YOU VERY DANGEROUS. ON NO ACCOUNT MY LOVE.

I folded my hands and sighed, stroking the bruises as if I could soothe them, and thought back, very firmly: *I know, believe me; I get it, I really do. I know. I just don't care.*

Nothing would ever be as bad as the Folly, after all.

I had to hold onto that assumption, until I proved it true.

Abbott's signature, and my own imitation of Gala's when the nurses weren't looking, got us through the discharge paperwork, though it took long enough I could see his doubts coming back. *Don't think I'm not grateful, Carra,* he murmured. *But I really don't know*

if this will help you get better. To which I'd simply given an annoyed scoff.

Maybe not, I said. *But sitting in that room doing nothing won't help, either—and better yet, it won't make me not me. Either I go out and find them, the dead, or . . .*

(*. . . they come find me.*)

Guess he took my point, since he didn't protest further.

Waiting in the museum's lobby, I looked around with interest. Gala wasn't much on spending outside of business investments, so I'd never actually been to the ROM before; I suppose if I'd thought about it I might have gotten nervous, given my sensitivity to things with long histories. For once, however, I was pleasantly surprised. The building's atmosphere was a lot lighter and clearer, metaphysically, than I'd expected, which made sense after a moment's thought—everything inside, however ancient or maliciously used, had not only been through dozens of hands to get here and had long exposure to thousands of minds, but almost all those minds must have been thinking something positive about what they saw: delight, fascination, genuine interest. Greed, boredom, or annoyance, at worst. Without refreshment, even the most toxic psychic stains rarely last long under that kind of sustained erosion.

On the other hand, that only meant anything that actually *had*—not survived, but endured—would probably be all the more dangerous for it.

My stomach roiled. The familiar, tingling chill eddied along my skin: DANGEROUS VERY DANGEROUS. ON NO ACCOUNT . . .

Shut up, I told them, silently.

"Dr. Abbott?" The olive-skinned woman who asked

kept her voice quiet enough not to echo, her handshake very quick as Abbott stood. "I'm Sam D'Agostino—Justin's colleague. He told me you wanted to see where he, um . . . where it happened." She shot me a look, half furtive, entirely curious. "Hi. Are you the . . . "

I held up a finger, tapping the side of my skull: "Wait, I'm getting something. Were you going to say 'psychic'?"

Her eyes widened. "I was."

I turned to Abbott. "See? Still got it."

Abbott winced, but hilariously enough, D'Agostino seemed far more impressed than insulted. She took us up to Lewis's former office, chatting along the way about how much everyone missed him, how useful his organizational skills had been. "We have to categorize untranslatable materials by imagery, mainly, and Justin's background in seals was *incredibly* useful. Have you ever seen any Proto-Minoan hieroglyphics before, Ms. Devize?"

"I really haven't."

"Well, they're quite fascinating. Much like other Cretan art, they obviously draw very specifically on sea-life, plus other natural formations . . . everything you'd expect to find on a Greek island. But they also incorporate what seem like various body-parts, stick-figures, and even what might be metaphorical images—an eye surrounded by rays that might signify the sun, a double swoop that might be a scribble signifying a flying bird's wings. But because we don't have the equivalent of a Rosetta Stone, we're basically not even sure how they should be presented: The 'eye' might be a sun if shown horizontally, but something else entirely if shown vertically. Justin suggested it might even represent the vagina."

"Fascinating," Abbott cut in, starting to look just a little red around the edges again. "But if I might inquire—do you know exactly what Dr. Lewis might have been working on right before he had his accident?"

"Absolutely. It was this set of tablets and the accompanying seal, right here."

On a long work-table at the end of the office, cushioned on a quilted chamois cloth, lay three small clay tablets plus one much larger item: a wide stone cylinder long enough to be held at either end, like the world's heaviest rolling pin. Whatever it was cut from seemed semi-precious, greenish, lovingly polished. "Probably malachite," D'Agostino continued, "and if it was smaller, I wouldn't hesitate to identify it as a seal . . . someone's name or their title, used to mark objects, to make sure everyone knew who they belonged to. This, though—it's very intriguing. Almost as if someone inscribed a message that could be printed and re-printed on clay or even dipped in paint or dye, then rolled over a wall or a piece of cloth, over and over again."

"A royal decree, perhaps?" Abbott suggested. "Some sort of warning?"

"We just don't know."

I nodded, then put my hand out, not quite touching it. "Can I?" I asked; D'Agostino didn't quite wince at the implication. Then answered, carefully—

" . . . sure, I guess. But please, be *very* careful."

I tried not to laugh; *If I was being careful I wouldn't have come here,* I thought. Instead, I simply nodded, settling my fingertips on either end of the cylinder. The greenish stone felt soapy, unpleasantly slick; almost greasy.

The thing that spilled up through my fingers, an

instant later, had the same feel—like cooking oil so old and filthy it had turned rotten or a decomposing jellyfish, squelching out from under a careless step. Nausea hit the back of my throat, even as my muscles locked stiff all over in reflexive, useless resistance, the invasion all the more ghastly for its painlessness. And then, in the next instant, signs came blooming across my skin, all up and down my arms, not cursively scribbled into being but *soaking* themselves into visibility, my skin tissue paper pressed down over pictures drawn in bruise-coloured ink.

D'Agostino let out a ludicrous, high-pitched sound (*yeep*!?) and leapt backwards, both hands clapped over her mouth. Abbott only grabbed Lewis's chair and wheeled it behind where I stood tottering, just in time to let me collapse into it, then slid me neatly back up to the desk where a roll of paper and a pre-sharpened pencil lay waiting, his video camera already set up and running, pointed at both. My hand—left, not right, so anti-dominant—grabbed up the pencil, launching into my own barely-legible scrawl in reply: *who are you who who who who*

(*I really wanna knoooooowww*)

A stuttering-skip interruption, one I felt in my heartbeat. Then: Three indecipherable symbols, each with a clear family resemblance to the tablets; I caught one of them circling around my forearm. A pause, then the symbols repeated. My knuckles, fingers, and wrist were already burning. A third time, harsher, sloppier, as if frustration was setting in, and I finally overbore the pain in my arm and forced out English words: *whats that mean show me show me your NAME.*

"Priest!" D'Agostino blurted, pointing at the first

symbol, a thick circle with a zigzag line covering the bottom and a gap at the top, like a torc. "Some scholars think that's the sign for a priest."

Priest, I thought at the thing inside me, hard as I could, dumping a flurry of images along with it; the other thoughts first seemed bewildered, then gave something like a shrug, accepting the term for lack of anything better. My hand bore down hard, leaving gouges: *tell what you want tell us tell me*

More hieroglyphics flowed down my arm, divided along each finger, replicated themselves onto the paper—no English, nothing so useful. But images burst behind my eyes with each new symbol, at the same time: Faces like smears, places like rain-dissolved watercolors; half-second brushes of scents like oranges, salt air, sweat. So old. So incoherent. I felt the thing's fury rise, its thoughts—the echoes and spasms which were all it had left of them, at any rate—bouncing uselessly off mine. Only the *wanting* remained clear, the ache, the need. A hunger not just for flesh, but specific flesh.

him him him, my hand scribbled, *him him him.*

WHO, I forced my hand to write back.

At which point my muscles seized up, my hand deftly twitching the pencil up into a dagger-grip as my arm swept up and around, a slicing arc that ended with the point jabbed inch-deep into my other wrist. D'Agostino screamed. Abbott shouted my name, infused with a fear I honestly hadn't thought him capable of; would have been sort of endearing if I wasn't in such agony, unable to scream myself through the Priest's grip on my body, squeezing me like a paint-tube. My arm jerked the pencil back out and threw it away, blood spurting over the paper, then smacked my hand palm first into the pooling scarlet and began to draw with it.

Maybe it was the blood. Maybe the pain had kicked my sensitivities up a gear or two, or connected me and the Priest on some universal level, beyond words: *Everybody hurts,* as R.E.M. once sang. But As I stared at the symbols my fingers smeared into shape, I saw the patterns in them. That tilted oval, like a heart; those overlapping circles—a chain, forever-binding. Concentric squares, a passage receding into distance. Rising lines, the spreading branches of a tree . . .

As the sword to the smith, so you to me.
Who holds you owns nothing.
As rain to the earth, you return, always,
making me bloom again. As you to me,
Me to you, each other's. There is no death.
The seed renews itself in burial,
The name in writing, the soul in burning.
No lord no god no thing will separate us
For long. Nor can you ever choose
To set me free: I am yours, always. This shadow
Forever following your light.

A poem, I realized. That was what the symbols on the cylinder meant. *A love poem . . .*

The pain was fading; so was the room around me. I felt my heart begin to stutter, then reminded myself how that was very much not a good sign. Blood loss.

A love poem. But that wasn't the right word, exactly. This was about what happened when devotion turned to madness, when people cursed laws and gods and oaths if they stood between lover and beloved. This was when everything inside you turned into something so immense it washed away everything else. Memory. Sanity. Self.

The office was almost gone now, and me along with it; somewhere at the edges I felt a vague fumbling, a gnat's whine of voices. Abbott and D'Agostino, probably, calling for help, or trying to give it—Abbott must have *some* medical training. But me? I was inside-out yet again, a flipped negative version of myself, afloat in my own shiny blackness. The only other thing I saw nearby was a shapeless, faceless smear of light, something that smoked and hissed with anguish like metal heated white, on the edge of dissolution.

Tell me your name, I repeated, still clutching myself together, if barely. And heard that voiceless voice answer from inside me, so paper-dry and very, very old, cooked from the inside with its own sheer idolatrous frenzy. So coagulated-feverish after all these years with—well, *love,* I guess. The only one way we have to say it, sadly.

(*such a tiny word for such a huge and hungry thing*)

. . . I don't remember, the Priest told me, finally.

Show me your face, then. Make me over. Make me you.

I . . . don't remember, anymore.

What DO you remember, then?

HIM ONLY *HIM* ONLY *HIM HIM HIM*

A poem is a prayer, I said. *You made him a god, and prayed to him. Did they kill you for it? Execrate you? Destroy your face—your name?*

WHAT THEY DID TO ME MEANS NOTHING, IS NOTHING. THIS LIVES, YET. MY WORDS. HE LIVES IN THEM.

You're dead, I told it.

I KNOW

Your lover . . . the one you wrote the poem for . . .
he's dead too.

NO NO NO NO NO NO NO—

Yes. Four thousand years dead, maybe more.
Suns, stars and moons flashed by overhead in blinding
timelapse speed. Stone shrank underfoot, became a
track worn in the earth. *Thera exploded; Knossos no
longer stands.* So many dead things. *The ocean
overheats. The whole earth sheds its cosmic shield.*

I SAW HIM I TOUCHED HIM

HE KNOWS ME

HE WANTS ME STILL

*No. He's not the one, and the one who was—he's
gone. Long since. Like you should be.*

LIAR I KNOW HIM HE IS MINE

Then what's his name?

Silence met this, sudden, awful. Anguish,
extinguishing the still-burning wreckage of what had
once been a person. Horror like slow quicksand
mounting up, dragging down, down, and down.

*You can't remember, can you. Which means . . .
you might be wrong.*

I'd never met Lewis, but I'd seen a photograph,
read his words, heard D'Agostino's affection for him
in her voice, seen the room where he did the work
that was his life. If I was lucky, that'd be enough. I
pulled all of it together and crafted the best image I
could, setting it to float before him, wiping away the
name-symbols the Priest-thing no longer
understood.

See for yourself, I said, aware that I was losing my

grip, even here. *Is this him?* No answer. *Why would he reject you, if it was? Make you hurt him?*

I never meant
You did, though.
YOU LIE
I don't. I can't.

Quieter: *All lie. A gift the gods gave us—to say a thing into being. Poem, prayer . . . lie. All lie.*

Not all, I repeated. *Some have had that gift taken from them, violently. Come inside, and see.*

I remember—opening. Not my arms. That strange sensation of furling, then unfurling: I'm familiar with it now. I've had years, since, to become familiar.

Outside the furl were Abbott and D'Agostino, visible now, clear and fine-etched against the anti-halo of my darkened vision: D'Agostino ushering in the paramedics, Abbott shirtless and barking orders—I could see how he'd stripped it off and ripped it in half, used his belt to tourniquet my arm at the elbow, one part of the shirt to bandage my wound. So much blood, so many bruises, eddying up and down every inch of visible skin except for my head—that was a mass of ectoplasm, a shifting body-junk jellyfish sculpting and re-sculpting itself, growing features at random, then wiping them away impatiently: this; no, *this*; no, THIS, gods-damnit. I've always vaguely thought that making ectoplasm probably unstrings proteins, coagulates included; that's why the stuff dripping out of me was so pale, so impossible to stem. Not long now, for me, unless—

(unless)

This is the oddest part of it: Sometimes you have to trust them, and it's hard, because . . . they're dead. Most of them don't care what happens to you, or anyone. But some—some do, surprisingly enough. Even if they have to remind themselves to.

Even when *you* don't.

Inside the furl, meanwhile—the ectoplasmic bag—I felt those dry, hard lips press against my ear, that searing breath scar my cheek. Five long fingers tipped in wound wire, maybe gold, printing themselves into the soft meat of my arm, insistently. Like they were holding me back from furling ever further, further, further . . . slipping down inside myself so far, all of me converted into nothing but a personal darkness full of constant motion, a Lethe-like torrent offering total forgetfulness. No ghosts. No gift. No memories. No *me*.

Seer-girl, the Priest said, quietly. *You saw me. Now I see you.*

I remember . . . wanting to laugh. No energy left to do it with; no mouth on my inside-out self, my black and shiny no-face. *There's nothing left of me,* I think I thought, then . . . and felt five more of those weird, sere invisible fingers reaching up on the opposite side, slipping beneath the bag-mask's writhing rim and lifting, ripping. Peeling it away from my face, my *real* face, like he was shucking petals from a squirmy, sticky flower, something that died as it came apart: shrunk to slime, to goo, to sparks. To nothing. Just those fingers pressing against my mouth in a last strange kiss, my vision beginning to lighten, the furl unknitting itself around us. And that voice, breathing itself inside my ear's whorl, a final dying breath from something dead longer than . . . a long, long time.

I said, I see you. Here you are.

You, *I remember.*

(*remember me, now*)

(please)

For the loss of love is death, and worse than death.

Long after 1993, Dr. Guilden Abbott remains very good at pissing people off, including myself. But moments like the one I caught when I woke up in the ambulance, on the way to Mount Sinai Hospital, help a lot when it comes to forgiving him. He was jammed in the corner by the door, his shoulders shaking, doing his best to keep his sobs silent lest he distract the paramedic leaning over me. I admit that I enjoyed it a lot more than I should have when I saw both him and the paramedic jump at my sudden rasp: "Your scientific detachment's gone to crap, Doc."

He swallowed, and it was enjoyable in an entirely different way to watch him cycle through half a dozen different expressions before finally settling on a semblance of his usual bland deadpan. "An endemic hazard of the parapsychological vocation," he husked, at last.

"Big words."

"That's why they pay me the . . . really not very big at all . . . money."

He didn't ask any questions about what had happened at the museum, so neither did I. It wasn't until a couple of days later, when sleep, food, and blood transfusions had brought me back to something like my old self, that he wheeled a TV-and-VCR stand he'd evidently persuaded the hospital staff to lend him into my room. "I thought you might be interested to see how things resolved," he said. "From the outside, I mean."

I pushed myself upright, being careful to keep my weight off my bandaged wrist. "I actually missed a lot of the end," I admitted, and told him—briefly—about what I'd learned, before that.

"A poem? Really." Abbott looked impressed, which was rare. "Do you remember any of it? Sam—that is, I'm sure Ms. D'Agostino and Mr. Lewis would both find the wording extremely . . . helpful."

Sam? I shrugged. "Well, I remember my own translation of it, roughly. I don't think I could break down the symbols for them, of anything. Besides which—it doesn't exactly hold up as research, does it? Academically, I mean."

"No, of course you're right." He slotted a tape into the machine, then paused. "If you're ready, then . . . "

"Maybe fast-forward some parts."

He obliged. The camera hadn't been pointed at the seal, so we didn't see the moment of possession, only the frantic movement as I was wheeled into place and began scribbling. It all went startlingly fast, even before—on the screen—I abruptly stuck the pencil in my wrist, and Abbott started speeding through the resultant frenzy of activity: me flailing around in a growing crimson pool, then collapsing face-down; Abbott flipping me over and D'Agostino recoiling as the bag rolled itself over my head, ectoplasm frothing beard-like first down, then up, milky and grotesque; Abbott almost too intent to notice, doing his best to tie up my wrist. After a moment, he paused the tape again, checking me quickly before continuing.

"I think this next part is what you'll want to see," he told me. "We enhanced it for volume and UV-infrared frequencies, then ran it again, here." He hit play. I could see the lips of my screen image moving. My face went oddly out of focus just as I realized I could hear my own voice, low and urgent: "*Yes. Yes. Yes.*" Then, suddenly, my movements and voice all stopped together, going so completely still my throat closed up to see it.

"I will," my image breathed, through still, white lips. "I . . . promise."

A few seconds later, the camera jerked to one side, focus resuming; I caught a brief glimpse of an EMS jacket the second before it ended, with an abrupt cut to a full black screen.

"And now, the enhanced version," Abbott murmured.

The sound leaped upwards into a harsh hissing clatter, and the image turned into a surreal, green-purple negative inversion of itself. Now the blur over my face was clear for what it was: ectoplasm, seeping from pores, eyes, and nostrils, formed into the translucent mask of something like a face—angular, gaunt and virile, empty-eyed.

The terror of some sounds is that they're there, then gone, without a trace left behind except inside your own skull, echoing. They suggest, more than confirm. They collaborate. I get that it's creepy, for most people. But me? I'm used to hearing other people's voices coming from my mouth.

For me, it means things are getting better.

"Tell the one . . . I hurt," came a barely audible whisper, following the movement of my lips. *"My words live. To study them is prayer, whether or not they know that. It is . . . enough."*

Again, the screen went black.

"I showed that to Mr. Lewis, yesterday," said Abbott. "I don't know if he quite believed it, but it was enough to get him to go back to his office. And he hasn't reported any incidents since, even after working with the cylinder-seal again. I think we can classify this as a successful resolution."

I nodded, turning away.

On the very edge of sleep, my heart sometimes jumps up into my throat, hammering, to choke me. As if allowing myself to sink down in dreams only serves to remind me of what death might be like: delirium, then dissolving. No real knowledge of how you got from one state to the next, nothing to judge against; simply a plunge into dark, forever, with no waking. A lid blinks, and everything you are just . . . falls away.

And even if some part of what I am endures—dancing and babbling, missing me without the ability to say so—the whole, of *me*, is gone. All that work, that fear, that passion. All.

A box of darkness is a gift, my mother used to say. Because there could be anything inside it, I suppose . . . or nothing.

But. If the passage into death is as unconscious as

haunt me

the descent through dreams into sleep, then maybe, just maybe, what waits on the other side isn't any less real for being unimaginable. Maybe the leap from death into life is just as sudden. Maybe we only have to let go of those we've loved precisely so that whatever eventual reunion we have is all the more joyous.

I'd like to believe that. But I can't know. And I'm out of practice at taking things on faith.

What I do know is that so much of what haunts us does so because, on some level, we want it to. We yearn for it, as much as it yearns for us, or what it thinks is us.

Come in, into me. Come inside. I'm empty. I'm a haunted house.

(*say that you want me, come back and haunt me*)

I remember the Priest, like I remember them all. Whether they choose to stay, or not.

Whether or not they choose to pass through, and leave me alone again.

Because haunting, in essence, is the refusal to let go, on both sides. The refusal to forgive something for changing, or leaving. Even if—even when—you can't remember what you're holding on to anymore. Or why.

One day, I'm going to be faced with that choice myself. We all are.

The best we can ever do is work on getting ready.

the happy medium

HELEN MARSHALL

Ossian *Gil has* strict rules.

The first is she'll only do it for time-and-a-half. The normal Park pay won't cut it, not for what they're asking of her.

The second is it's only for kids. No one older than ten, no one younger than five. Adults make too much of a fuss, Ossian knows. How many times has she been through those great blubbering tears and someone pawing at her, trying to clutch at her hand, searching for skin—searching for something *human*, she thinks—beneath what they make her wear?

Ossian doesn't like that.

(Ossian, pronounced *Aw-shin*—though no one ever says it right.)

She doesn't like it when people want to touch her.

No one is allowed, not even Ivo her boyfriend, except when she asks him to. The Park makes sure everyone signs a contract spelling this out pretty clearly but when push comes to shove the contract never seems to matter. Grief makes people behave in all sorts of weird-ass ways.

And the third rule? The third has to do with the costume.

The boy's name is Chris McLaren.

He's nine years old which is okay then. He's got a rakish dart of black hair like one day he'll be pretty handsome. He could front a boy band, Ossian thinks—like The Bees She Sees or Mad Magnolia—with those kind of almost-good looks.

Today Ossian is suited up as Gentleman Grover.

Gentleman Grover: half-cat, half-something else entirely—half-gentleman, she guesses. He's a minor Park character, nobody's favourite, local color in The Enchanted Forest. He wears a fancy top hat and tails. (The top hat is heavy, two-feet tall. It makes Ossian's neck hurt to wear it.)

In The Enchanted Forest, it's forty degrees—the Florida humidity thick as cream of mushroom soup—but still it's snowing: weightless polystyrene flecks that land like ash from a crematorium. It's always snowing in The Enchanted Forest, always snowing and every house is a little gingerbread cottage nestled in a marshmallow mound of snow.

In The Enchanted Forest, Gentleman Grover's top hat has a quiet dignity. Anywhere else and he'd be ridiculous. But not here, not in the Park. Here, he's the Loyal Companion you'd whisper your worst secrets to.

And they do, don't they?

Ossian can't count how many times she's slipped her arm around the shoulder of some grinning, damp-bottomed bub only to find a yoga momma with her ass jiggling like two puppies in a plastic bag, close beside her, whispering: "I fucked him—the plumber—twice. I wanted to. I wanted to so much but I'm sorry now and that matters, doesn't it? It matters that I was sorry?"

"Hey," says Ossian to Chris while her handler shoots daggers at her for breaking character.

She should be saying "Greetings, son of Adam" but she can never be bothered. Ossian has a smoker's voice, wasted to almost manliness, though she's never smoked a day in her life. She's eighteen years old and beautiful inside her Gentleman Grover costume.

"Hi," says the boy, staring at her hard, staring at Gentleman Grover, and his post-weepy eyes are the grey-green of gator skin. "I want to talk to my sister."

"I know," says Ossian. Trying to be good now, she gives a dandyish little flourish.

"Her name is Maya. My sister. She's . . . " He sniffles noisily, then gives her an angry-at-himself look.

Grief.

"I *know*," says Ossian again. She hates this part—the build-up.

Somewhere in the distance Ossian can hear a snatch of screaming. Elated howls from Galaxy Mountain, which towers in the distance. It's the Park, one of the problems of the Park. Noise carries here. It seeps through the dense thicket of artificial oak, ash and thorn, even this deep in the Enchanted Forest, in the Dale of Unexpected Encounters.

"Can you hear her then? Maya? Can you speak to her? Hello? *Hello*?"

This is Chris again.

Ossian blanked out for a moment. Sometimes it happens.

"She's here," Ossian confirms.

And it's true.

She can sense the Maya-ghost slipping in close beside her, a smell like peanut butter—cloying but distinctive—mingling with the suit's microfibre and her own musky sweat.

"I need her to hear this," says Chris. His face is scrunched up and red like he might start crying. "You're sure she's listening?"

"She's listening," murmurs Ossian.

Sure, there she is, something warm and sticky inside the costume. Ossian feels it slicking against her stomach, down her thighs, tickling the tender insides of her arms.

"Good," says Chris. "So how does this work then?"

"How this works," says Ossian, slipping into character, her voice dropping an octave lower, filling up with wisdom and benevolence, "is that you tell me a story."

That's enough for him apparently. Mostly it always is. He fixes his gaze on Gentleman Grover's heavy-lidded, gleaming eyes, double blinks in rapid fire, and then he gets into it.

Dear Maya (he says).

It's strange to start this way but I don't know how else to start so I guess I'll start like this.

Dear Maya, I'm sorry you're dead.

Mom thought this would be a good idea. I didn't

want to. I wouldn't . . . well. You know. But she's always had a thing about this place. The Park. I mean, she thought *you* had a thing about it but . . . we both know it was always *her*, don't we?

How many times did she bring you here, huh? Like, a hundred?

Every time she thought it'd be the last time. She'd smile with that smile she uses sometimes—I dunno—when she's taking little pictures in her mind. Like, "Okay, here's Maya with the Mouse, the Bird, and the Sausage. Isn't she so beautiful? Isn't she happy?"

You were sixteen and dying, then, and I'm sure you didn't give a crap about any of it. But still. You pretended. I always thought that was pretty cool of you.

Anyway. I don't need to tell you. You know how Mom is.

She misses you pretty bad.

I just thought I should say that. You know, I think that's what she *wants* me to say here. This isn't really for me, is it? She says it is . . . but it isn't.

She shouldn't have done this. I told her I didn't want to speak to you, that I knew you were dead now. That you and I had talked about it before and I was okaaaaay.

We talked about it a *lot* really, didn't we? Like the day you were supposed to go to prom and then after you'd got yourself ready and put on your dress Mom wouldn't let you go because you couldn't even make it down the stairs, remember?

"Next year, honey," she told you, just like she was always telling you about everything you wanted to do. "Next year you can go."

And: "Mu-*um,*" you said like it was maybe even possible she would listen to you this time. But of course she didn't.

And that night I crept into your room with that flower thing—a corsage?—after Mom had gone to bed. Even though the little white flowers were all wilted you still pinned it to your pyjama top. You were so pale and bluish, like the Lagoon Princess Mariella—it was supposed to be "Under the Sea" and you said your friends had spent weeks making little tinselly fish and crepe seashells but there in your bedroom you looked like you were, I don't know, shipwrecked or something—but I helped you with the corsage anyway because your hands were shaking . . .

And you smiled at me, Maya. I remember.

You would've gone out in your wheelchair, I think. It wouldn't have mattered to you if you couldn't dance to Mad Magnolia or The Bees She Sees. But, well. You knew you were gonna die and I knew you were gonna die and at least when it was just the two of us we didn't have to pretend.

Do you remember that?

Do you remember anything, Maya?

"Dying doesn't mean anything," you told me. "You shouldn't be afraid of it. It isn't what Mom thinks it is. It isn't what anyone thinks it is, Kit, and I *know.* I know because I'm so close to it now it's like I can flip to the end of the story and peek early . . . "

And I believed you, Maya. The way you talked about it. You knew what was coming and you were okay with it.

Then after . . .

After.

the happy medium

Mom kept saying you had gone to a better place.

I guess it's just weird that the better place turned out to be *here*.

And now I—

"That's enough," chirps Ossian's handler with a faux-happy Park smile. "Break time for Gentleman Grover."

Chris double-blinks again but this time it's like he's coming up for air.

But the break is part of the contract too. Ten minutes on, thirty minutes off for cool down. There are no fans in the costume even though all the guests think there must be. No one believes the Park would make teenagers wear that crap when everyone else is slathering sunscreen on, still dying in the shade . . .

"Wait, I—"

The kid has tears in his eyes and the Maya-ghost is writhing around inside the suit: an awful gumminess rubbing up and down Ossian's flesh.

But then her handler bustles her away through a secret tunnel that passes underneath the Naiad Lagoon and five minutes later Ossian is in the staff room, popping off Gentleman Grover's head and stripping down. She breathes in the fierce air conditioning.

"Hey," says Ossian's handler. "You're s'pposed to stay in character out there."

Ossian wants to flip her handler the bird but she doesn't.

Instead, she takes out a peanut butter sandwich. She hates the taste of peanut butter but the thing is that when she's doing her job all she can smell is peanut butter and who wants to eat, say, tuna fish, or ham, or even egg salad, when all you can smell is peanut butter? So she brings in peanut butter and even if she hates it at least it doesn't make her retch.

"You gotta follow the rules, Ossian. They're for your sake too. You *know* that."

Her handler says her name like it's *Ocean* so Ossian ignores this as well.

The Maya-ghost is still with her, not close-close like before but close enough that Ossian can feel that tickle of presence. It's worse with the costume on. The Park knows that but they say the costume is important, it's what turns the whole shebang into an *experience*. And what's she going to do? Unionize?

But still it's hard. The Maya-ghost doesn't know Ossian is on break and so . . .

"Hey," says Ossian. "Hey, babe. You listening?"

She can feel the Maya-ghost pressing closer against her, sinking into her crotch and her armpits, vibrating the little hairs that cover her, seeping into her sweat glands like reverse osmosis.

"Don't do that," hisses her handler.

Ossian rolls her eyes and focuses on the sensation. She hums the opening lines to that song she's always hearing on the radio. She thinks it's Mad Magnolia but she's never been good at knowing those sorts of things. Ivo her boyfriend does. He's in a band too.

"Duh, dum, di duh, yeah, it happened on a stupid Sunday morning . . . "

Ossian had wondered after she heard what the boy said if the Maya-ghost would be any different than the others—most of the time it's a sudden death situation, something unresolved, something nagging and left over like a spiritual hangnail—but the kid said his sister *knew*.

Still there's that same old feeling there, the same crazy hunger . . .

"*Make me a holy city cause I know I could be so good . . .*"

"Not cool," says the handler with an anxious look.

"It's my break," Ossian croons. She holds out the peanut butter sandwich: an offering.

But that's not what the Maya-ghost wants, it seems. So Ossian shrugs and eats it herself.

Now break time's over and she's back in the Dale of Unexpected Encounters with Chris McLaren.

The boy's sitting underneath the shade of a crossroads sign, playing something on his console. Wizard Frog, it looks like. He's jamming his fingers at the buttons. It looks like he's losing. *Blam, blam, blam* goes the console before it shrieks with the sound of heavy braking, there's a splat, and it falls silent.

Ossian has tipped the mask back over herself and now the smell is a hundred times worse.

"Not yet, babe," she whispers to the Maya-ghost. "C'mon. Hold out for the kid. He's your brother."

Ossian doesn't really believe in ghosts. Sure, she's felt them and all, she can smell their sugary reek inside the costume, but that's not really the same thing. "Smelling isn't believing," she's told Ivo her boyfriend who loves to get high and talk to her about all the Gnostic crap he found on the Internet because he figures with her job she's tuned into, like, some higher plane.

Like last night.

"So you know there's these books they say that Jesus wrote?" Ivo was telling her. "But these books, they're not in the Bible. It's crazy because they're, like, all the best bits, you know? The fairy tales of Jesus of Nazareth. Like he said, if you bring forth what's inside you, what you bring forth will save you and if you don't bring forth what's inside you, what you bring forth can destroy you and that sounds a lot like he was talking about you, Ocean."

"*Aw-shin*," she told him like she always tells him but he was grinning a dopey pothead grin and getting on with his dopey-ass questions.

Like do they ever talk to her? The Park says they talk to her but the Park says a lot of crap, so do they talk to her? Like, can she hear them? And does she get to choose, ever? Like could she talk to John Lennon or Alex Trebek? Could she talk to Leon Trotsky or Pliny the Elder or Marilyn Monroe?

Ivo thinks she looks a bit like Marilyn Monroe. He likes to say it's a fucking crime that they put her in the Gentleman Grover suit when she should really be playing Princess Menechella who gets to show her face at least.

And then of course Ossian has to tell him she *likes* playing Gentleman Grover and all the girls who play Princess Menechella are bitches because it's, like, a requirement for the job or something, and besides, the Princess Menechellas never gets extra breaks so *fuck you*.

What she doesn't tell him is that also there's the third rule. The thing about the costumes.

See, you can't haunt a fucking Princess Menechella

get-up, that's the thing. The ghosts like a snug fit. No one knows why, but they do. So Gentleman Grover, it is.

Besides, it makes it easier for the guests. What the guests all want is a *sign*, something solid-but-not-too-solid they can fit their expectations around. They need that bulbous, joyful costume as much as the ghosts do.

And now Chris's eyes are darting up toward her and he's put the fucking console away. "So how'd you get this gig anyway?" he asks her.

"My great-grandmomma was Irish," she says with a smirk. "Some things travel in the blood."

"And the Park?"

"The Park's good at spotting a niche, you know?"

He half smiles like he wishes he did. But then the smile slips. "So, does Maya want to say something to me, or what?" he asks her.

"Keep talking, kid," says Ossian.

The smiles slips further. "I don't want to."

Deep down Ossian feels like she sort of likes Chris McLaren. She likes what he said about his sister, how gentle he seems. Gentlemanly. And liking one of the Park clientele, that's not a bad thing, is it?

"All right," says Ossian, "how about I tell you a story instead?"

Once upon a time (she says) there was a Princess named Ossian.

Ossian wasn't your regular princess. She didn't live in a castle and she didn't have any money because the Queen—her mother—had split with the crown jewels and the King—her father—had locked himself away in the tower so no one knew whether he was alive or dead. But, see, they kept leaving TV dinners outside the tower at night and in the morning they'd find empty trays with half-chewed vegetables and a whole mess of gloopy gravy so they figured he probably was alive but for sure he wasn't any help.

But the Princess.

The Princess couldn't turn straw into gold and the Princess didn't have a fairy godmother but she did have a second sister. "Beauty attracts the divine eye," said her sister unhappily, like she was reading the same Gnostic crap online as Ivo. See, her sister wasn't beautiful and so was maybe a little happier because the possibility of princes never really occurred to her.

Second Sister was worried though. She was worried about how Princess Ossian was always out there trying to find a prince. How she was chasing after all sorts of beasties like toads and slugs and mice and wild sausages just in case one of them happened to be a prince.

So one day after one of these not-quite-princes had been round and had hurt her sister a little because that's what happens when you invite a wolverine into the house, she said, "Well, Ossian, enough is enough."

So Second Sister made for Princess Ossian a mask of panned mud and witch grass. And Princess Ossian wore it outside every day until her face took on the folds and the crevices of the mask, the ugliness of what Second Sister's hands had made.

Then Second Sister made Ossian walk with a limp.

She taught her how to spit.

She tore a hole in Ossian's right eye so it wept blood.

She threw away Ossian's razor so her armpits grew

as shaggy as thistledown.

"Hush now, Ossian," my sister used to whisper to me. "Don't you see how it's better this way? How it's so much better for both of us? We'll always be together."

But it didn't matter how crooked the second sister made the first, how ugly and unlovable because something had got into the first sister and was already doing its own work. See, her belly was getting bigger and bigger and her skin went red and splotchy and her thighs slapped together when she walked and her breasts grew as pendulous as wasp nests.

It was too late then. Too late for Second Sister. Too late for Princess Ossian.

But the thing is, Ossian was *happy*.

Oh, she knew the prince or the beast or whoever it was wouldn't be coming back. She knew that, sure, but that didn't seem to matter to her so much.

Before that she'd felt, like, this emptiness inside her, this thicket of rage and pain and darkness. Second Sister had felt it too, and maybe the King and Queen had and maybe the not-so-much-princes had, which is what had drawn them to her in the first place . . .

But now she was filling up with something.

She'd never trusted love but this wasn't love exactly, it was something else. And now she wasn't just a princess, she was an anchor maybe, a lightning rod, a holy city like in that Mad Magnolia song Second Sister was always listening to.

"*Duh, dum, di duh, yeah, it happened on a stupid Sunday morning . . .*"

"What happened after that?" says Chris McLaren.

He's fiddling with the console, not turning it on but tapping against the buttons as if he expects something magic to appear.

"Nothing happened after that," says Ossian.

"What do you mean nothing?"

"I mean, the baby came out of her too early. She was barely more than ten weeks old, which meant it wasn't a baby at all, you know? It was just like a clot or something, a bit of stuff inside her that suddenly wasn't inside her anymore which meant it couldn't live."

She doesn't know why she's telling Chris McLaren this story. Maybe it's how gentlemanly he is, maybe it's those long handsome lashes of his . . .

Or maybe Ivo her boyfriend is right. If you bring forth what's inside you, what you bring forth will save you . . . but then that's never really worked, has it? Not for Ossian.

"What happened to your sister?" says Ossian as the handler signals wildly from behind Chris McLaren.

But it's too late for that because now the Maya-ghost is moving against her, which means it's time then, just like on Galaxy Mountain where you go up and up and up and all the while the terror is getting bigger and bigger inside you until you tip over the edge . . .

. . . and Ossian *remembers* that feeling, that feeling her sister said she couldn't have: a feeling of something rushing into you, something soft and membranous. How for month after month afterward Ossian had dreamed it was still there, that something was growing inside of her. How it was like her whole body had become a wildwood filled with breadcrumb trails.

And the ghosts.

The ghosts felt it too.

They followed those breadcrumbs her daughter had left, didn't they? Ghosts of hunger, ghosts of want. Ghosts of broken promises and failed trials and hidden secrets. Because what else were you once you stripped off your skin? What else could you be, except naked and alone?

The Park knows this. The Park knows this is how it works.

"What happened to your sister?" Ossian says again because Chris is staring at the console, not even looking at her now.

"*Nothing* happened to my sister too," mutters Chris. "Nothing happens to everyone, I guess. In the end."

"But you miss her."

"She said I shouldn't."

"But you do anyway, don't you?" she prods, and all the while the Maya-ghost moves and moves and moves, unfurling against her. "So I guess I better tell you something."

"Not for me," he mutters. "For my mom."

"For your mom, yeah," says Ossian.

And the Maya-ghost is just about ready, it seems, which is good because now Chris is ready too. His face is tipping upward and even though he said he didn't believe—which is what Ossian has said too, has said a thousand times to Ivo her boyfriend—it seems the living are just as full of hunger as the dead.

"Okay," says Ossian.

She knows the words she's supposed to say. She knows the script.

What you should say is this:

Dear Chris. I can feel your sister. I can feel Maya close to me now and there's something she wants to tell you. She wants to tell you that you shouldn't be worried about her anymore, and neither should your mother. She loved you both very much. She still loves you. Of course, she does.

The fairy tale—she wishes she could do it. She wishes she could do better than that.

She wishes she could peel the poor boy down, through the layers of obligation and need, of good behavior and kindness and chivalry, peel off the panned mud and witchgrass until he was as naked and gleaming and unborn as his sister.

Instead, she says:

"I think your sister was lying to you, Chris. That's what she's telling me. Your sister was lying when she said she could see what was coming because no one can really see what's coming. No one wants it. No one can see it."

Now his hands are clenched into little fists and his face is red and grotesque. "And if she did?"

"If she did . . . I don't know, Chris." She feels helpless now, unsure of what it is she has started. Only Ivo had said if you bring forth what's inside you . . . "I didn't know your sister," she tries, backtracking.

"Okay," he hisses, "that's what I'll tell my mom then."

"Don't be an idiot," Ossian snarls though it's getting hard now, it's getting really hard because the Maya-ghost is thrashing around, pushing and pushing and pushing. And her handler is waving her fingers and rolling her eyes and threatening all sorts of silent lawsuits.

"So, why?" he wants to know. "Why's she coming back?"

The truth is that Ossian doesn't know. It's the thing she wonders. It's the thing she wondered when she could feel the baby moving inside of her. *Why are you here, babe?* she wanted to ask it. *What do you want from me?*

But all she could feel was the hunger, the insides of her body moving around, being rearranged to make way. Something peeking through: mindless, thoughtless, but not unloved—that's the crazy thing, how much you can love a thing that's barely anything at all.

The Park says they can't be loved, not as they are. Not half-formed—or decomposed, really—and that's why she needs to wear the costume. That's why they need the performance. It helps the living let go.

But what if that's all so much bullshit, just like everything else in the Park is bullshit? What if you could love—really love—whatever it was that loved you so much it kept coming back? Kept hanging around, trying to find the space inside you where it knew what it was to be safe?

In a flash her gloves are off and she's gripping Chris's hand with her own. Flesh to flesh, nothing between them.

And then she feels it, like a kind of movement or pressure. For a moment, the Maya-ghost is against her skin, and then suddenly the pressure lifts and the ghost passes away from her, drawn like a lightning rod to the thing she wants. Ossian shivers with something that is neither pleasure nor cold.

"Tell your momma this," she hisses when it's over. "Tell her Maya was loved. Tell her she's at peace."

And now she's staring at Chris and she sees a new look in his eyes: half wonder, half terror.

"Maya?" he whispers. "Maya?"

And then their time is up and her handler is hauling her away.

Later that night, Ossian is heading home from the Park. She walks with a stagger, her hands buried in the pockets of her over-sized jersey dress.

Most of the Florida heat has burned off but still her skin feels clammy and wrinkled, as if she's spent the day drifting on the River of Ataraxia. She passes mommas pushing their strollers but now they don't give her a second look.

Why should they? Without the costume, Ossian Gil is nothing special. Ossian Gil is nothing at all.

Besides, her ass has been fired.

Well, she knew it was coming, didn't she? "The rules are there for a reason, Ocean," her handler told her, "and so what if there's a complaint? I'm gonna have to tell Madison . . . "

Madison is Ossian's line manager.

Was Ossian's line manager.

Madison had worked her way up from playing Princess Menechella a few years back and so she could be a real bitch when she wanted to be. And she'd never much liked Ossian. Well, fuck *her*, Ossian would say when she got home tonight. She'd find another job. Ivo would understand. Ivo was good that way, undemanding. He'd run her a bubble bath, then she'd sink into it, the perfume washing over her, her body almost weightless in the water . . .

And she'd let Ivo rattle on and on, him lying on the unclean bathroom floor, resting his head against the tiles, smoking a joint and maybe sharing it with her if she wanted.

This is what he'd say:

He'd tell her how in Cyprus the remains of horses were found in the necropolis of Salamis. How they'd dragged in the chariot of the dead, then been butchered while still yoked to the cart.

Or in ancient Greece you could drape a flayed donkey hide beneath the corpse of the newly slain and compel their spirit to do your bidding.

Or in Britain even now if you searched the chimneys of certain old buildings you'd find the skin of a cat stuffed with salt to ward off bad luck.

And she'd nod her head drowsily as the water crept between her legs and over her breasts and the bubbles piled up like snowfall on her nipples. Then she'd sing to herself:

"Duh, dum, di duh, yeah, it happened on a stupid Sunday morning . . ."

And somewhere, she'd know, Chris would be going through the photos his momma had snapped of the Park: Naiad's Lagoon, The Enchanted Forest, Galaxy Mountain looming overhead, the two of them arm in arm with Princess Menechella.

And maybe, if his momma was looking closely, she'd see something blue and shimmery between them, something shipwrecked, something naked and loved come home at last.

Ossian touches her belly then, feels the ripple of almost-movement beneath.

"*Make me a holy city cause I know I could be so good . . .*"

the marble lily

KATHE KOJA

Honored gentlemen and judges, judge for yourselves, *consider* for yourselves: all the wrong I did was clasp her hand. And for this I am separated from my useful work, and my dear family, and subject to a confinement more solitary and cold than that which this poor girl, this so-called "Désirée," or "Marble Lily of the Seine," lay for so long unnamed and unmourned.

Nor am I mourned. My wife steadfastly refuses to admit to the merits of my case; she has gone into seclusion in Cluny, at the home of her sister, Beatrice. Beatrice has never cared for me; from the very start she opposed our marriage because, she said, I had dreams above my station, I was irreligious, with "scientific ideas." Of course I am a student of science! It is what brought me here to Paris and the Morgue, to learn more of the great and secret marvels of the body, while employed to provide much humbler sanitary aid. My wife, were she able to listen with an open heart, would understand that what I have done was done in that hope of knowledge. All else—the hysteric crowds, the chants, the filthy accusations—oh! so filthy! The human mind, gentlemen and judges, is the greatest cesspool in the world—all of that denies the truth of what happened in this room.

Explain myself? Shall I not begin where the story itself begins, with water? The effects of water on the human body are quite wonderful and well-documented, from the wrinkling and swelling that is called "washerwoman's skin," to the gooseflesh we all experience from a dash of cold liquid—even the living feel so, the living are not so very different from the dead—to other, more grievous changes produced when a body floats for days, such as this girl's had.

I have seen many such cases, gentlemen and judges; though I am but a servant, I have—I had—the confidence and approbation of my superiors, who marveled at my facility with the bodies, and how I keep the viewing glass so clean. The greasy hands and fingers of the public—! They are ravenous, those crowds who come to view the mystery of death, it is well-known that hundreds of them pass through our doors in a single day, during the sensation of the "fillettes de Suresnes" there were ten thousand here in less than one week! I had situated those bodies on draped chairs, not the slabs, so that the viewers might be able to offer better aid in the sad case of the little drowned girls. I myself affixed the identity numbers to their tunics, and as I did so I said a prayer to the Virgin, whose tender heart is surely touched by the lost children, now gone home to Paradise . . . And Beatrice calls me irreligious!

Though I admit that prayer was not my first

response when I saw this girl. Still garbed in her servant's apron, pulled from the river by a pair of fishermen and carried by them to the Morgue: a female, aged perhaps sixteen, with fair hair that, when loosed and dried from its sodden plaits, hung nearly to her hips, and the still, calm face of a marble Venus— it is what the crude fishermen called her, that and much more, and swore that they had done their utmost to revive her, though "revive" was not the word they used, those rogues!—who were bought cups of wine for their so-called heroics, their names were even printed in the newspapers . . . *Her* name, let it be noted in the records, is not "Désirée," any more than it is "the Water Lily of the Seine" or "The Marble Lily," as she came to be called once she was arrayed upon the slab; it is likely that her true name will never be discovered. So many people have passed before her, avid to gaze and remark, yet none of them could say with certainty who she was.

Yet the moment I laid eyes on her, I knew her.

I see by your expressions that this admission suggests to you something untoward, unwholesome as those fishermen were unwholesome, but may I remind you, with all deference, that my own superiors at the Morgue were always more than willing to rely upon my vision: *Ask François*, they all said. *François has an eye for the dead!* Is that not why they allowed me, a mere janitor, so often into their forensic examinations, why they allowed me to take notes—you have my notes, my copybook there on the table before you; may I read to you, read that "the case of Female Subject so-called Marble Lily was"—Yes. Yes of course. Only demonstrate that it was science that drove me, to learn further the mechanism of death: Was she lost before or after she entered the water? Was the cause truly drowning, or was she the victim of an assailant, and her body thus introduced into the river to cover the foul crime? And how long had she been in its currents and deeps, for the normal rhythms of decomposition are disrupted when—My apologies, gentlemen and judges, *I* only seek to demonstrate that my interest in this young woman was entirely scientific, to begin.

But the more I looked upon that lovely, lifeless face, alone in the dawn peace before the crowds—for I am the first to enter in the mornings, I am here before the orange sellers on the avenue—the more I considered her, the more the spiritual dimension of her situation began to press upon me. One hears tales of the saints taken from their tombs still incorrupt; and to find a young woman who had been so sunk—her clothing bore the marks of it—yet remained untouched by the grosser mechanisms that must attend a death in the water . . . Even my wife was moved to remark, at first, that the girl might be "a sort of miracle."

Do you know what a miracle is, gentlemen and judges? It is a gift from God to the brain.

And it was my brain that I put to work; it was that silent, unravaged face, that furled bud of a girl arrested forever in her blossoming, that I circled, with my thoughts and my vision, though busy always about my daily tasks. Thus it was that in those earliest mornings, I sat beside her—on the workers' side of the glass, not the viewers', why should I not avail myself of this proximity, as I sought the proximate cause—not of her death; of *her*, the girl herself, this nameless slip of flesh and pale hair, alive in the fact of the question she posed: What is Life? when death takes the animation from a body, but leaves it still so beautiful, and, when closely inspected, seemingly ready to live again? Why did we not, with her, need employ any means of preservation? for she did not decay; she lay there day after day with her eyes closed and her lips parted, as if, watching closely, one might almost see her soft breast rise and fall once more with respiration; as if she only dreamed of death, in a sleep so complete as to mimic its depths.

And yet in another sense it was as if she had never been alive at all, for though her photographic likeness was in all the newspapers, from the penny broadsheets to the *Herald* and *The Metropolitan*, and bruited from the salons to the streets—they even heard the tale in Cluny; Beatrice saved all the sheets—even thus so *known*, she remained unknown: without name, family, employer willing to come forward and claim her, nor even themselves to be found. A reward, yes, was offered, and what a sad farce that spawned: the woman who claimed to be her twin, and the oldster from Lyon, that antique fraud—! It began to seem as if she had drifted down the river from someplace farther than the countryside, farther even than France, from a place one can visit only in faith or desire. As the fourth week passed into the fifth, some of those who came began to leave offerings in her honor—heaps of lilies, picture postcards of the Virgin, notes, packets of sweets—*those* brought the rats—praying aloud, imploring her succor and aid.

Meanwhile I continued to watch, though importuned with increasing agitation by my wife, who demanded to know why I stayed, each night it seemed later, there beside her slab with my notebook, watching—for what? I cannot say. Is a mystery named before it is deciphered? I only knew that a process was at work, and that my own diligence was essential; perhaps some witness was required to bring forth what was to come, humble and obscure though he may be? Were there not angels present at the tomb of the Resurrection, stationed there by Christ Himself? For perhaps kind hands were needed, to help Him pass back between this world and the next.

So I watched; I made my observations and my notes, I drew diagrams. And as for those curbside chants, and filthy accusations—that alone in the morgue I touched this girl improperly, impurely, made sport with her poor slim body, that they found me in positions that—oh, it is painful even to recount the slanders, one can understand my poor wife's anguish if not her flight! But me! Whose interest was so pure— When first Monsieur le Directeur questioned me, I laughed!

No, M le Directeur did not laugh.

No. When M le Directeur heard the rumors, heard the orange sellers making sport of me outside our very doors, he summoned me into his office, and *François, he said, you have been at the Morgue for nearly six years now, is that so?*

It is so, sir, I said.

And your superiors say your eye is a keen one, that you notice details that others miss. Is that not so?

It is so, sir.

What do you make, then, of this "Marble Lily"? So I showed my copybook, that very copybook upon the table, and told all that I had seen in the watches of the night, I even shared my speculations that something miraculous was at work. I withheld nothing from M le Directeur! He is himself a man of science, I felt sure that he would believe and understand.

But it was he who instructed me that, for the good of the institution, for the reputation of the institution, I must no longer *stare and hover about this girl, what more can be gained by that? You see it is becoming a scandal. Do you wish the Morgue to be tainted by scandal?*

Of course I did not. Of course I do not! But—yes, I disobeyed him. That is true, and I accept all blame and punishment. But when M le Directeur told me, then, that there would be no more public viewing, nor any viewing at all; that there was to be an autopsy, that that butcher Dr Grenouille was to take the girl apart, piece by piece, as a clumsy child might break a watch, to learn its mechanism—in my heart I saw her secret processes soiled, I saw her holiness destroyed; I was in such a state that I confess I did not know what to do, gentlemen and judges! To disobey one's superior is a very serious matter. But the girl and her mystery still unborn, what other friend had she in this place but me?

Before I did what I knew I must, I did the only wrong to which I may confess: I took her hand, that cold curl of palm and fingers, and clasped it as a brother might, or—as if we were both young together, in some strange Eden, light and fragrant as the Morgue is dim with odors—as a friend, I clasped her hand and promised her my aid. And despite what the penny papers may say, that is all that I touched, and all that I did.

The rest was easy.

I have—I had—access to the bundler and the dead carts, I know every hallway and corner of this great Morgue, and I know, gentlemen and judges, that now the girl, "the Marble Lily," named at last by me as the true daughter of Death, will never be found. For that, gentlemen and judges, *that* is the fact that came to birth, that is the secret that flowered for me alone, a momentous and dreadful fact whose contemplation brought me—through my vision, yes, that misses nothing, *François has an eye for the dead—to a* place beyond all dread, a place where death is as plain and good and necessary as flowing water, nothing to be marveled at, nothing to be feared: and she herself its emblem and ambassador, this girl whose body lay, as if on an altar, on the borderland, always dead, yet somehow still alive. She will stay so thus, she will stay that way forever, she is of both worlds and neither, and we meant to be her keepers and friends, and venerate her as one of the great mysteries given to us by God until such time as we will, by science, understand her pale unmoving animation, and use what we learn to help all who must suffer and die; which means all of mankind. If a miracle is a gift from God to the brain, then let the brain use it! Let the brain and the eyes—

Forgive me, gentlemen and judges, but what you say is as unfair as it is unkind. And may I state that whether or not my "eloquence is equal to my madness," I am not mad, the girl is Death's daughter, and until such time as you find it good to release me from my own morgue of death-in-life, that jail cell so dire even the rats refuse to enter, she will remain in the hiding place I chose for her, inviolate and clean,

the marble lily

until God Himself calls her forth as he will call us all, to answer the Last Call—a day at which you, gentlemen and judges, may quail as fully as the rest of us. My wife and Beatrice, too.

And beyond that statement, gentlemen and judges, all I may say is that I ask of your mercy, the mercy of my copybook returned to me, and a pencil with a point that I may sharpen, for the lead I have now is beyond all earthly use.

[End testimony of François Undine, former janitor and servant of the Paris Morgue, found lifeless in his cell on 8 Mai 189–. The copybook was empty. Undine had never learned to read or write.]

the bone eater

LEE MURRAY

You *were down south*, near Mahana, picking
apples on some old lady's orchard, when you
got the call. Not an actual call. Not a text or a
letter or anything like that. You didn't hold with that
technology stuff. Couldn't be bothered, couldn't afford
it, and your fingers were too clumsy to work the
buttons. No point anyway, since by now, you were
estranged from everyone who counted.

But there it was: a strange niggle, like an omen of
bad things.

It started out vague, like a persistent tickle at the
back of your throat. Demanding. It reminded you of
crooked pūriri branches grinding and clacking high up
in the forest canopy; you know there's nothing there,
but still you're forced to look up. You let it simmer a
few days, but you couldn't ignore it. You'd been
thinking of getting out, anyway. You were getting too
old; everything hurt. So you crammed your stuff into
a plastic bag, stopped by the farmhouse to let the old
lady know you were heading out, and got on the road,

turning right at the crossroads, and sticking your thumb out for the journey north.

It took a weekend to work your way up to Picton, and another couple of days to get the fare together by scrubbing out plastic boxes at a fish warehouse—honest work but bloody pongy. You split a ten dollar note, spending five at the laundromat and the remainder on a cheese and onion toasted sandwich and a cup of tea at the ferry terminal.

You chose a seat at the front of the ferry, away from the other passengers, where you huddled against the gusting wind, cradling your warm paper cup in your palm, and rejoicing in the call of the gulls, the crash of the waves on the hull, and the shouts of nearby children. That kind of noise didn't bother you. For the first time in weeks, your mind was quiet. Massaging your aching leg, you savored the distraction.

The quiet in your mind lasted only a few hours: the moment you stepped off the ferry at Kaiwharawhara, the clamor erupted again. You'd come to expect it; the further north you travelled, the more urgent it became. Muffled voices. Shrieks. You strived to hear them, screwing up your eyes and clenching your teeth to make sense of the incessant buzz. But the words eluded you.

It was getting so you couldn't rest. And you were growing thinner. Thinnest you'd ever been. Before hitching a ride out of Wellington, you stopped at a second-hand store, paid a gold coin for a decent leather belt, then used a nail you found on the road to poke a hole in it and tighten your waistband. It would have to do. You'd understand soon enough.

At least, you hoped you would.

the bone eater

Forty years you'd been waiting to understand.

All that stuff about you being a matakite when you were a kid: it'd been so long without any inkling; you were starting to think it was a crock of shit. Back home, up north, they insisted you were a seer. A speaker for the dead. A sorcerer. Your great-uncle had been convinced you had the gift—same as him. Your mother thought so, too. That was back in the days when you were still speaking to them. Those days, you were more interested in getting a motorbike so you could leave that dead-end place, in wasting your Friday nights drinking—and your Saturdays wasted. You'd thought they were dreaming. And that your great-uncle was off his head. But even you didn't say those things about your elders back in those days. Not out loud.

"How will I know?" you demanded. You'd been fourteen and at Great Uncle's place, sent by your mother to wash the pink weatherboard house with sugar soap after getting yourself expelled from school for shit-talking the teachers.

"You'll know," he'd said.

You'd wanted to scream. It was like trying to find the answer to the cryptic crossword. And not the everyday one, the fucking *hard* one published in the Sunday paper.

"When exactly?"

The old man waved a hand absently. He shuffled inside to put on the jug and make a cup of tea.

You dumped the cloth in the bucket, stripped off the yellow rubber gloves, and followed him in. "Well, can you at least tell me how it is for you? What does it look like? When you get a call from beyond, I mean."

Great Uncle gazed out the grubby window. You

hadn't gotten to that side of the house yet. "It doesn't matter," he said. "It's never the same. Every matakite finds their own way of reading the signs." He poured boiling water into the pot over the leaves—the old guy didn't believe in tea bags—fitted the lid and stepped back to let it steep.

"Then how do you know I have the gift?" You pulled two mugs from the cupboard. "I've never seen anything. Never felt anything."

Sighing, your mātua sat at the table and picked at the Formica that was peeling off the corner with a gnarled finger. "You won't believe me."

"Try me." You put the mugs on the table. Dragged out a chair.

He turned his milky eyes to the window. "It was the sixties, just after you were born. I was up north at Te Rerenga—Spirits Bay—at the tip of the country."

You nodded. Everyone knew where that was.

"I'd walked there, from Te Hapua, gone to wave farewell to an old friend. It's a long way, so I was resting on the bluff near that gnarly pōhutukawa tree, the one that marks the jumping off place where the wairua-spirits of the dead leap into the sea."

You nodded again, impatient. Yes, yes. The pōhutukawa. The dead begin their final journey there. You knew the story.

"That's when the pīwakawaka flittered from the branches. Bold as anything, it was. It flew around my shoulders a bit, then landed on my shoe, fanning its tail feathers. When I didn't move, it spoke."

Your eyes widened.

The old man shook his head. "Not like that. Not the way you're thinking. It didn't actually speak; the words

68

were in my head. That little pīwakawaka poured its pain into me until my bones ached with sadness. The bird's message stank of death, of desolation. I figured the little fellow was foretelling an accident: a mountain erupting, or maybe a pile up on the motorway. I needed to get back to town and check the radio to find out for sure, so I scrambled to my feet, frightening the bird which flew into the branches." He chuckled. "I was as impatient as you are now." He fiddled with the handle of the mug nearest him. "Only, the pīwakawaka said my part was to prepare the way. And that's when your face popped into my head. Weird thing, it wasn't your face from back then; you were much older and skinnier. But then some people came, holidaymakers off the bus with their cameras and their plastic drink bottles, and the pīwakawaka flew away."

You watched the steam spooling from the spout of the battered teapot, waiting for him to elaborate.

The old man said nothing.

"That's it? Really? A little bird told you?" You scoffed. "You're right, Uncle; that's fucking hard to believe."

"Language." He tapped the table with his fingernail. "This is still my house."

You looked down at the orange linoleum. Curled your toes. "Sorry."

He breathed deeply, thin shoulders lifting then slumping. "I should've waited to tell you. You're still too young, too busy swaggering around acting tough. But some day, if you get the call, you do the right thing. Whatever happens, you do the right thing, you hear?"

"But—"

He grunted. "Stop asking. I've told you all I know.

Now pour me a cup of tea, will you? Those leaves have steeped enough."

By the time you got to the outskirts of Auckland, three days later, you'd poked another notch in the belt and your leg was hurting from all the walking. The voices— definitely voices—were killing you now. Your head was pounding with the noise. A constant migraine of pressure. You kept on. Caught the bus on the Great South Road, getting off in the heart of the old city, in Symonds Street.

The wails were so close now. Dreadful inhuman shrieks that chilled you to the bone. You turned. The screaming was coming from near the bridge. You ran-hobbled up the street, stepping through the broken gates of the old cemetery, or what was left of it after they dug it up to make way for the motorway.

It was cool in the shadows, a small mercy. You followed the moss-pitted path among the twisted old trees. You took in the soggy leaves, the crooked, cracked headstones, and the broken brickwork. The iron latticework, rusted and bent. The place was a mess: two centuries of a formal cemetery, dug up and displaced, with the city grown up around it like a vine, the remaining tombstones abandoned in the neglected pockets between the spaghetti junction of roadways and construction, the council coming along later and adding paths to make it look like a park.

Yet this was the place. This lonely patch of green.

A bell rang out, and you jumped aside as a cyclist passed by on the lumpy asphalt. He was gone in a flash of Lycra. Alone again, you shuffled down to the overpass and sat among the discarded railings and broken headstones, your back to a concrete wall. Cars and trucks whizzed by overhead, the vibrations pulsing down your back and rattling your bones.

Well, you were here. *Bring it on.*

You splayed your feet in front of you. Maybe a pīwakawaka would sit on your shoe.

But there was no new message. Just the never-ending noise. Maybe it wasn't a call at all, and you were just going mental like your crazy great-uncle. Exhausted, you strained your ears for something distinct. Despite the cacophony, you dozed.

Someone kicked your foot. "Hey man! Wake the fuck up. You don't wanna sleep here." Bone-tired, you squinted into the dazzle of the afternoon sun. The speaker was around thirty, wearing a scruffy bomber jacket with grimy cuffs. When he grinned, he was missing a tooth. "You're too close to the road, to the cycleway; the cops will move you on. We got some mattresses and stuff a bit deeper in. They don't bother us there."

"Thanks." Using the wall to steady yourself, you clambered to your feet and gestured for him to lead on, but he shook his head and pointed back the way you'd come.

"Not yet, man. We gotta leave now if we want a hot tucker. There's a soup kitchen up the road a bit. Potatoes and sausages, and peas if you want them. And they have hot showers. They give you a free kit to brush your teeth."

You hesitated. Your stomach was as flat and empty as a Canterbury plain, but you didn't want to leave. More than anything you wanted answers, a way to stop the relentless screaming. But a hot shower sounded good, so you ignored the roar in your head, and the ache in your leg, and followed him up the road.

You hung about in the cemetery all through the next week, reading the tombstones and the historical plaques in the daytime, and, at night, laying on the damp and pungent mattresses under the bridge with Marty, Jake, and the others. Unable to sleep, you would stare up at the concrete girders, waiting for the sun to rise. Where was the fucking pīwakawaka? You couldn't take much more of this; you were going out of your head with the noise.

Then, one evening, you were sitting, leaned up against an old headstone, when Marty and Jake walked by.

Marty waved a grimy cuff. "You coming for dinner, Rawiri? We're heading up to the kitchen now."

"Not tonight," you said. You flicked your head at the mattresses on the gravel ledge under the bridge. "Gonna try and get some sleep."

"You should eat something, man. You don't look great."

"Tomorrow," you murmured.

Marty lifted his eyebrows in acknowledgement. "Okay, man. It's your funeral." The pair of them shuffled off.

They'd only been gone a few minutes and you regretted not going with them. Why had you said no? It was a long time until tomorrow and already your stomach was knotted.

You rested your head on the stone as the shadows

lengthened. Meters away, a tiny shard glinted, captured by the dying sunlight. You crawled over and picked it up. It was a sliver of bone, the interior honeycomb all but crumbled away. You don't know what made you do it, but you popped it to the back of your mouth, crunching down hard with your molars. You swallowed it, grit grazing your throat. Dry, the bone had tasted chalky with a tinge of rot. You almost chuckled. Who did you think you were: a bloody wine expert?

You sat back on your haunches. Why the fuck had you done that? Eaten a bone, and off the ground, too. And yet you were filled with a strange sense of relief.

You fell forward on your hands and knees, frantically scratching in the dirt, your fingernails filling with sand and cement as you searched for more. You wanted to stop, but you couldn't help yourself. You kept scratching, digging.

There! Another piece of bone, larger this time, squeezed in a crevasse between two marble headstones. Your teeth clenched, you pried the morsel out of its hidey-hole with a stick and gobbled it up, heedless of the dirt. You gagged down the macabre bolus, suddenly feeling lighter.

Was the noise less? Your head was pounding, the roar still there, but it felt different.

There had to be more . . . This whole area was full of bones. You'd read the plaques; the council had dug up the cemetery in the sixties when they constructed the motorway, disrupting thousands of graves. Identified remains had been dumped in a shared sarcophagus, but many more skeletons were simply ground up or covered over.

You lay your head on the ground, squinting, scanning the surface. Aha! Was that a stone or a bone? You crabbed your way over to the pebble, pain shooting through your bad leg. A bone! A big one. You stuffed it in your mouth. Your stomach contracted as you forced it back, willed it to stay down.

Again, the rush of noise cooled.

Another! You needed another. But it was dark now, shadows crowding at the edges of the park, the streetlights up on the bridge too distant to penetrate the gloom.

"There's a bone over here," a voice called. "Under this stone."

You glanced up. Rubbed at your eyes.

The man was waiflike, ghoulish, with hollowed cheeks and wizened clawed fingers. "It's my sister," he said. His voice was formal, old fashioned. "We've been here so long, waiting to be rescued. Ever since they ripped us from our family grave."

He's dead? So now you were seeing things, too.

"No one's come looking for us before." A different voice.

You whipped your head around.

"Henry McKenzie," the man said, raising a dusty hat. "Formerly of Scotland. I landed in Wellington in 1839 on the *Bengal Merchant*. Made my way up here after that. Died in 1856 of the influenza."

"I can't find my mother," a little girl said.

"My sister. Please," interrupted the man with the clawed fingers. "She's this way."

You got up and hobbled over to where he stood. The newcomers followed you, crowding around.

"Angus Masterton. It's my sister, Verity. She's

trapped under this little block wall. It's the largest piece of her left. The poor girl's been displaced so many times, there are fragments spread everywhere."

"They desecrated our graves," Henry said, shaking his head. "Thousands of us. Anyone with no family left to advocate for them, they churned up with their machines. Spat us out. Left us to find our own way . . . "

"Please hurry," Angus groaned.

You used your good leg to kick down the bricks, exposing worms and dirt. You pushed away a web of white roots.

"Deeper," Angus said.

Picking up a brick, you used it to scoop a hole where the wall had been, then sifted through the dirt, uncovering a fingerbone. A pang of hunger engulfed you, and you longed to wolf it down, this relic of Angus's sister. Lifting the chipped fingerbone to your lips, you hesitated.

"Do it," Angus said. "Please. I beg you."

So you extended your tongue, curling it around the bone, then chomped down on it. When you'd crushed the tiny limb to mash, you swallowed it.

A thin woman materialised in the shadows.

"Verity!" Angus exclaimed. "Thank the Lord." He lifted the woman into his arms.

Incredulous, you wiped your face with your hands. Was this your calling? To resurrect dead colonists by devouring their bones. But why? To what end?

Verity broke away from her brother. "Please, there are others. So many of us. My friend, Margaret is below where you found me."

"Is it my mother?" the girl asked. "Her name is Marie, too. Like me."

Bending, you scraped again at the hollow, Verity urging you on. You seized on the scrap and devoured it, the salty morsel making you gag. Another woman appeared, dressed in a ragged tunic.

"Margaret!" Verity said. The ghost-woman burst into tears.

Breathing hard, you sat with your back against the concrete wall. "I don't understand what's happening."

"It's obvious, isn't it?" Angus replied. "There's no rest for us here." He gestured around the group at the dilapidated cemetery. "No solace. Now you've freed us, we can go somewhere peaceful where we can rest."

"Where will you go?"

Angus paused, gazing down at you from empty eye holes. "I don't know."

You looked at Henry, who shrugged.

Puzzled, you scrunched your nose. What? How could they not know where to go? You stared at the ghosts—Angus, Henry, Verity, Margaret, even little Marie, and it dawned on you that none of them were Māori. If they had been, their wairua-spirits would know instinctively that they should head north, to the jumping off place in Spirits Bay at the tip of the country, to begin the long journey home to Hawaiki.

And you realised with a start why you had been compelled to come here. "I know the way," you said. "It's near my home. Or what used to be home. I could show you . . ."

Margaret scrubbed at the spot where her nose had been with the hem of the ragged tunic. "You know a place where we can rest?"

You nodded. "I know where the journey begins, at least. The voyage ends on a beautiful island in the sun."

the bone eater

Verity clasped her hands together.

"And we'd be welcomed?" Angus asked.

Would they be welcome in Reinga? They weren't Māori. You hesitated. Pressed your fingers to your temples. What did it matter if they were Māori or not? Freed of their flesh, weren't people all the same? Hawaiki, Valhalla, Heaven, Elysium—whatever name you gave it, it was the resting place for wairua-spirits. The end of the line.

You smiled at Angus. "Of course."

At that moment, Jake and Marty ambled down the path, heading for their beds under the overpass.

Jake was munching on an apple. "Who you talking to, Rawiri?" he mumbled through a mouthful of fruit.

"Angus," you replied, gesturing to your new friend.

Jake spat out a pip. "Crazy fucker's talking to himself now."

Marty frowned. "You feeling okay, Rawiri? I thought you were going to grab some kip."

"Can't sleep now," you said. "Too busy."

Using his finger, Jake drew a circle in the air near his head. "Come on, Marty. Let's leave him." Marty glanced back over his shoulder as they moved off, heading for the stinking mattresses.

"There are more bones over here," Henry urged.

Yes, already the bones were singing in your head. You turned away, following Henry to the spot where you would carry on digging.

You woke in the public hospital with a vague memory of collapsing. The crowd of concerned cyclists had gone, replaced by a circle of heavy curtains in dull purple. Your wrist ached.

A guy in a white coat stepped into view. "You were severely dehydrated," he said. He slid the needle out of your wrist and taped the wound. Then he pulled up a chair and sat down. "Your blood work came in, Mr. Manawa. It shows you're dangerously anemic and you've picked up a parasite." He cleared his throat. "This is consistent with your living on the street."

You clucked your tongue. "Okay."

He leaned forward, steepling his hands, his elbows resting on his knees. "Sir, the tests reveal that you also have bone cancer. Osteosarcoma."

The noise roared in your head; so loud you could barely hear him. You let your eyes slide away, focusing dully on the purple fabric as you rolled the word around your mouth. *Osteosarcoma.* In a strange way, it made sense, as if you already knew it deep down in your bones.

"I expect you'll have a lot of questions," the man said. He was far too young to be a proper doctor. "There are things we can do. Perhaps you'd like some whānau with you, so we can go through some treatment options?"

"All my family are up north."

The doctor sucked air over his teeth. "We have some excellent care facilities here in Auckland. You're going to need some imaging, a PET scan . . . "

"I'm from the north," you said. "I'm on my way there now. I just have to do something first . . . "

The doctor nodded. He handed you a script, a card stapled to the top. "We can't keep you without consent. I've written you a prescription in the meantime, and that's my card, attached. When you get home, please get in touch and we'll transfer the results to your doctor."

You turned the documents over in your palm then stuffed the lot in your pocket and swung your legs over the side of the bed.

The doctor got to his feet. "Mr. Manawa. Please. Don't leave it too long."

A bit later, your leg throbbing, you snuck in the back doors of the bus. The driver waggled his eyebrows, letting you know he was on to you, but he didn't stop. You got off on Symonds Street. Gave him a wave. You longed to head down to the Britomart hub, to catch a train or a bus north like you'd said you would, instead you trudged up the hill. The tsunami of sound pummelled you even before you stepped through the cemetery gates.

"Where have you been? You promised to help us!"

"I'm so tired. When can we go to the island?"

"My cousin. He's over here. Please . . . "

Marie tugged at your trousers. "I thought you'd left me."

Your shoulders drooped. You couldn't go north yet. Not yet. There were too many of them still to rescue. Crouching, you set to work.

After that, you didn't attempt to sleep, not that you could anyway. Not with the clamor still roaring in your skull. Instead, you hunted the park for more bony remains, searching every nook and cranny, bashing at concrete and upturning brickwork. A bizarre vampire, you slurped up the night soil.

And with every bone you consumed, every tiny relic, the dreadful noise softened.

You're not sure how much time had passed, only that you'd released hundreds of desperate souls, so many the noise in your head had dulled to a persistent hum, like the drone of a mosquito or the overloud tick of a clock, and you knew the hour was close.

Soon, you would lead them all north. Soon. There was just this last little bone . . .

It was crammed under the bridge, way back in a piece of concrete pipe.

You'd grown so thin—three more holes poked in the leather belt—it was easy enough to squeeze your frame into the pipe.

The bone sang to you as you advanced. Deeper and deeper you crawled.

Nearly there.

It was so close, just ahead—you reached out with ragged bleeding fingers, pinching through the dirt.

Another centimeter . . .

At last, you seized it: a crumbling black tooth, barely bigger than your fingernail. There was no space to bend your arm, so you let it go and shucked off your shoes, wiggling your toes to inch forward like a worm. Sweat stung your eyes. You craned your neck, puckered your cracked lips, and scooped it up.

Yes! With no saliva to speak of, you gulped it whole. Like a firecracker, it scraped and burned your oesophagus. Your stomach roiled. You would've doubled over if the pipe had allowed it.

Wait.

Quivering in pain, you listened.

the bone eater

The screaming had stopped, leaving only the quiet whirr of the traffic on the bridge. A couple of drunken students shouted in the distance.

The screeching was gone.

Flooded with relief, you breathed out.

The search was over, although you'd never found Marie's mother. It seemed likely that she'd been ground to dust, with no bone large enough to sing to you. No bone for you to absorb, to carry with you on the journey north . . .

All at once, you realized your arms were pinned.

Your heart thundered despite the lack of space. No one knew where you were, not even Marty or Jake. And you were too far in, too out of sight, for the police to find you.

You would die here, never mind your promise.

No, no, no. How could you lead these people north to the jumping off place if you were stuck in this stupid pipe? You were the only one who could *see* them. What would happen to Angus and Henry? To Marie? They'd be prisoners here.

You had to get out. You *had* to. You tried to shout, but your breath was too shallow, your voice barely a whisper. You wiggled and squirmed. An hour dragged by, and another. It wasn't until the morepork owl hooted somewhere in the cemetery, its song full of mourning, that you finally understood.

Cold crept up your spine.

You would lead them north.

You just had to die first.

LEE MURRAY

It was sunset when you reached Spirits Bay. Your great-uncle, long dead, was waiting for you beside the craggy pōhutukawa. You embraced, the two of you sharing your death-breath in a tender hongi.

The old man clapped a withered hand on your shoulder. "So skinny."

"You knew, and you waited here for me. Postponed your own voyage to Hawaiki."

"Was it hard? At the end?"

Your lip trembled as you recalled the pain: the four long days it had taken you to die.

"You did the right thing," your mātua said softly.

"Did I? Will they be welcomed?"

Great Uncle smiled. "Of course. These lost souls needed some place to call home. You opened your heart and offered ours."

Home. You'd been gone so long. It would be nice to rest a minute. But the ghosts you'd led here had already been waiting years for a place to rest, some as long as a century. They were impatient to get on their way.

Crinkles formed at the corners of Great Uncle's eyes. "I can take them from here," he said, resting a bony hand on your arm.

As darkness shrouded the peninsula, you farewelled them, waved as those displaced souls plunged into the ocean on their journey to where they might rest their bones forever.

Marie slipped her fingers into yours. "I can't swim," she said.

"Then we'll go together."

"Now?"

"Not yet. Let's wait until morning."

She rushed away to play in the pingāo grass while

the bone eater

you sat cross-legged on the bluff, looking north to the horizon, the bones no longer singing in your head.

Instead, you listened to the calls of the gulls and the gentle break of the surf.

a feather for mrs. edmond

DAVID DEMCHUK

he day **1** met her, I was sitting at the back of St. Andrews as I did every Saturday afternoon, on the aisle in the rearmost pew. This was my office, where people came to find solace, and possibly a glimmer of hope, after a loved one had died. I sat in the shadows and watched elderly Father Mulgrew as he scuttled around at the front of the cavernous church, and I waited, and I smoked. There was an issue with the hymnals apparently, he had received some new ones that didn't match the old ones, and he was flapping and fluttering like a big black crow.

From where I sat, I could hear a newsboy shouting about the arrival of the city's first talking picture, at the Tivoli, some travesty called *The Terror*. Really, the actors in those things were dreadful enough—who needed to hear them speak? I drew deeply on my cigarette, held the smoke in for a moment, then tilted my head back and released a long bluish plume up into the rafters. Mulgrew jerked his head and scowled at me, then turned his disapproving face back to his stacks of books. He muttered to himself—something nasty about me I'm sure. He may have been appalled by my presence, but he did love my money.

The heavy oak door behind me swung open with a squeal; a tall, thin, nervous woman hurried down the aisle, late thirties, owlish glasses, tweed coat, black silk scarf pulled tight over her hair, handsome in her grief. Mulgrew caught the movement out of the corner of his eye, pulled the woman off to the side. I watched them confer, exhaled another stream of smoke, then dropped the butt to the floor and ground it under my shoe. He guided the woman by the shoulder back to the aisle, gestured in my direction. She peered into the darkness. I held up my hand, encased in a white silk glove. She could see me now. As she approached, I could see the tears shining on her cheeks. Time to get to work.

"Hello. I'm Ruth Edmond. Are you the woman with the boy?" she asked.

"My sister's son," I replied. "She died last year, along with my mother. I'm all he has left in the world." I extended my hand to her. "Helen Bradford."

She took my hand, clasped it lightly, released it. "I lost my husband and son, just three months ago." She turned away slightly.

"I'm so sorry," I said. "It is a terrible hardship."

She looked back up at me, hesitant, maybe fearful. "Is it true, what Father Mulgrew says? Can your nephew really help me?"

"I'm sure he can." In a different world, I would have taken her hand in mine, lent her my shoulder to cry on, perhaps even something lower than my shoulder. "He has helped many people over the years," I added. "I'd say it's his calling."

a feather for mrs. edmond

"It must be wonderful, having him with you, being able to communicate with your mother and sister on the other side."

I opened my purse, pulled out an address card and a pen. "That has never happened, sadly. He has tried, of course, many times, but . . . it seems we are destined to help others in ways we cannot help ourselves." I turned the card over and began to write. "Well then, Mrs. Edmond. Are you free tomorrow? We can see you at one." I jotted down the details of our appointment, plus the required fee, then handed the card to her. Her eyes widened when she saw the figure, but she did not return it. Instead, she tucked it into the inside pocket of her coat. There was something else mixed with her grief. Guilt, perhaps, or shame.

"Thank you, Mrs. Bradford."

"Miss," I corrected. "Or you can call me Helen." I closed my purse and stood up from the pew. "My nephew's name is Rodney."

"Thank you, Miss Bradford. Helen." I saw that Mulgrew was approaching, with a particularly sour look on his face. It was time for me to go.

"My condolences, Mrs. Edmond," I said, as I stepped out into the aisle. "I'm certain that Rodney will be able to provide some consolation." I fastened my coat collar, drew down the thin web of veil over my face. "Be sure to bring cash when you visit. And please, don't be late. The spirits don't like to be kept waiting." I took a few bills from my coat pocket, pressed them into Mulgrew's waiting hand. "Good afternoon," I said to them both, then walked up to the heavy church door and out into the sharp winter sunshine.

The following morning I was with Rodney at the dining table. I had forgotten that it was his birthday, turning 12, and he was quite annoyed with me. I had hurried round the corner to the bakery and brought back a custard slice that he now demolished sullenly with his fork. Little specks of pastry were scattered everywhere. I was reminded once again that adolescence and all its trials would soon be upon us. "I'm sorry that I am asking you to work today. It won't be for too long, I promise." Taking care not to ladder my new silk stockings, I crouched down beside him and tried to encourage him to bring us a suitable contact for the afternoon's session.

"Remember," I said, pushing a wayward brown curl off his forehead, "the happier we make Mrs. Edmond, the more likely she'll return. That's how we pay for all the things we enjoy." Rodney nodded, peeling away the hard white icing that coated the cherry almond pastry. "Do you think that Angela might visit us today? She always has kind things to say." Rodney shook his head. No Angela today. "Oh, that's a shame. What about Little Kevin? He's such a sweet, gentle boy, he brings such pleasant news of the other side."

Rodney shook his head. No Little Kevin. I watched as he lifted up the top layer of pastry smeared with fruity jam and stuffed it into his mouth. The crisp flakes crunched between his teeth and coated his upper lip. He was still of an age when he was in constant need of a brushing-off and a wiping-down.

a feather for mrs. edmond

I smiled. "Well, who do you think will join us today, Rodney? Someone bright and charming I hope."

"Eddie," Rodney answered through the thick beige mush now gumming up his mouth.

It was difficult for me to disguise my reaction. Eddie had been one of Rodney's earliest contacts, a boy who had passed from typhoid fever right as he turned 15. I remembered my sister Carole mentioning him when Rodney's talents first emerged, and how troubled she was by his presence. Of course, everything troubled Carole back then. But still: sly and boisterous and full of mischief, he was a peculiar companion for a five-year-old child. After a while he drifted away as other, younger spirits found Rodney's light. But now he was back, his return seeming to coincide with the accident that took my sister and mother from us. I had to admit that Eddie was invaluable in helping Rodney through his grief. But he had a dark, unpredictable edge whenever he appeared at the spirit table. "Oh, Rodney," I said cautiously, "it's not that I don't like Eddie. But—I think Mrs. Edmond needs someone gentler, more sensitive to her situation. Are you sure Angela isn't nearby?"

Rodney shook his head, swallowed, then rasped: "Eddie." He gulped from his glass of milk, then lifted the next layer, launched it into his mouth, and began chewing noisily.

"I know who we haven't heard from for a long time," I offered. "Little Peggy!" Peggy was a six-year-old who had been struck by a horse and carriage some decades ago. She had a limited understanding of the modern world, but she was lively and endearing and a welcome addition to the spirit circle.

Rodney kept chewing. Either he wasn't paying attention, or he was choosing not to listen.

I drew a deep breath and stood up from the table. Time to get ready. I stepped into the vestibule between the kitchen and dining room—a tiny butler's pantry— and unlocked and opened the tall mahogany cabinet. I took down the green glass bowl from the second shelf, and in it placed the small brass bell that Angela used to signal her presence, Little Kevin's tarnished tin whistle, and, from the back, Peggy's blackbird feather, its rich lustrous darkness deepening along the length of its vane, all items that Rodney had chosen over the years as conduits for their individual spirits. I made a point of leaving Eddie's tiger's eye marble on its little nest of black velvet.

"Rodney, please go wash your face and change your clothes," I called back towards the dining room. "And could you cast your mind about for Peggy? She really is a comfort, and that's why people come to us." I heard the chair legs drag away from the table, the tap-tap of his footsteps into the hall. "Your jacket and tie are on your bed." Feet clomping up the steps. Had he heard me? He did seem to feel I was ruining his day. I would try to think of a way to make up for it later. I reached up to the top shelf and brought down the carefully folded grey satin cloth, its flashes of gold peeking out to tease the eye. There was an element of the theatrical to this business. I placed the cloth over the other items in the bowl, took them in my hands, and locked the cabinet doors.

I returned to the dining room, pushed his chair in, set the bowl with the satin cloth on the sideboard, then gathered up the lunch plates and tablecloth and carried them into the kitchen. This past year had obviously been difficult for him, and here it was, his birthday, with no father and now no mother here to see him grow. Of course he was upset. He had doted on his mother as if she was the most beautiful woman in the world, even as she grew more uncomfortable with him and his talents. He had been terrified of her rejection, of losing her, and how sad it was that those fears came true in such a horrible way.

Carole had been three years younger than me and had squandered her looks and figure on a series of shiftless young men. Rodney's father was supposed to have been some slick-talking horn player she spied at a club where his band had played. They only spent a few hours together, but that was all it took for Carole to end up pregnant and abandoned, living in our mother's basement until Rodney was born, and then several years after. Mother quickly noticed that Rodney could see things no one else could; he would chatter excitedly with playmates that were more than just imaginary. As he grew older, he recited names and birthdates of these invisible friends, the cities and neighbourhoods and streets where they had lived, and sometimes how and where they had died. Eddie had been among them, as had Angela, and a clever little boy named Jerome who had long since vanished.

At first, Carole nervously dismissed her son's chatterings as childhood nonsense. Our mother, however, saw in Rodney an opportunity to provide people in distress some solace—and make a few dollars in the bargain. She began to visit strangers' funerals, to sit at the backs of churches, to present herself as someone who could help a grieving wife or mother say a few last words to someone they'd lost. Many of them would never have considered visiting a medium, but were intrigued when they learned they'd be communicating not through some bespectacled table-tipping matron, but through her innocent grandson. Those first few years had been highly lucrative, with Rodney's spectral contacts providing words of consolation to numerous grieving women. My sister, however, was insecure and ill-suited to the rigors of parenthood, and grew increasingly frightened by her son and his talents. She was convinced that the boy's father had cursed her somehow. She became paranoid, volatile, sometimes violent—drinking, sleeping, smoking, seething. More than once she had lashed out at the boy, thrown things, accused him of being a monster, a devil, while our mother protected him, taking the brunt of my sister's blows. I stayed well away. I felt badly for Rodney, but past interactions with my sister and our mother had taught me to avoid getting involved.

Then there was the night when I woke to a thunderous banging at my front door. The police. Rodney was in a hospital downtown. Carole and our mother were dead. As the officer described it, the three of them had been in a terrible automobile accident on one of the city's major streets. Mother had taken Carole and Rodney out for dinner to a restaurant that hoped to host informal psychic readings during their Sunday tea service. Carole was furious at the suggestion and cut their meal short. On the drive home, the two women were in the front seats of Mother's year-old Buick Roadster, arguing loudly, while Rodney sat curled up in the rumble seat, drifting

a feather for mrs. edmond

in and out of sleep. He awoke to see them shrieking and flailing, as if something was loose inside the car with them. Carole apparently lost control—the car rolled across the sidewalk and into the plate glass window of a haberdashery. Rodney was thrown from the back of the Roadster onto the pavement, bruised and scraped and sobbing but otherwise uninjured. Mother and Carole, however, were killed instantly, their faces and bodies slashed, their necks broken in mid-scream. Poor things. Rodney was resting in the children's ward, in an apparent state of shock. The officer advised that if I was not in a position to take responsibility for him, he would be consigned to an orphanage, and then put up for adoption.

I didn't even think for a moment, of course I said yes, I would take the boy in and raise him as my own. Rodney and I barely knew each other but he was family, after all, and now an orphan. I would receive the house, and my mother's modest estate. I was sure that we would ease out of our mutual grief and into a fond and faithful guardianship. Besides, I knew that Carole was foolish to be frightened of her son's gifts, and inattentive to their potential rewards. I would not make the same mistake.

I heard Rodney's voice from upstairs, a murmur at first and then louder, sharper—then something that sounded like a slap. A sudden thud above my head made me jump. "Are you all right?" Silence. "What's going on up there?"

Another ringing silence, and then: "I was putting my pants on and I slipped."

Slipped. I stared at the spot above me. The boy could be clumsy sometimes. Growing pains, I hoped.

"Be careful," I called into the hallway. "And don't get those pants dirty." I stepped back into the dining room, took the satin cloth from the bowl, and spread it out onto Mother's rosewood table. The embroidered letters and numbers formed a variation of the talking boards that had been popular since I was a child. It was more decorative than functional. Rodney's clients came in with certain fanciful expectations. I emptied the bowl, placed it in the center, and set the various items around it. Just as I placed the silver bell onto the words "Good Bye" at the bottom edge of the cloth, the doorbell rang and then, seconds later, a series of sharp knocks rattled the front door. *Oh for Pete's sake.* It had to be Mrs. Edmond. Rodney hadn't even come downstairs from dressing. I cast my eyes around the table, then gave the parlour one last look as I headed into the hallway where I was greeted with another burst of ringing and knocking. I pulled the door open abruptly, catching Mrs. Edmond with her knuckles hanging in the air. She nearly jumped back off the porch and down the icy front steps. *Good.*

"Mrs. Edmond," I said crisply. "Is it one already? I was *certain* we had a few more minutes before our meeting."

The poor woman was blushing so fiercely that I could feel the heat from where I stood. "I'm sorry I'm so early, I walked around the block twice and then stopped at the corner shop, and even now I've arrived much too soon. Does your nephew like toffees? I brought a few for him, if he is allowed to have them." I could see she had one lodged in the corner of her mouth.

"Please come in," I said, holding the door open.

a feather for mrs. edmond

The woman was positively tremulous. "Rodney's not quite ready but he'll be down shortly. Come join me in the parlor." Mrs. Edmond handed me the small paper bag and I peered into it. Half a dozen cream toffees, in an assortment of colourful wax paper wrappings. "So thoughtful of you," I told her, handing it back. "I'm sure a sweet or two wouldn't hurt. You can give them to him after our little session. It is rather arduous, making contact with the other realm. He'll be exhausted for hours."

"Oh my, I had no idea," Mrs. Edmond replied, pocketing the bag and frowning as she stepped into the next room. "My, how cozy." I forced an agreeable smile onto my face. Much like the rest of the house, the parlor was worn and tired, in dire need of refreshing: the sage-green wallpaper now muddy and dull, the walnut mantle with its carved medallions sticky with old French polish, and the once-pretty beaded chandelier forever clouded with a halo of dust. It was like being wrapped in an old, mouldering mitten. Though I never regretted my decision to take my nephew in, I did wish that I could travel, see the world, live my life freely. But it was not meant to be. Whatever money we made would bind us tighter to each other, at least till he was grown.

Mrs. Edmond perched herself on Mother's favourite chair, cream damask with a tufted back, closest to the small round table with the silver-framed photos of her and Carole and Rodney. None of me, of course. "Rodney simply loves interacting with the spirit world," I assured her, "and of course helping people with whatever insights he's able to glean. It's just that, well, he is very young and—oh, here he comes."

95

Mrs. Edmond leaned forward to see Rodney making his way down the stairs in his smart brown blazer, red clip-on bow tie, corduroy pants, and Buster Browns. "My, what a sharp young gentleman!" Mrs. Edmond exclaimed.

"Rodney," I called. "Come say hello to Mrs. Edmond."

Rodney hopped down off the second last step, then turned and walked into the parlor and held out his hand. "How do you do?"

Mrs. Edmond took his hand and shook it. "I'm very well, thank you, Rodney. And thank you very much for seeing me this afternoon. I'm—wondering if we could . . . begin? If you're not ready for me, I can wait right here—"

Rodney turned to look at me. I forced a tight smile and nodded. "Please, right this way." I stepped aside and drew the heavy red velvet curtain that led to the dining room. Rodney held it open for Mrs. Edmond while I took a wooden match from a small silver tray on the sideboard, struck a flame from it, and lit the large maroon pillar candle that Mother had ordered years ago from the De Laurence company in Chicago. The odor of sulfur and woodsmoke briefly filled the air, quickly replaced with the fine fragrance of sandalwood, frankincense, and myrrh. Encouragements to the spirits. Mrs. Edmond paused over the array of objects on the table's surface before Rodney pulled out her chair for her. She seated herself as Rodney took his place at her left, and I at her right with the candlelight flickering behind my shoulder.

I saw Rodney cast his eyes across the table's surface, frown, then with narrowed eyes start to ask, "Aunt Helen, where is—"

a feather for mrs. edmond

"Rodney," I replied, perhaps too sharply. I made an effort to soften my tone. "I trust we have everything we need. Now, who will be joining us today?"

Rodney glared at me from across the table, then glanced back down at the embroidered green satin, the bowl, the various objects. His eyes landed on the feather. "Peggy," he whispered.

"Oh, excellent!" I said, relieved. I turned to Mrs. Edmond. "Peggy is a sweet young thing, plucked from this earth at a most innocent age. Rodney, has Peggy entered our circle?"

Rodney closed his eyes, pressed his palms to the cool green satin cloth. "Peggy, are you with us?" he asked. A moment passed. He furrowed his brow, bowed his neck slightly. "Yes," he said quietly. "She's here."

A light breeze seemed to whirl towards the table's center, and at that moment the blackbird feather stirred, lifted itself, stood upright on the table's surface in front of Mrs. Edmond. She gasped and pulled back. I reached over and patted her hand.

"Please, don't break the circle. It's only Peggy, come to say hello." I moved her hand towards the quivering feather. "Now, take it and place it in the glass bowl. No need to be frightened. This will establish contact."

Nervously, Mrs. Edmond grasped the feather between her finger and thumb like some alarming insect, and dropped it into the bowl. It lay there for a moment, then once again shivered and rustled and righted itself. It spun at the bottom of the bowl like a tiny ballerina, and then paused in front of Mrs. Edmond as if it were looking at her intently.

"Peggy welcomes you," Rodney began. "She tells me you had a husband, and a child. A boy, not much older than her."

Mrs. Edmond's face crumpled in sorrow. "Warren was my husband, and our son was Theo." She took a handkerchief from her clutch and wiped at her eyes. "They both died just over a year ago. We all fell ill, but the two of them . . . "

The feather danced once more in a tight little circle. "They are here with us now," Rodney stated, in an oddly icy tone. "Peggy has brought them to us. They are together, and smiling, and watching us. Just outside the circle."

"Are they? Oh my! Can we speak to them?" Mrs. Edmond asked. "Can you tell us what they say?"

"They can speak through Peggy," I explained, "and then from Peggy to Rodney." Just then I heard one tap, and then another, like tiny stones tossed against a window. How odd. Where had that come from?

"Please, tell them how much I miss them," Mrs. Edmond said, clutching the handkerchief in her fist. "Tell them how sorry I am."

The blackbird feather twirled. "They miss you too. Peggy tells me it was your husband's birthday, you cooked a special dinner: a Waldorf salad with chicken and apples and almonds, and a potato and celery soup. But something went wrong."

Once again, Mrs. Edmond was overcome with tears. "The almonds," she cried, "the grocer sold me the wrong almonds. They were bitter, not sweet, they were meant to be used for poisoning rats. I had no idea, not until the end of our meal. First Theo collapsed, and then Warren. I felt dizzy, my heart was racing, I ran to the telephone and told the operator we needed a doctor, and then I fell to the ground, gasping for breath. The ambulance came—but it was already too late for them. I was rushed to the hospital, and they were taken to the morgue."

Once again I heard that insistent brittle tapping sound. I looked around the corner towards the kitchen. The pipes, the radiators? I turned back to the table and saw that the feather was lazily turning at the bottom of the bowl like the spinner in a children's game.

"Peggy wants to know how it is that they died," Rodney stated pointedly, "and you did not."

Mrs. Edmond looked quite disconcerted by the question. "I, well, that is, surely they know the answer to this. They didn't care for the soup, though it was perfectly lovely, so I had a second helping while they ate the salad. I tasted it of course, but—"

"You knew they wouldn't like the soup."

"Well, I *hoped* that they would," Mrs. Edmond replied. "What a strange thing to say."

"Rodney," I cautioned. The conversation was starting to worry me.

"Peggy wants to know about the cake," Rodney said flatly. The feather stopped spinning. Mrs. Edmond recoiled slightly. It was pointed directly at her.

"I don't know what you're talking about," she replied, flustered. "There was no cake."

"Why not?" Rodney said. "It was your husband's birthday. You were having a special meal. You often baked cakes for your family. So, what Peggy would like to know is—when did you decide that you wouldn't need to bake a cake for your husband's birthday?"

The room grew still. I heard another tap-tap from

behind me, and then a soft aching creak. Something fell to the floor, and then quietly rolled into the dining room, puttering over the parquet tiles. It came to a stop underneath Rodney's chair. I didn't even try to look, I already knew. It was the tiger's eye marble.

The spirit in the room with us—it wasn't Peggy.

Mrs. Edmond stood up, shoving the chair back from behind her legs. "I don't know what you are trying to insinuate. I've a mind to speak to the police about this little business of yours, and about your thinly veiled accusations."

"Mrs. Edmond," I said, reaching for her, the knot in my stomach pulling tighter.

"No, thank you, I have heard enough," Mrs. Edmond said sharply, and the feather sprang up from the bottom of the glass bowl and shot like a dart into the corner of her left eye, in beside the bridge of her nose and winnowed and burrowed into it ferociously. I screamed and jumped back against the sideboard, singeing my hair on the red candle's flame. Rodney watched, fascinated, as Mrs. Edmond threw her head back, jerked it one way, then the other, as the feather squeezed and squirmed and pushed itself in behind her eye until it vanished through the rear of the socket. She stood clutching the chair, her eyes rolling upward, her throat forcing out stifled squeaks and choking gasps like a chicken being held down against the chopping block. I could feel my lunch rising into my throat.

Rodney calmly stood up from the table, walked around to the woman's clutch, picked it up and opened it. "Rodney! What are you doing?" I demanded. He held a quieting finger to his lips, then reached into it, pulled out a pressed tin money clip stuffed with tens

a feather for mrs. edmond

and twenties. He removed the cash and returned one folded ten back into the black satin folds of the purse. He turned to look up at Mrs. Edmond for a moment, then reached into her coat pocket, pulled out the bag of toffees and inserted the clutch purse in its place.

Mrs. Edmond lowered her head and locked her gaze upon me. Her eyes were wide with terror. Her mouth dropped open, and a trickle of drool slid down from one corner. Her jaw rocked and shook, and then snapped shut again.

"Aunt Helen," Rodney announced. "Could you please see Mrs. Edmond out?" As if on command, the quivering woman turned on her heel and tottered out of the dining room through the parlor and out into the hallway, dragged about like a broken marionette. I hurried after her, then fluttered around her, afraid to touch her. She scratched helplessly at the door and I opened it. She stuttered out across the porch and down the steps, one-two-three, and onto the sidewalk—then farther, over the boulevard, and out into the street.

"Oh my God, no," I whispered—then shouted, "Mrs. Edmond!"

Mrs. Edmond jerked her head round at the sound of my voice. Her eyes were blind with blood. A horn guffawed, tires screeched, and a shiny black Dodge coupe drove at top speed into the woman, crushing her head under the far front wheel, splashing the slush-covered asphalt with crimson and flecks of white and pink. Instantly the street was filled with screams and alarms and shouts for police.

I stood in the doorway and stared at the spectacle, scarcely able to breathe. "Aunt Helen," Rodney said. "Don't be upset. Her family is very excited to see her."

He reached into the bag of toffees, unwrapped one, and popped it into his mouth. Then calmly closed up the bag and headed toward the stairs. He stopped, knelt down, and picked up the tiger's eye marble which had rolled out to greet him. "Oh, Eddie is coming to live with us. He wants to make us lots of money. He says you're right fit for an old bird, he'd like to come see you one night and tickle you with a feather too."

"That's disgusting," I said, trembling. "I ought to slap you for that."

Rodney smiled. "I wouldn't do that, Aunt Helen. Eddie's keeping a close eye on things, now that we're going to be family." He placed the marble in his pocket and began his ascent up the stairs, the legs of his corduroy pants scuffing against each other as he climbed.

meeting katie king

LISA MORTON

1.

March 4, 1874

As the carriage pulled up before the house at 15 Stanley Street, Brompton, Thomas McKenzie looked out the window and muttered, "Here we are, and not a spirit to be seen."

His fellow passenger, Annie Spencer, tapped his arm playfully. "Not *yet*, you mean. I warrant you'll see some soon enough."

Thomas smiled and shook his head, but didn't respond. He knew that Annie was a confirmed Spiritualist, and he had promised himself that he wouldn't mock or challenge her. After all, it was due to her good graces that he was here tonight, at the home (and principal workplace) of the esteemed scientist William Crookes, about to watch the great man's pet medium Florence Cook in action. The teenage Cook and her spiritual skills were the talk of London society; Thomas guessed that getting an audience with the

Queen would have been slightly easier than securing a seat at one of Florence Cook's séances. But Annie had used her connections with James Burns, who ran the popular Progressive Library and Spiritual Institution, to garner them both invites.

Annie's companion for the evening was listed as "Tom Kent, visiting from Liverpool"; it wouldn't do to have them connect him with the Thomas McKenzie who had skewered Spiritualism before in the pages of the weekly magazine *All the Year Round* and who fully intended to skewer it again tonight.

"Come, Mr. McKenzie," Annie said, as she opened her carriage door and leapt out, not waiting on Thomas to be gentlemanly, "we don't want to be late!"

Her excitement made Thomas grin, even if he didn't share it. Truth be told, *many* things about Annie Spencer made him grin; since she'd begun working for *All the Year Round* three months ago, the publication's offices had seemed far less dingy and uncomfortable. She was vivacious, attractive without being strictly beautiful, and Thomas had recently spent far too much time mulling over visions of her light brown hair and large grey eyes.

He reminded himself, as he offered his arm, that tonight was a work night; he was here to write about Florence Cook, not succumb to the obvious and plentiful charms of Annie Spencer.

They reached the door, rang the bell, and were admitted by a servant who led them to a spacious, well-appointed sitting room already occupied by nearly a dozen people. Thomas recognized the bearded, imposing, forty-one-year-old Crookes, holding court before the hearth; when a man with kind eyes and possibly the fullest beard Thomas had ever seen approached Annie, he guessed that was James Burns.

"Annie," Burns gushed, barely noticing Thomas, "I'm so happy you're here. Have you met Mr. Crookes?"

"Not yet. Mr. Burns, this is my friend Thomas Kent. He's a distant cousin visiting from Liverpool."

Burns turned from Annie to Thomas, his enthusiasm dropping considerably although he politely extended a hand. "A pleasure, Mr. Kent. Are you a Spiritualist, sir?"

"I've only recently become interested in the belief, Mr. Burns."

It was a good answer, because Burns smiled at him in a congenial manner. "After tonight, Mr. Burns, I've no doubt you'll be a full convert."

Burns led them over to Crookes, and Thomas couldn't help but notice the appraising look the eminent scientist cast upon Annie. He'd heard the rumors about Crookes and young Miss Cook—that Crookes had more than a merely scientific interest in Florence, despite their age difference and Crookes' standing as a married man and father of six (whose wife was even now pregnant)—and after seeing Crookes' obvious interest in Annie, he gave more credence to such whisperings.

Annie knew several of the others in attendance and introduced them; she assured Thomas they were all well-known in Spiritualist circles, but he was unacquainted with the names. He was far more interested in seeing Florence Cook, the evening's star performer, but she didn't seem to be present.

A handsome, ginger-haired man who couldn't have been out of his teens struck up a conversation with Thomas as Annie chatted with friends; Annie had introduced him as Frank Podmore, and assured Thomas that they'd have much to talk about because Mr. Podmore, who was a student at Oxford, was also new to Spiritualism. "Have you attended many séances, Mr. Kent?" he asked.

"A few. Last year I was lucky enough to have a sitting with D. D. Home."

Podmore's jaw dropped. "Indeed? How fortunate. That's an opportunity I've yet to gain myself. It was an impressive event, I trust?"

"Oh, to say the least." Thomas had actually written a scathing satire of Home for *All the Year Round*. He'd found Home, often touted as the greatest medium of all time, to be little more than an overly-theatrical charlatan with gifted toes, which he used in secret beneath the séance table. "It was . . . " Thomas searched for the right words, " . . . a most intriguing spectacle."

Podmore peered at Thomas for a moment, and Thomas realized this man's mind was disciplined enough to catch an unbeliever. "Ahh," Podmore said, then added, "Well, I daresay you may find something altogether different in Miss Cook's mediumship."

"Have you witnessed it before?"

Podmore nodded. "I have, and it was most extraordinary. That night, her spirit guide Katie King treated us to a shower of glowing orbs. It was the most astonishing thing I've ever seen."

"Well," Thomas answered, "I hope for a similar display, then."

meeting katie king

Podmore was called to another conversation, and Annie murmured to Thomas, "Are you starting to be just a little intrigued?"

Thomas was saved from responding when Crookes called them to order and led the way out of the sitting room to the dining room. As befitted a man of Crookes's wealth and standing, the room was large and extravagant, the walls papered in red brocade, the long mahogany table easily seating all twelve of them, display cabinets holding elegant bone china placed along the walls. Thomas, who was seated near the middle of the table, noticed that the room had three doorways: the one they'd entered through, one leading to the kitchen, and a third that was curtained off in a makeshift way. Crookes stood near the head of the table, but the ultimate seat was left vacant.

After they were all seated, Crookes addressed them. "Ladies and gentlemen, please permit me to introduce our medium for this evening, Miss Florence Cook."

The woman who appeared through the hastily-erected curtain and moved to the head of the table was just as charismatic as what Thomas had heard. At eighteen, Florence Cook was small, with alabaster skin and long curling dark hair, unconventionally pretty with chin and nose that were slightly too pointed, dressed in a black brocade dress; she possessed an intense gaze that she turned on each guest. "Good evening, dear friends," she said simply, still standing.

A few of the others offered hushed responses. Thomas saw their shining gazes turned on the medium and knew they were in awe of this teenage girl.

Crookes stood beside her, almost paternally. "In

case any of you aren't familiar with Miss Cook's method of calling the spirits, permit me to explain: we will begin the evening with the usual singing, at which point Miss Cook will enter into this area . . . " He gestured to the curtained-off room, " . . . a small parlor that will serve as her spirit cabinet tonight. While in the spirit cabinet, Miss Cook will enter a trance state and will call on her spirit guide Katie King. If all is in alignment, the spirit will materialize for us and walk among us as we remain seated. At that point we may ask Katie King questions, and the spirit may even *touch* you, but don't be alarmed.

"The one thing that you must all agree to is that at *no point* is Miss Cook to be disturbed; to suddenly break her trance state could lead to the medium's death.

"If there are no further questions, please clasp hands to form a circle and we'll begin."

Thomas had to stifle a laugh. *Oh, I have many questions, beginning with: how can thinking adults allow themselves to believe this gibberish?* But when he felt Annie's hand in his, other thoughts fled.

A servant moved quietly around the room, turning the gaslights down until nothing was visible but dim shapes. From the darkness at the end of the table, Florence said, "If you'll now proceed with the singing, I will adjourn to the spirit cabinet."

As Crookes led the sitters into "Blessed Assurance," Thomas barely made out Florence rising and stepping behind the curtain.

Beside him, Annie sang loudly, her voice a pleasant soprano. Thomas mumbled the lyrics because he'd always been embarrassed by his singing voice, but he found himself pulled into the energy of those around him; they swayed in their seats as they sang, hands joined. The whole gathering felt more like an enthusiastic church event than an attempt to contact spirits.

By the time they were halfway through "I Stood Outside the Gate," he became aware of a new sound: jingling, somewhere above him. One of the sitters broke off singing to gasp out, "Look!" Turning his head, Thomas just made out a tambourine floating near the ceiling, a few feet from the spirit cabinet, tinkling as it leapt in space. Beside him, Annie inhaled sharply; Thomas, however, knew of the telescoping rods that mediums used in séances to "levitate" objects. *Miss Cook will have to do better than that,* he thought.

The tambourine was joined by faintly shimmering orbs, four in total. Thomas thought of what Mr. Podmore had said earlier, wondering how a few balls of cotton dipped in phosphorescent oil and flown overhead on wires could possibly be perceived as "a shower of glowing orbs." The credulity of true believers never ceased to amaze him.

The singing had ceased altogether, and from the chorus of low mutters, a shrill, "I see a hand!" suddenly broke out. Indeed, Thomas now saw a pale hand located near what he thought was the hanging curtain. A few seats away, he heard a man utter excitedly, "That must belong to Katie King!"

A slight feminine voice sounded from the other end of the room. "I come to you from the Summerland, friends." The sitters turned as one and got their first look at the spirit, Katie King.

Thomas had to admit that both her surprise appearance at the opposite end of the room (*clever misdirection, that*) and her dress were impressive: she wore a long white gown with a headdress that wrapped around her head, leaving only her face exposed. In the darkened room the white fabric nearly glowed, giving her an appropriately ghostly effect.

The face, though . . . it was clear enough even in the dim light that it was Florence Cook's. The same eyes, nose, chin . . . how could anyone possibly believe otherwise?

"Good evening, Katie," Crookes said. "We thank you for blessing us with your presence this evening."

Katie/Florence walked forward, slowly and gracefully circling the table; even though she'd mastered the art of moving in a way that suggested supernatural gliding, Thomas made out the sound of her rustling skirt.

"There is one here tonight," the "spirit" said in sonorous tones, "who has lost someone dear to them—"

A middle-aged woman across the table from Thomas blurted out a single, half-stifled sob, drawing the attention of the strolling spirit.

"Ahh, yes," Katie said, "that would be your—"

Again, the woman cut her off: "My brother Harry!"

She's making the medium's job terribly easy, Thomas thought.

The séance continued for the next thirty minutes, with Katie/Florence guiding the sitters through questions that connected them to Mum, Da, Uncle Jack, friend Lucy, Shakespeare, and, in one case, a golden retriever named Sugar. Some of the onlookers cried, others gazed in wonder, and Thomas marveled at their gullibility, their *need* to believe that a spirit was providing messages from beyond the veil. The whole thing seemed openly preposterous—Florence Cook garbed in white, passing herself off as "Katie King," using a stage magician's tricks and a bad mind-reading act, while the sitters gobbled it all up like starving men at a Christmas feast. Even Annie, sweet Annie whom he thought about far too much, took it all in with shining eyes and mouth agape.

Katie/Florence had just finished conveying greetings to Mr. Podmore from a beloved long dead childhood playmate when she said, "There is one here, though, who does not believe . . . "

She turned to look at Thomas.

He felt a momentary jolt before telling himself that he had failed to respond to her offered communications from beyond, so it was easy to guess his skeptical nature. "The gentleman from Liverpool . . . "

Thomas almost corrected her—he was born and raised in Wembley—before remembering his cover. "Yes," he said. "It's not exactly that I don't believe, but that I remain unconvinced."

"And also not really from Liverpool," Katie said, surprising Thomas until he realized he didn't have that area's distinctive speech.

"I've only recently relocated there."

"What would it take, sir, to convince you?"

Thomas thought for a moment before answering, "To begin with, you could pull that curtain back on the spirit cabinet and show us where Florence Cook sleeps in her trance state."

William Crookes half-rose, angry. "Sir, you are impertinent—"

Katie cut him off. "It's quite all right, Mr. Crookes." Turning to Thomas, she gestured toward the curtain. "That will convince you?"

"Let's say it would open the door."

"Then come, sir, and look beyond the curtain."

Thomas blinked in surprise, then glanced around the room to see all eyes on him. Abruptly self-conscious, he said, "Very well," and rose.

The spirit stood back to allow him to pass. "Please remember that you cannot touch or otherwise disturb my medium in any way. I'm quite fond of her, you know."

"Of course."

His heart beating fast, Thomas reached the curtain, grasped one end and drew it back.

Beyond the curtain was a small parlor, containing little more than a fireplace, a few tables and chairs . . . and the body of Florence Cook, motionless on a divan.

Thomas's breath caught in surprise. The parlor was lit only by the dying fire, but it was enough for him to see that the woman on the divan wore Florence's black dress. She was face down, but Thomas recognized the mass of curling hair. He was just wondering whether the figure might have been a mannequin when it emitted a light sigh.

"Are you satisfied, good sir?"

Thomas let the curtain drop and turned to peer at Katie's face in the darkness. He stammered, "But you—you look just like her . . . "

"Of course—I draw energy from my medium to attain the form you see before you. It's only natural that this shape will bear her resemblance."

Still stunned, Thomas returned to his chair. He

paid little attention to the remainder of the séance, which ended with the spirit bidding them farewell as Crookes led them in a final song, and a few minutes later, as the lights were turned back up, Florence Cook emerged through the curtain, looking fatigued. Crookes rushed to her side to support her, and together they bid the sitters good evening so Florence, exhausted by bringing up her spirit guide, could retire for the night.

In the carriage, Annie couldn't stop talking about the wonders they'd witnessed. When Thomas failed to respond after some time, Annie said, "But surely you *must* believe now! After seeing Miss Cook in her trance state while the spirit stood nearby . . . "

Thomas was abruptly jolted by awareness. "I saw *someone* in that other room, but I never saw the face . . . there's no reason it couldn't have been some other girl dressed as Florence had been."

Annie huffed, exasperated. "Oh, you've simply decided you'll *never* believe!"

Smiling, Thomas said, "I do believe in one thing: that I'm quite famished and we should have dinner."

"Oh, Mr. Kent, it's late and I have to be at the offices early, you know. And besides—don't you have a story to write?"

Thomas tried not to let his defeat show. "Yes, I suppose I do."

They drove in silence for a time until the carriage pulled up at Annie's building. After Thomas helped her down, she paused before going in to say, "Try not to be *too* harsh in your piece about tonight, will you, Thomas?"

With that she was gone, and although she'd turned

down his dinner invite, at least she'd used his first name, leaving him with a shred of hope that carried him home on a small but buoyant cloud.

11.

March 6, 1874

Two days later, Annie looked up and grinned as she saw Thomas enter the offices of *All the Year Round,* his case clutched under one arm. "Good morning, Mr. Kent," she said, cheerfully, before nodding at the valise. "Got a story in there, have you?"

Inwardly, Thomas squirmed, knowing that the story—about a séance that took place at the house of a "crook" and was guided by one "Frederika Cooked"—was anything but a heap of glowing praise. "Yes . . . is Mr. Dickens in?"

"He is."

Thomas passed Annie's desk, made his way down a short hallway, and knocked on a door labeled "Charles Dickens Jr., Editor." "Come," sounded from inside.

As Thomas stepped into the cluttered office, already opening his case to remove the story, he couldn't help but wish again that the man behind the desk was a senior, not a junior. Although Charley had managed to keep *All the Year Round* going in the four years since his father's passing, he possessed neither the elder Dickens' fine editorial eye nor his interest in gleefully jabbing at beliefs in the supernatural. He'd taken the piece on D. D. Home only after insisting that Thomas hide true identities behind even more obfuscating layers, and as he glanced through the pages Thomas had just handed him, his brow furrowed. He turned to the conclusion before laying the sheets down with a slight sigh.

"Is it that bad?" Thomas asked.

"No, not at all. It's perfectly fine, but . . . I'm not sure our readers want one more piece that savages ghosts and those who believe in them."

"Oh. I see."

Charley tried to offer a reassuring smile. "I'll take it, Thomas. But I'd really like to see something different from you—maybe something on superstitions of another country. The readers quite like those pieces, it seems."

"I understand. I'll see what I can come up with."

Dickens wrote Thomas a cheque, but it was accepted without any real happiness.

To make matters worse, Annie turned down a second dinner offer; she was going to a Spiritualist gathering at Burns' bookstore on the night Thomas had suggested.

He left the offices of *All the Year Round* almost wishing he *could* believe.

III.

April 2, 1874

Thomas scanned through this week's issue of *All the*

Year Round until he found his piece, "A Crooked Séance." He noted without surprise that the piece had been rewritten, emphasizing the comedic elements. However, it still retained enough critical commentary of Spiritualism overall that he was more satisfied than he'd expected to be.

It was midnight when he finally set the magazine aside, finished the glass of brandy he'd been sipping, saw the fire in his small flat was dying, and decided he'd had enough of the day. He was about to head into his bedroom when he felt a small, chill draft. Turning curiously, he was shocked to see a woman standing in a dark corner near the dingy window that looked out over London's East End. He recognized her immediately, and his initial surprise turned to anger. "Miss Cook, how—what are you—?"

"I am not Florence Cook, but Katie King."

Thomas uttered a small, sad laugh. "Oh, really, Miss Cook, enough of that nonsense. No doubt you saw the article today and you've come to upbraid me, but I'm afraid I'm not interested in playing along. I don't know how you got in, but please remove yourself or I shall be forced to call for assistance."

"Yes, we know of your article. It's why I'm here."

"The door," Thomas said, pointing, "is *that* way—"

He broke off in shock as she abruptly disappeared, simply vanishing in an eye-blink.

Her voice came from behind him. "There's something I want to show you, Thomas . . . " He was turning, saw her white hand reaching up to his arm, felt something impossibly cold hit his flesh—

And he was falling, not to the floor but *through* it, into a great black void. He flailed, his mind overwhelmed, feeling as if he was pinwheeling. He struggled to right himself, and saw that he was no longer in a lightless abyss but sailing toward a pinprick of bright light, rapidly expanding as he approached it. He didn't want to go through that light—some part of him silently screamed, *No, it's not my time, no No NO* . . .

Then he was inside the light, blinded even through closed eyes, his body still plummeting, the fall endless—

A soft voice in his ear said, "Open your eyes, Thomas."

He did—and what he saw stilled his internal chaos. He (no, *they*, because Katie King was beside him, it had been her voice) now glided above a landscape of astonishing beauty: gently rolling valleys, between low hills covered in pristine woods, clear blue streams meandering through sunlit groves, fields of blossoming flowers in yellow and orange and vivid magenta, and towns that were just as beautiful, with houses that combined the best architectural styles from a hundred different places and times, placid and serene people wandering the streets, some in groups, some alone. The air was scented with a thousand pleasing aromas, the temperature ideal, the sky deep azure and cloudless.

"Is this heaven?" he asked, not even feeling ridiculous.

"We call it the Summerland," the spirit beside him answered. She took his hand (her grip was not cold, but warm and comforting) and they floated down to a sun-dappled plaza where a man waited for them. Because the man was young and robust, it took Thomas a few seconds to realize this man was his father, who had died ten years ago, withered away from consumption. Thomas felt a joy he'd never experienced wash over him as he and his father embraced while Katie waited. "Father," he said, between sobs, "I can't believe you're here. There's so much I want to ask you, to *tell* you—"

"And you will," his father said, releasing him to look at him proudly, "but not today. Now you must return."

"No!" Dismayed, Thomas turned to Katie. "We can stay for a while, can't we?"

She smiled at him, an expression so warm he felt it on his skin, and then said, "You don't belong here . . . *yet*. Now, we must return."

She gripped his hand again, and Thomas knew it would all be ripped away in seconds. He instinctively reached out for his father, who took his grasping hand long enough to say, "Do what's right, Thomas."

Then he was slingshot into darkness. His last words to Katie King, as the universe streaked by him, were, "Am I going to remember this?"

"Yes," she answered.

She was right—when he awoke in his own bed as London's grey morning light began to filter into his cold bedroom, he *did* remember.

All of it.

IV.

April 3, 1874

When Thomas entered Dickens' office a few hours later, he had a new story on Florence Cook to propose.

meeting katie king

He'd practiced the scene all morning, how he'd tell his editor that he'd made a terrible mistake with the first piece. Dickens looked up and smiled as he saw it was Thomas. "Ahh, Mr. McKenzie, I was just chatting about you with Leo at the press. He said he quite enjoyed your séance piece, especially since he has a great friend who was rooked out her life savings by a crooked medium."

Thomas felt blood rush to his face as his mind whirled through possibilities: *But the vision of Summerland . . . could she have drugged me? I was drinking brandy when she arrived . . . Mesmerism? Is she capable of that?*

"Did you want something, Thomas?"

"No. No, I . . . it's nothing."

Dickens peered at him briefly before returning to the stacks on his desk. "Yes, well, if you'll excuse me, then . . . oh, and don't forget: give me something on legends and superstitions."

"Of course, sir." Thomas wandered out of the office.

Do what's right, Thomas.

But what was right? Accepting the existence of spirits and a girl's ability to communicate with them—a notion which violated every principle Thomas had lived his life by—or believing that a teenage girl had somehow gotten access to drugs (*Crookes could have gotten her something, no doubt*), broken into his flat, and caused him to experience a guided hallucination?

"Are you quite all right, Mr. McKenzie?"

Thomas started as he realized he was standing in the front office of *All the Year Round* and Annie Spencer was addressing him. He smiled gently, abashed. "Oh, yes, just . . . " He approached her, earnestly, needing something solid and earthly to cling to.

"Annie, have dinner with me. Tonight, tomorrow—any night of your choosing."

Annie lowered her eyes. "Oh, I'm sorry, but . . . I'm seeing Mr. Burns now."

Thomas nodded and started to walk away, but Annie called him back. "Thomas—" He turned, hoping for something else, but she said, "Is there nothing that would make you believe?"

He considered a few moments, then answered with his own question. "Is there nothing that would make you cease believing?"

She gazed at him sadly. "I've made my choice and you've made yours."

Thomas nodded silently. As he left the offices and stepped onto the crowded, noisy, acrid-scented street, he felt the ground falling away from beneath him again, a black pit waiting, but this time the light was too distant to ever reach.

the mad monk of the motor city

GWENDOLYN KISTE

he ghost of Rasputin is hanging out in the tenement hallway again.

I sneak past him every morning on my way to the bus stop, my long hair in my face, a heavy bag slung over my shoulder. When I return in the evening, exhausted from my shift at the dry cleaners, I always hope he'll be gone.

Unfortunately, I'm never that lucky.

Tonight, he's standing on the top floor, his beard a tangled wilderness, his hulking body blocking my way. My hands clasped in front of me, I shuffle past, never looking right at him. It doesn't seem safe. But without glancing up, I already know he's looking at me.

His breath hot on the back of my neck, I fumble with my keys and shove open the door. Inside, the apartment's dark, the only light glowing from the old tube TV in the corner.

I flip the deadbolt behind me, pretending it's

enough to keep him away. "Something's out there," I whisper.

"Like what?" My mother's voice like gravel and steel rises from the living room.

"Like a ghost."

My mother chokes up a laugh. "Does this ghost have a name?"

"Rasputin," I whisper. "His name's Rasputin."

Another thin laugh in the dark. "Don't be a little fool," she says, and clicks up the volume on the television. This is how most of our conversations go these days. That's to say we have conversations at all.

I cross to the kitchen and lean against the sink, piled high with dirty dishes.

"Have you eaten?" I ask, but she doesn't answer. She just holds up her empty TV dinner tray. I take it from her and drop it in the heaping trash bag that should have been emptied two days ago.

This is it, all we've got. An apartment that's one step up from an efficiency, not that I can see what's so efficient about it. A leaky radiator, a leaky ceiling, hand-me-down furniture spewing yellow foam from every seam. A couple years back, they almost condemned this whole building. The newspaper called it a flophouse, and heck, they were probably right, but we rallied alongside our slumlord to save the place, because what else were we going to do? This is home. You're supposed to fight to save your home.

Aren't you?

"How do you know it's Rasputin?" my mother asks the next morning.

the mad monk of the motor city

I gaze down at my bowl of generic Cheerios, the milk halfway to sour. "I just know," I say with a shrug. "And anyhow, I recognize his face."

"Maybe it's only a ghost that looks like him."

My eyes flick up at her. "So you believe me about the ghost?"

"No." My mother lights another cigarette. "Why would a spirit end up here in the first place?"

I finish slurping my last spoonful of milk before stacking the chipped bowl in the sink. "Maybe because we're halfway to ghosts ourselves."

We've certainly been forgotten like ghosts. The city's turned away from us. Sometimes, it feels like the whole world's turned away. All of us in the building are still living and breathing, but it's mostly perfunctory. Maybe that's what he sees in us.

Kindred spirits.

Easy prey.

Out in the hallway, Rasputin's waiting for me again. I try to slip past him, but I'm not fast enough. As I edge by, he reaches out for my hand. It's the first time he's ever tried that, and his thin fingers go right through me, passing into the bone and sinew.

I pull away and scurry down the steps. I tell myself he's not quite whole. He's not quite real. That means he can't do all the terrible things he did before.

At the bus stop, I fidget in my worn-out sneakers and slacks, thinking about how Rasputin doesn't even belong here. Not in this city, not in this country. He lived and breathed and died in Petrograd. My mother and I live and breathe (and will probably die) here in Detroit. Ours is a city with more smog than hope, somewhere that's a far cry from Saint Petersburg, a place that's got marbled palaces and ornate cathedrals by the score. All we have are the Penobscot Building and old steel mills as empty as cicada husks.

But then again, Rasputin always fancied himself a wandering prophet, didn't he? Maybe he's ambled his way into the Great Lakes region for a change of scenery.

At the dry cleaners, the day's a blur of pressed suits and steamed skirts in clear plastic bags. This is it, my whole life. I've been here for fifteen years and will probably stay for fifteen more unless this whole city decides to close up shop before then.

Plenty of places have already vanished. Plenty of people too. It's been almost a decade since cigarette tar and cancer gobbled up my father from the inside out, leaving only a shell for us to bury beneath a discount headstone.

"Now what are we going to do?" my mother asked, her heavy eyes shifting to me, and I knew exactly what she meant. She wasn't able to work, not for long—there was always some excuse, some reason her jobs didn't take. She never seemed to mind lounging around the house in her threadbare slippers and pink terrycloth robe when it was my dad bringing in the rent. But now that it's me, all she can do is sneer. It's like she can't forgive me for being the one to take care of her.

When I get home, it's already dark, and I trudge up the tenement steps alone, shadows tracking my every move. There aren't many of us left here. Forty units in the building, and not even a quarter of them occupied. It's mostly widows now, too set in their ways to flee. A lonely building filled with lonely hearts. We've only got one family left in the whole place, with a frail homeschooled daughter who doesn't get out much. Of course, none of us in this building get out much.

I reach the third floor, when a splintered door creaks open.

"Hello, Ingrid," a small voice whispers, her face obscured in shadow.

I grin back. "Hi, Lorelei."

Another creak of the door, and she peeks a little farther into the hallway, giving me that sad smile of hers, all the melancholy in the world hanging over her like a thin shroud.

Lorelei says she lost her husband to the war. Which war, I'm not sure, but she's got the gray look of someone who's been alone longer than life ought to allow. That's never stopped her from trying though. She's the one person who always says hello to me, the one who used to bake me peanut butter cookies when I was growing up and would let me play in her living room on the days my mother forgot and locked me out of the apartment.

A nearby radiator grunts, a drop of water spilling to the floor, and I start to say something else, to ask Lorelei about her day, to ask her *anything*, but her door lurches closed again, leaving me alone with only a bare bulb flickering above me.

Sighing, I finish climbing the stairs to the top floor. My floor. His floor too. But this time, there's no phantom waiting to greet me.

"Are you there?" I ask, but nobody answers.

My mother doesn't bother to look up when I come in. "How's your ghost?" she asks.

"Gone," I say, and hope it stays that way.

In the morning, Rasputin still hasn't returned. I take this as a good omen. Today will be an all right day.

But things never turn out the way you plan. Work's busier than I expect, and by the time I close up the register, I'm five minutes late to the bus stop, and that's all it takes. In the biting night air, I stand there, waiting for a ride that won't come. There's not another route going through here until tomorrow. That means I'll have to walk three miles in the dark.

Detroit's not like other cities. It's a skeleton of its former glory, all bare bones and bare lots, entire city blocks left in ruins like an ancient civilization. Abandoned houses with their façades wasted away, their roofs sloughing off into darkness, gloom watching you from every corner.

By the time I swing open the front door of the tenement building, my breath twisted in my chest, I can't help but wonder which is worse: being haunted by Rasputin or being haunted by Detroit.

On the first floor, I spot another familiar face. Mrs. Stevens hanging out in her doorway, curlers in her hair, matted slippers on her feet. "You're late, aren't you?" she says, as though it's any of her business.

"Good night to you too," I say as I shuffle by, her door still open, her eyes still on me. From inside her apartment, the stale stench of pine cleaner and zealotry seeps out into the stairwell. Even from here, I can see her collection of kitschy crosses and Virgin Marys on the far wall. Mrs. Stevens firmly believes enough faith can cure anything. A broken heart, a broken arm, even our leaky radiators.

"We're going to need a contractor for that," I've tried to tell her as she gripped a figurine of the Virgin Mary and waved her hands near the gathering puddles.

"You've just got to believe harder, girl," she always says to me, and I want to remind her it's been at least twenty years since anybody had the right to call me "girl." But I just let her and the Virgin Mary do their worst. They certainly can't make this place any less bearable.

On the top floor, the hallway's still empty. Maybe our haunting's got a brief half-life, the same as Detroit. I drift toward the door, and I hear my mother inside, murmuring a lullaby I haven't heard her sing in years. Tonight might be okay after all. Smiling, I open the door, and everything in the world seizes up.

Rasputin is sitting at our kitchen table, sipping a cup of Lipton tea.

I gape at him. "He's got no right to be here," I say, my index finger jabbing accusingly in the air, as if my mother doesn't already know exactly who I'm talking about.

She clucks her tongue at me. "That's no way to behave, Ingrid," she says, shaking her head before regarding Rasputin. "That girl of mine has always been trouble."

"Trouble," I repeat, my voice dissolving. My mother honestly believes I'm the problem.

Rasputin rises to his feet and whispers something to her, his chapped lips pressed to my mother's ear. She giggles like a schoolgirl. I don't know how long he's been here, but apparently it's been long enough.

"You can't—" I start to say, but my mother waves me off like a gnat.

"Leave us for now," she says, and I want to charge at her, to beg her to stop, to tell her what he really is. But she's already laughing again, pulling him toward her bedroom, and before I can reach her, she slams the door behind them.

The lock clicks on the other side, and I stand here, alone in a way I never expected.

All night, they're in there. Though I cover both ears, I can still hear them through the vellum-thin walls. The violent grunting, the quiet begging. Hers, never his. A ghost is fucking my mother, and she seems to be enjoying herself.

I can smell him too. They say he never bathed. It turns out they were right.

Except I shouldn't be able to smell him. My mother shouldn't be able to touch him. He's only a ghost, something less than dust. But then again, he was always a man with a trick up his sleeve. Now his greatest sleight of hand is simply reaching out for ours.

In the morning, I slip out of my room and creep into the kitchen. My mother's already at the table, smoking her bottomless pack of Marlboros.

"Is he gone?" I wheeze.

"For now," she says with a smirk. "But he'll be back again tonight." Her long fingers drum back and forth on the table before she adds, "He'd like to talk with you, Ingrid. Get to know you better."

At this, my flesh tightens on my bones. "I'm not

sure I want to get to know him," I say. At least not the way he'd like to know me.

My mother scoffs. "You've always been such a rude girl."

I stare at her, at the way she's pretending this is just another of her useless boyfriends instead of the man who spoiled the Russian empire.

"This isn't right," I whisper, "and you know it."

"Did I ask you?" Her gaze set on me, sharp as thorns. "Besides, my love life's none of your business."

"You're right," I say, and with that, I'm out the door and rushing to the stairs. There are whispers down the hall. I wonder who else in this building has met him.

Another day, another endless carousel of business suits and satin. My head heavy, I invent stories about the people who wear these clothes. Who they are, what they do, how they've probably never met a ghost like mine. All these lives, these easy lives, right at my fingertips but always out of reach. I could never figure out what to do with myself, so I did nothing at all. Now I'm simply something that belongs to my mother. A useless appendage. The noose around her neck, as she likes to call me, as though she's the one paying the rent every month and not me.

Rasputin certainly figured out what to do with himself. A mesmerist. A mystic. A bonafide charlatan with colorless eyes that would gobble you up if you'd let him. That's what happened to Tsarina Alexandra. I remember my freshman year in high school when we watched some grainy documentary on the fall of the Russian empire. Even back then, I never could understand how silver-tongued men like him could get away with it. How could the world let him become so powerful?

At home, he's waiting. The moment I unlock the front door, he's there, his long shadow draped over me.

"Good evening," he says, and up close, he's shorter than I expect.

With a flourish, he reaches out for my hand, and I hold my breath, waiting for him to pass right through me again. Only he doesn't. He's stronger now, more substantial. This place is making him that way. The attention he craves is turning him into something almost alive, almost flesh and blood. The tips of his fingers slip into me, and I feel him, caressing my skin from the inside out, his touch as moist and slippery as an eel.

I heave up a sob, but he only laughs.

"We could have much fun, you and I," he says and leans closer. I nearly gag. He's got the scent of a barnyard animal, and bits of old stew and fatty meat crusted in the tangles of his beard.

It's not enough he has my mother. He wants me too. He wants everything. This mad monk, a man who could devour the whole world and still be ravenous for more.

I turn away and search my mother's face as she leans against the doorway of her bedroom. She looks like a stranger now.

"This is nonsense," I whisper, as if that's all she needs to hear to break the spell.

But I already know it won't be that simple. Nothing broke the spell for Tsarina Alexandra. She was pied-pipered to her death, along with the tsar and all their children. And of course, Rasputin was sent to his demise too. He went into the darkness first, carrying a prophecy in his bones, promising the end of an empire. Though from the looks of it, his own end didn't take.

the mad monk of the motor city

With a sly grin, my mother crosses the room and takes Rasputin's hand, his fingers slipping deep into her, as she leads him off.

"Please don't," I say, but it's too late.

In the morning, he's gone again, and my mother reclines in our ragged La-Z-Boy, languid as a cat.

"Have fun at work," she says as I lock the door behind me. For all the good it'll do.

Out in the hallway, his vile scent lingers in the air, and there are strange whispers behind closed doors. Shuddering, I realize he could be anywhere, with anyone.

On the third floor, I start to take a detour. To Lorelei, with her sad smile and sad heart. I want to talk to her, to find out if she's seen him too, but it's quiet in her apartment, and I decide not to bother her so early.

The steps groan beneath me. I'm almost to the front door when Rasputin's voice rises up like smoke.

"Don't listen to the doctors," he's saying. "They won't help her. Not like I can."

I hesitate, as his words keep leaking through the wall. He's with the family, counseling them on their daughter no doubt. The same way he counseled Alexandra about her sick son.

This is what he's always done. Making false promises like the false prophet he is, pretending he's got what we so desperately need. And when all we have is nothing, it's easy to find something to offer.

"What are you doing?" Mrs. Stevens is looming next to me, materialized from nowhere, curlers still in her hair.

I stare back at her. "Have you seen him?" I ask. "Have you seen anything?"

"Nothing except a young woman who should be on her way to work," she says with a snuff, the Virgin Mary gripped tight between her fingers.

I don't trust her not to use that thing as a weapon, so with my heart in my shoes, I back away. By the time I drag myself down the block, I've missed the bus again and have to run the last half mile to punch my card in time.

All morning, I slump behind the counter. I don't know how to stop him. The police won't come even if I called, and why in the world would I ever want to involve them? They wouldn't help me, because they wouldn't believe me. Their heavy boots pounding up and down the rickety stairwell would only make everything so much worse. Plus, so far as I know, there's no law against being a ghost.

That means I'm on my own.

On my lunch break, I sneak down the block to the library and check out a book on Russian history.

"Research for a project?" the librarian asks as she stamps the card, and I nod, because she's not wrong.

Outside, an ambulance blares by, loud as an air raid siren, and I tuck the book in the bottom of my bag before disappearing out the back exit.

In the back room at the dry cleaners, I flip through it, the spine cracking, Rasputin's haggard face staring up at me from the yellowed pages.

In the appendix, there's an autopsy photo, his eyes closed, his body cold and damp. That was how he finally met his end. After the poison and the bullet holes and the bludgeoning, it was the dark water of the freezing Neva River that swallowed him whole.

the mad monk of the motor city

Tonight, I don't want to go home. At least not to my own apartment. I'm shaking when I knock on Lorelei's door.

"Can I come in?" I ask when she answers, my cheeks burning.

She gives me that same sad smile. "What's wrong?" she says, and motions me inside. But as I start to cross the threshold, something knocks me back a step. That smell. It's everywhere in her apartment. It's seeped into the carpet, the ceilings, even the bedsheets.

I edge backward, my chest constricting. "He's been here too."

Lorelei won't look at me now. "Don't judge me, Ingrid," she whispers. "You don't know what it's like."

"To be alone, you mean?" The words nearly evaporate on my lips. "He's a ghost, you know. He isn't even real."

A sharp sigh. "Your mother told me you'd say that," she says and closes the door in my face.

Nobody's safe from him. Of course, we're not. This has long been a building of lonely hearts. Maybe that's why he chose us. We're easy pickings for a man like him.

Up on the top floor, my mother's waiting for me in the kitchen, a Marlboro perched between two fingers. Nearby, Rasputin's kicked back in the La-Z-Boy, a ghoulish grin on his face, the stench of his body more acrid than a ton of garbage.

My head down, I start to pass by him, desperate to get to my mother, desperate to reason with her, but Rasputin won't let me go that easily. Without even glancing up, he stretches like he's only yawning before reaching out for me, his fingers clasped tight around my wrist. In an instant, his hand pierces into me, further than before, my body contorting at his touch like a sock puppet. I let out a strangled moan, but his hand only goes deeper. It feels like he could keep reaching into me and never stop finding new places to break apart.

Grimacing, I wrench away at last, stumbling back a step. Then I turn to my mother.

"Why are you all doing this?" I ask, my voice splitting in two. "Why is he so much easier to believe than me?"

She only rolls her eyes. "Just go to your room, Ingrid," she says, and this is what I've become. A grown woman who still gets grounded by my own mother. She's under Rasputin's thumb, and even after all these years, I'm still under hers.

But as he inches closer to me, I do as my mother says. I retreat to my bedroom, and with the door latched, I hide in the dark, listening to the leaky radiator plink-plunk on the floor, silently praying the water might wash this whole place away.

Unfortunately, I'm never that lucky.

The next day at work, I tell myself how I could leave. How I could start walking across the barren landscape of Detroit and disappear into the night. Nobody would probably even notice. Not my mother, not until the rent came due anyhow.

Instead, at sundown, I tally up the register like usual and lock the shop door, pulling down the metal grate behind me, before running down the block, my bag slung over my shoulder. I won't miss the bus again tonight. I won't run from this.

the mad monk of the motor city

When I get home, I don't make it past the foyer.

"Come on, Ingrid," he says and ushers me into one of the second floor apartments.

Apparently, Rasputin's holding a soiree tonight, and everyone's invited. My mother and Lorelei and that family from one floor below. Faces I've seen before and faces I hardly recognize. There's boxed wine and tarot cards and chime candles lit on every windowsill.

This probably isn't so odd. Rasputin always loved parties, somewhere he could be the center of attention. The center of the whole world, in a way. He'd hold séances and read fortunes and pretend he could peer into the unknown. As though knowing the future ever saved anybody.

Mrs. Stevens is here too, her hand on Rasputin's shoulder, as he blesses her Virgin Marys. She giggles, the same way my mother does, and as though he's collecting his payment, his fingers slide up her arm and disappear inside her.

I shake my head. "You too?" I ask.

Mrs. Stevens sneers at me. "Don't you say a word, Ingrid." She shakes the Virgin Mary at me. "Godless girl, thinking you understand how the Lord works."

"I don't think he works through a man like that," I say, as he slips his moist fingers out of her and moves on to the homeschooled daughter from the first floor. This girl isn't like the rest. Her arms folded in front of her, she backs away from him. But Rasputin's not a man who takes no for an answer.

"I'll cure you," he whispers to her, his hands on her now, as she starts to weep softly.

"Stop," I say, but he won't listen to me. None of

them will. I'm invisible, a nothing in plain sight. These days, I'm more of a specter than Rasputin, and he's been dead a hundred years.

The girl's still sobbing. Nobody else moves to help her. Not her father or her mother or my mother or even Lorelei who's standing with her head down against the far wall.

They'll go along with this. They'll go along with anything he says. He's given them what they wanted. An escape—from doctors' orders, from the loneliness, from the long nights in Detroit.

Except for me.

With my jaw set, I step between him and the girl. "You don't belong here."

He grins, his teeth blackened. "Sure, I do," he says before advancing on me. The others fall back, their gazes blank as tidepools. They won't stop him. They'll smile and mingle at their party and turn their backs while he's unraveling me.

He reaches out, but I surge toward the door, headed for my apartment. Headed for home. But he's right there, tracking my every step. When I finally get to the top floor, my body's gone numb, and I'm so very tired.

Rasputin senses this in me, the way my resolve's withering to ash.

"What do you seek?" he asks, and we both know he could offer me something. A different future perhaps. A promise he'll break in a heartbeat. But that almost doesn't matter. Sometimes, a candy-coated lie is better than the truth.

Another step forward, and he's so close I can taste his breath. Like curdled milk and endless winters and something darker and stranger than the grave.

the mad monk of the motor city

"I can help you," he whispers, and it would be so simple to close my eyes like the others, to drift away, to believe him. It's always easier to give in than to fight.

He backs me up against the leaky radiator, and both his hands are on me this time. My feet give out beneath me, and I glance down at a thick puddle that's pooled in the corner of the hall. Rasputin's standing in the center of it.

Dark water. His end came in dark water.

His hand slips in deeper now. He wants to help himself to me, but something twists inside me, and I realize I can help myself to him too. With all my strength, I open up, my bones shifting, my flesh making room for something new. A deep breath, and I guide him into me, his body soft and malleable. His body belonging to me now.

First his fingers, then his hand, then his entire arm, writhing and warping and vanishing.

I don't stop there. I just keep yanking him closer.

His eyes go wide, and he tries to wrench away, but I won't let him.

"You can't," he seethes, all his limbs tucked inside me now, his figure contorted beyond recognition. "You know what happened before. I ended the crown. I'll end you too."

I let out a sharp laugh, as I slide him in a little deeper. "You're too late," I say. "We're already doomed here."

One final tug, and I absorb the rest of him. Then I stand alone in the hallway, the water pooling around me, my body heavier than it's ever been.

And a little lighter too.

After he vanishes, my mother cries every night for a month. She curls up in the La-Z-Boy, the shapes on the television flickering lifelessly on her face, as she clutches filthy sheets that still smell like him.

"Are you sure you don't see him in the hallway?" she asks, thick tears staining her cheeks.

"He's not here anymore, Mama," I say, and do my best not to laugh while somewhere deep within, he squirms silently.

I go to work each day, pretending everything's the same. As I trudge down the stairs, all the doors are slammed shut, and there are no more whispers leaking through the walls. No more phantoms mussing up the hallway. No proof he was ever here at all.

Soon, there will be no proof we were here either. There aren't many of us left, and we'll be losing a few more now. Lorelei's planning to leave at the end of the month. Mrs. Stevens too. It won't be long until even the slumlord won't bother with us anymore. Then the city of Detroit will finally come and condemn this place once and for all, fulfilling Rasputin's prophecy.

That mad monk might have been our last shred of hope, and I took him away. Maybe that was wrong of me, or maybe it was right, or maybe right and wrong have got nothing to do with it.

Once the bulldozers come, I don't know where we'll go. Where *I'll* go, alone this time.

But for now, we're still here, my mother and me exiled to the top floor.

When I get home, she hasn't stirred from the

the mad monk of the motor city

La-Z-Boy, the TV gone to static, so I put the last frozen dinner in the microwave for her.

"Are you sure you don't know where he's gone?" she asks.

"I'm sorry, Mama," I say, as Rasputin twitches beneath my skin, wordlessly mouthing a prayer no one else can hear.

Outside, in the hall, the radiator is still leaking dark water, and I smile as I pass my mother her lukewarm dinner, my bones humming a melody all their own.

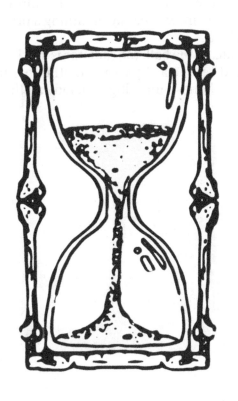

the one word i can't say

S. P. MISKOWSKI

*M***y sister Chloé** is such an asshole. Another Sunday morning, seven a.m. All I want to do is postpone being fully awake. I'm not even asleep, haven't slept for days.

Chloé stands next to the bed watching me. Not speaking. Not moving. I can feel her presence, close and senseless. Not breathing. She doesn't need to breathe, does she?

An hour ago, she was jiggling the handle on the front door. Making that noise deep in her throat, half whine, half growl, like a dog demanding a walk.

It's stupid because she doesn't need my help. To get outside. To do anything. She doesn't need me. I don't know why she's here at all. But I know I need to be alone, soon. I need to be free of this.

I can't foist her on relatives. Our parents are gone.

When I was twenty-five, Dad passed away in a hospital with only a night nurse in attendance. This year, a week before my birthday, Mom drank two pitchers of margaritas during her usual happy hour with friends, fell asleep on the floor in the ladies' room, and died clutching a handful of toilet paper. Happy birthday.

Chloé and I have nothing in common. We were opposites growing up. I was the one who saved quarters in a sock, for a year, to buy a pair of gold earrings. Chloé was the one who "borrowed" and lost them at a party in a house whose address she couldn't remember.

"Serves you right," Dad said. "Why did you let her wear them?"

God, he was a pain in the ass. So was our mom. But at least they both had the dignity to lie down and shut up when they died. Maybe it matters that they fell asleep and passed while they were calm and quiet. Maybe that makes a difference.

Here's how Chloé met her fate. At the upscale coffee shop where she worked, most of her fellow baristas were sporty types. Chloé wouldn't know a soccer ball from a volleyball, and yet she was always signing on for these insane activities with her co-workers. They would go out and slog for miles, in the mud. Or they would climb gigantic trees using ropes and saddles, wearing helmets painted with the coffee shop logo. On the day Chloé died, four days before Christmas, her boss closed the shop early so they could all go ice skating.

No one in our family skated. Or played tennis. Or went camping. Or hiked in mud. I barely survived the P.E. fitness requirement in high school.

Yet on that afternoon, ignoring her DNA, Chloé laced up a pair of skates she'd borrowed from a woman whose feet were two sizes larger than hers, went gliding out onto the ice with her legs slowly spreading in different directions, and fell. Flat on her back, her head landing with a loud thump.

Everyone laughed, because that's what people do. The sporty ones always urge and cajole and insist until we, the entirely un-sporty, agree to gear up. Next thing you know, we crash into a mountainside and sprawl on the snow like an insect dashed against a windshield. Then the sporty ones laugh and ask why we did it.

None of my sister's co-workers could tell the difference between a little accident and a fatal one. They believed her when she said she was fine. Two of them hoisted her up and held her by the arms and skated her around the frozen lake a couple of times until her eyes closed and she slumped between them.

"Epidural hematoma," the coroner explained. "You see, her head hit the ice pretty hard, and there was a lot of swelling." He showed me an x-ray of my sister's skull, where the blood had pooled around her brain tissue. He said it's sometimes operable, but not when the symptoms are ignored by idiots on an outdoor adventure.

The sympathy bouquet from Chloé's employer was shaped like a coffee cup on a checkered tablecloth, white carnations on a surface of red-and-white roses.

We are so sorry for your loss. Chloé will be missed!
As in:
We didn't know your sister was such a klutz. Please don't sue us.

The following Monday morning, I stumbled into the kitchen and found Chloé waiting for me at the breakfast table. She was dressed in the black and ivory organza I'd chosen for her funeral and for all eternity. Apparently confused by its luxuriousness and perfect cut, she kept picking at the fabric, and plucking at her skin. Although she'd worn patent leather pumps to her grave, she kept gliding everywhere as if she were still wearing skates.

I sat there, sipping unsweetened coffee, as bitter as I could stand it, wondering if I might be hallucinating, wondering if I might be sick. Then I went back to bed and closed my eyes, hoping I was only running a fever or dreaming while awake. A few minutes of quiet rest would make it go away.

Soon I could hear my sister humming beside the bed. After a while she started bumping against the nightstand. When that didn't provoke a reaction, she picked up each item on the nightstand, one-by-one—the novel I'd been reading, the alarm clock, the Xanax—to hurl across the room.

The prescription bottle hit the wall, and its contents scattered over the room. That was it. This was real. I sat up. I said her name and watched her do a jerky little dance. Her hair was lustrous, as it was in her coffin, a dark ring encircling her face. I could even smell the irritating cologne she wore, some citrus-y, cheap spray.

This wasn't a dream. This was exactly what my asshole sister would do, choosing to hang around and make my life hell.

She wouldn't go away. She lingered and followed me. Haunting. Stalking. Growling. Crawling up the walls. Leaving windows and doors open. Breaking appliances. Emptying potted plants onto the floor.

For a while I thought I could lose her. I'd shower,

get dressed quickly and dash out the door, slamming it shut and locking it before she could catch up. I hurried downtown to a department store, ran up an escalator and into women's shoes, then ducked around a corner into an elevator—and there she was, inside, smiling and waving like a toddler. Waiting for me.

I went out for drinks with a friend. Two dry martinis into the evening I let my gaze wander to the next table and saw Chloé wedged between a drunk couple, her arms linked with theirs, eyes bloodshot to match them, smiling like a fiend when they tried to make out.

Granted, she was always a pain in the ass. Pulling pranks, helping herself to anything she wanted and never saying thank you. Death only made her less considerate, sillier, and more selfish.

For example, posing with mannequins inside display windows. Or jumping in front of taxis and laughing hysterically when the drivers heard the "thump-thump" and slammed on the brakes to find out what was happening. It took practice to ignore the results of her interference, to walk away as though the accident in progress had nothing to do with me.

Maybe it wouldn't have been so bad, if she had gained some positive or helpful quality from being dead. But there was no improvement I could see. If anything, Chloé had regressed since she died. Her grade school habit of chewing on a strand of her hair had returned. Disgusting. I broke her from it when she was nine by duct-taping her mouth shut. Dead, she took every opportunity to chomp away.

I told her to stop. I reached out to slap her hands. She slipped away, crammed another strand into her mouth and chewed while a nasty grin spread from ear to ear. I could hear the crunch of it between her teeth. That sound, as much as anything else, drove me crazy.

Eventually the long winter passed. Trees began to sprout tiny leaves again. The cherry blossoms opened little by little until a windstorm stripped their limbs clean and spread the pink and white petals in the street to rot.

One day I stood before a window, studying the dead flower petals in the gutters outside. Chloé appeared next to me, munching a strand of her dark hair. I didn't even turn to face her.

"What the fuck ARE you?" I screamed. So loudly the windowpane rattled in its frame.

In answer she reached up, grabbed a fistful of her hair, and tore it out by the roots. I shook my head, told her to stop, but she kept seizing her hair by the handful and tearing it out, three, four, five times. She lay the pile of hair on the floor at my feet, the way a pet displays a dead rodent to its owner.

Her appearance hadn't changed. None of her hair seemed to be missing.

That day, I accepted the situation because, really, what else can you do when your dead sister comes to stay? But I began dreaming of new ways to free myself. This was honestly my only thought after admitting to myself that I was being haunted by the last person I ever wanted to see.

Once I was sure Chloé wasn't leaving, I started looking for more serious and reliable ways to get rid of her.

the one word i can't say

The bell above the door tinkles too merrily. A recording plays in the background, either a gargantuan sea creature keening, or a cello string being scratched with a wooden splinter. The odor of patchouli, faintly alluring and then sickening, catches in my mouth. The moment I inhale that spicy musk my throat muscles tighten. I control the gag reflex with shallow breathing. My vocal cords are as dry as they might be in a nightmare, one of those in which escape depends on the ability to scream.

These irritating sounds and fragrances are meant to greet customers and envelop them, to convey that we are in the presence of a person operating on a higher spiritual plane, someone for whom smelly herbs, jingling bells, and high-pitched whale songs are perfectly natural. I try to imagine a sane human who would find all of this comforting.

"Have a seat, and allow yourself to breathe freely, my dear," says the medium. This time she's a tall, pale woman dressed in a knit pantsuit with a lavish brooch at her shoulder, a turquoise and ruby octopus. She smells of talcum powder, and the roots of her blond hair are solid white.

I sit at the table. Chloé stands behind me. Her heavy, unbrushed hair hangs over my shoulder. We watch the medium go through the familiar motions. The meaningful pauses, the deep sighs, the squeaky voices. Later she holds my hand and tells me not to fear the darkness because my parents, two dear people who love me very, very much, will always be nearby to guide me.

I pay the medium the amount agreed upon, but I leave no tip. She tries to sell me a pack of tarot cards and a candle she guarantees will soothe the itchy spirits. I ignore her sales pitch. With Chloé trailing after, I manage to exit the shop onto the busy street. I practice restraint. I sidestep the next customer and watch the door close after him, without ever calling the medium a charlatan.

This was our fifteenth consultation. Not one of the "psychics" we've visited has ever mentioned my dead sister gliding around the room on invisible skates, chewing at a strand of her hair. Because they couldn't see her.

In fairness, I don't know whether all of these people are phonies (although some of them definitely are), or if Chloé is somehow evading their detection. But if they're not able to see her, how can they make her go away?

I need a hot shower when we get home. I crank up the water pressure, adjust the showerhead, and let the steam roll around me, releasing the tension in my naked limbs. Chloé stands outside the glass door, forehead pressed against it, oblivious to the heat, staring at me.

When I have dinner, she pretends to eat too. She's amazed at not being able to taste wine. She guzzles the deep red liquid, frustrated, gurgling and blowing bubbles until she's soaked in it. And just as quickly, it fades from her dress and her skin. She can cause a truck driver to plow into the side of a building, but nothing sticks to her. Nothing changes her.

the one word i can't say

The childhood memories she evokes with her antics are not pleasant. I remember being late to class, missing exams, sitting on the sofa in our bland living room while the threats and complaints of both drunk parents rained down on me.

I don't like to linger over the past. I really don't. Some things are beyond the pale. Some things are truly fucking ridiculous and not worth remembering. Some things ought to stay dead.

Mom died pretending to be destitute. When a lawyer called to say I would receive the remainder of the funds in her bank accounts, I only hoped for enough cash to buy a six-pack of Belgian ale. Learning she had squirreled away tens of thousands of dollars in a bunch of CDs, two of which paid out enough cash every month for my rent and expenses, only made me hate her more.

I thought of the years I spent struggling to pay off student loans. The scruffy secondhand car that spent more time with a mechanic than trundling me to my dumb job answering phones and typing at a temp agency. The out of fashion dresses I treated like designer originals just to prevent fraying hems and cuffs. The view of two concrete parking garages from my one-bedroom apartment. The shameful excuses I made up to avoid parties because I could never afford a gift for anyone's birthday, anniversary, or baby shower.

"Fuck you, Mom," I said when I read the balance statements. Who knew she had the wherewithal to invest a portion of every week's pay in long-term, high-yielding accounts? The woman was incapable of preparing a sack lunch for an eight-year-old.

Naturally, I quit my job. It felt like vindication, a tiny victory over responsibility, over every wasted hour of a childhood spent running errands, babysitting, and lying to the neighbors.

Now I have days and nights free, but this place is too confining since my sister moved in. Twice a week I go looking for a bigger apartment, a more comfortable place to stay until I can free myself. Chloé tags along but she's such a nuisance, I can't trust her out of my sight.

I'll hear barking while discussing amenities with a manager, and through an open window I'll see Chloé following someone walking their dog. The alert canine bridles at every step, jumps at Chloé, and barks a warning. The baffled owner pulls at the leash, calling the dog's name and sputtering commands. Chloé loves this game. She loves playing with dogs. It's the only time I see her smile without a hint of malice.

When I'm not shopping for an apartment large enough to close a door and forget about my sister for a while, I'm still hauling her to one medium after another. Waiting. Hoping. Dropping hints, letting strangers hold my hands, staring into the eyes of all these "sensitive" people who think they have to convince me, to make me "believe": a former dancer whose knees are shot, a mother of three who lost her children to an auto accident, a music teacher whose school district decided her subject was a waste of meager resources, or any one of a dozen lonely idiots who think their shivers and discomforts are signs of the supernatural. All of them unable to sense the presence of my awful sister. It makes me angry, if you want to know the truth. These assholes are happy to take my money, and put on a show, and I can see they're lying. I know it. But what choice do I have? Someone somewhere has to be able to detect my problem. I must locate that person.

Of course, Chloé finds all of this hilarious. She hovers behind me, her feet several inches off the floor, arms raised. She makes Linda Blair noises and laughs that movie demon laugh, the one that sounds like a throatful of bile.

Sometimes she lies on the table between the so-called psychic and me, moaning until she makes herself giggle. Is she preventing the psychic from detecting her? I can't tell, but when she gets bored, she climbs off the table and wanders through the shop or the apartment, pushing books and pictures slightly askew. I imagine the charlatans later walking past these signs of my sister's presence, and I wonder if they will notice.

In all of these situations, I feel her mocking me. Nothing is taken seriously. No boundary is respected. I've become a secondary character in my own life.

Yesterday I reached my limit. My sister broke me, and now she has to go. No more games. No more bullshit. She has to go. As soon as possible.

I was eating strawberry yogurt with toast and coffee when Chloé plopped down opposite me, rested her chin on both hands, and grinned like the goddamn Babadook. Luckily my mouth wasn't full of yogurt, or I might have spat it all over the kitchen.

She was wearing my gold earrings. The ones I saved forever to buy. The ones she said were lost, the only truly good jewelry I ever owned. The bright, precious gold I'd given myself as a reward for all the garbage in our lives. She had sworn they were lost when we were teenagers. I was denied the pleasure of wearing them for the past twelve years.

If she had been alive, I would have killed her.

Cully Swift advertises herself as a *shamanic energy medicine practitioner*. She's sought after, the ad claims, for her superb crystal readings. Her secondary specialty, covered in the fine print, is clearing homes of negative or unwanted energy. Also known as unwelcome energy, or interfering spirits. Also known as Chloé.

The thing is, I didn't find Cully. She called me, out of the blue, and asked if I was in need of her services. This was the very day my asshole of a sister wore my earrings to taunt me. If there are signs, if people can sense the presence of something dead, or bad, or asinine like Chloé, this might be it. I decided to take one more chance.

I refuse to get out of bed at seven. No matter how she snorts and stomps up and down. I practice the relaxation techniques I learned from an app on my phone. Forcing nothing. Closing my eyes and taking turns, from one limb to the next, tensing muscles and releasing, letting go, sinking into soft weight, trusting the solid mattress beneath me.

Bliss nearly achieved, by the time I roll out at eight-fifteen, Chloé is draped upside down over the sofa, her head egg-shaped resting atop the pool of her dark hair.

the one word i can't say

She hangs by her knees like this, sometimes indoors or sometimes hooked over the windowsill, surveying the city with eyes as dark and green as they were in life.

I can almost remember a time when I didn't hate her, but it's a very distant memory. If you spend your life forgetting a thing you buried, you can almost believe it never happened.

Cully Swift's knock at the door breaks me free of this remembering nonsense. The cloud of indecisiveness my sister commands can surround me now and then, a warm robe tossed around my shoulders when I least expect or want it. A voice reverberates in my head:

We were almost identical, although not twins, one growing up fast and one still small, faces tilted together while reading, the shutters open to a blur of sunlight, the "torch glow" of bright fuchsia bougainvillea pressed against the window . . .

I have to step to one side and shake my head vigorously. For a second all I can see is fuchsia, a fog of it, billowing all around. I come to my senses and catch a glimpse of Chloé dashing from the room, hand over her mouth to disguise her giggling.

She hates me. She's crazy, always has been. She has to go. She has to go.

"Thanks for driving up," I say.

"I enjoyed it," Cully says. "The coast is at its most beautiful, I think, at this hour."

"Would you like coffee?"

"Yes, thank you," she says. "With cream and sugar, if you have it."

We take a seat in the cramped living room, where I've opened the blinds to catch the periwinkle sky. It occurs to me that darkness might be better.

"Would you like me to close these?" I ask.

"Oh, not at all," Cully says. "The lighter, the better. I love the morning sun, don't you?"

She isn't dressed like the other mediums I've consulted. Her A-line pink dress is an actual one, not a caftan, not a costume. Her smile is relaxed and easy.

While exchanging pleasantries I've been backsliding. I've convinced myself this will be a waste of time. There's no way this calm, friendly woman will be any more adept at ridding the world of unwanted spirits than all of those people in those little shops where singing bowls resonate and I try not to choke on the scent of bergamot and patchouli.

I'm just wondering how long it will take to finish our coffee and negotiate the awkward moment of payment for absolutely nothing, when Chloé comes gliding through from the bedroom, sputtering or "motorboating" with her lips, sailing around the room in a circle and out the door again.

I notice something I haven't experienced before. Cully is watching closely and listening. Her gaze follows my freak sister perfectly. When Chloé leaves us with our coffee and heads into the bedroom to "motorboat" there, Cully smiles pleasantly.

"Can you see?" I ask her.

"Oh, yes," she says. "She's talented, letting you see her while shielding herself from outsiders."

I knew it. I knew she was letting me go from one medium to another in vain. But now she's met her match.

the one word i can't say

"Did you name your sister, when she was a baby?"

I'm too stunned to handle my coffee cup. I place it securely on the table between us.

"How did you know?"

"Well," Cully says. "Now you've asked the unanswerable. Is this information in your thoughts, or hers? Is it in the ether, like a cloud of all the things we know about one another without knowing how we know? Is there a god somewhere—above, below, inside us—sharing the knowledge we need? I have no idea."

"But you can see."

"Oh, yes," Cully says. She laughs, lightly, happily. "In fact, what you're experiencing is more than the usual glimpse of a loved one, both the external form of Chloé as you prepared her for eternal rest and the unyielding nature of her soul."

Hearing my sister's name on her tongue gives me a shiver. "What else do you see?" I ask.

"How she was, alive and wild in your mother's arms," Cully says. "Her small face so bright and bunched up like a boutonnière. You were barely big enough to hold her. Your mother was tired, impatient, disinterested in raising another child. She asked you what to call the baby, didn't she?"

This is true. The recollection is cold as a knife between my ribs.

"You chose the name of a character in a book," Cully says. "Thinking this would be wiser than naming her after someone in your family. You disliked them so much."

"My parents were liars," I say. I haven't intended to talk about myself, but now it all comes out.

The drunken nights, the wrecked kitchen with its

empty refrigerator, and the baby shrieking for attention. She had to be weaned from my mother's breast and given a bottle in the first month. She didn't like being left alone. She was screaming when I left for school and screaming when I got home.

When she was able to take solid food, I was the one who fed her strained peas and custard and carrots and spinach, the bright gobs of food oozing out of her untrained mouth onto her chin. I burped her. I changed her diaper. I bathed her and dressed her. All my mother did was push Chloé out of her womb and buy the minimal supplies needed to keep her alive. I did the rest.

When she was old enough for school, I walked her there and back. In middle school I arranged my class schedule so I could be there when the bell rang, to accompany her home. I picked out her clothes and brushed her hair—the hair she gathered in large strands to suck on throughout the day. I took her to music lessons until the piano teacher asked me not to bring her anymore. I paid a couple of kids in the neighborhood to play with her. I strong-armed a pimply kid to go with her to the prom.

Then the drugs and all-night parties started. Then she stole my gold earrings and "lost" them. Then she broke into a neighbor's apartment and drank all of their booze and passed out on the doorstep. I tried to change her, to make her more like me and less like the assholes who claimed to be our parents. I taught her everything I knew about the world. I shadowed and sheltered her every day until I was finally old enough to leave home. And then I left.

"What does she want?" I ask Cully.

the one word i can't say

"You," says Cully. "She wants to be with you."

I close my eyes. I take a deep breath, and release it, startled by how ragged and exhausted I feel. A little extra rest has done nothing to alleviate my fatigue.

These weeks alone with my dead sister have been as trying as the first weeks of her life. She no longer needs help, in any physical sense. Nevertheless, she follows me at all times. More than a distraction, she's a nuisance and a hindrance to my plans. She sucks up space and makes it impossible to relax, to sit still and just *be*. While I'm trying to form these thoughts into words a stranger will understand, I can hear her "motorboating" from one corner of the apartment to another. Once she starts one of her games, she won't stop. She's entranced by herself, and it never gets old. She can go on like this all day.

"I want her to go away," I tell Cully. "I don't care how you do it. I can't stand this anymore."

Her expression is hard to read. Not smiling, and with the "br-br-br" of Chloé's vocalizations thrumming in the kitchen, Cully opens the oversized canvas bag at her feet and takes out a few items: a fancy writing pen, some thin strips of what appear to be rolling papers, a box of wooden matches, and a ceramic bowl shaped like a mushroom and small enough to hold in the palm of one hand.

"As a precaution," she says. "I must warn you that the process is irreversible. So long as you follow all of my instructions."

This takes a moment to sink in. Not because I'm concerned. I know what I want. I'm just not sure why Cully feels the need to say it.

"Good," I tell her. "I don't want her showing up again."

"Are you absolutely sure?"

"Of course," I say. "Would you want your dead sister crawling into bed next to you, in the middle of the night, freezing the sheets? I don't want to wonder if she's going to turn up at my table in a restaurant. Or appear in my shopping cart at the grocery store, picking apart the salad I just bought. I don't want to go up to the roof for a glass of wine and a smoke and find her planking on the ledge. When I try on clothes in a department store, if I turn my back to undress, when I look again, she's wearing all of the blouses and skirts I've picked out, right over her funeral dress. She ruins everything. You have no idea."

Cully's eyes are soft. She gives a slight nod and shows me how to use the items she's placed on the table between us.

"With this pen," she says. "Write her name on a slip of paper. Close your eyes and repeat it, silently, only to yourself. Open your eyes. Strike a match and light the piece of paper over the bowl. Drop the paper inside and hold the bowl in your left hand until all of the paper is burned away. One last thing. People find this difficult, but it's essential."

"Tell me," I say.

"When the ritual is complete, you must not say her name again," Cully explains. "Out loud, or in your thoughts."

I have only one thought in my head as I follow her instructions: *Make that incessant noise in the other room stop. Make it go away forever.*

I write Chloé's name. The paper catches fire as

though its only purpose on earth is to burn. The ceramic bowl grows warm in my hand. I wonder if it will become too hot to hold, and as I wonder this the fire goes out. The paper has curled into a black, thin strip of ash. The smoke drifts away and disappears. The quiet is dense and rippling, like waves of desert heat in summer.

I don't know how long we've been sitting here. I notice Cully has cleared the table and put away all of the items from her canvas bag. She shakes my hand and accepts an envelope with her payment and a generous tip, all cash. She slips the envelope into the canvas bag. At the front door she wishes me peace, and when I close the door after her I feel the silence like a warm breeze.

On the day my mother handed the baby to me and stumbled off to watch TV in the bedroom, I wasn't sure what to do. The squirmy bundle in my skinny arms barely registered the absence of its mother. It smelled of breast milk, the last serving it would ever receive. Its eyes stared up at me, opaque and quizzical. And when I asked, with a smirk and a heavy heart, "What are you?" it answered me with a grimace full of drool, followed by its first smile.

In a week I'll be moving into a new place. Much bigger, brighter, with a real dining area. I can invite friends over for a meal. There will be enough space for a queen-sized bed, and I'll be able to sleep late, if I want. Despite the quiet, this apartment now seems unbearably small. Every corner and piece of furniture is tainted with unwanted memories.

The money I inherited from my shiftless mother will carry me for a while. And then I'll figure out what to do next. I'm good at that. I've been making my own way, throughout my life. Nothing has changed, I tell myself.

All I have to remember is to not say or think about one little word. That should be easy enough.

knock three times

SEANAN MCGUIRE

San Francisco, 1906

"*The practice of* spiritualism is inherently counter to the will of God." Miss Beecher's voice was a sharp, shrill nail hammered through the wall of Florence's thoughts, somehow managing to be piercing and dull at the same time. It was a nice trick. Florence considered the value of pointing out that the transmutation of materials from one state to another—such as a voice into a weapon of aggression—was equally counter to God's will, and thus the both of them must be seen as sinners with no chance of redemption. It was an appealing idea. She dismissed it all the same.

Miss Beecher was of a breed, one Florence had become well-acquainted with over the past four years, ever since the spirits began to whisper in her ears of an evening, ever since she had realized that the world was greater than the limits of her eyes.

Miss Beecher had gone quiet. That usually meant she was waiting for some form of response and would, upon failing to receive it, report Florence to her father for daydreaming through lessons. Miss Beecher never seemed to tell him when Florence was insouciant, or prideful, or just plain rude, but silence was the one thing she could not tolerate. Florence rapidly reviewed the matron's last several words, settling on an appropriate reply.

"The idea that God would create immortal souls only to abandon them to slothfulness and indolence the moment their fragile flesh decayed is also counter to the will of God," she snapped. "The practice of spiritualism is an ongoing acceptance of God's will, and acknowledgment of His glories."

"Very well said, Miss Denver," said Miss Beecher, with unusual approval. Florence glanced to her tutor in surprise. Miss Beecher was actually smiling, expression foreign on her customarily dour face. "I believe we can mark today's lesson down as complete. You have earned today's riddle."

"Excellent," said Florence, who felt this paltry offering was anything but. She looked to Miss Beecher attentively. "Pray you, begin."

"Half a minute's warning you will have, and if you're able, get yourself to safety in the shadow of the table," said Miss Beecher, voice crisp and precise. "Class dismissed."

Florence rose, offering a polite nod to her tutor, and turned toward the door.

She was almost there when there was a whisper of sound from behind her. She glanced back, eyebrows raised.

The upstairs room where she took her lessons was, as always, silent and cold, furniture save for the lone chair she sat in for classroom review covered in plain white sheets and kept meticulously clear of dust. The lights were down, the ashes in the fireplace long since chilled and reduced to grayish powder. It was a clean, presentable, dead place, and no others among the living walked here, nor had in years, nor, if Florence had the choosing of it, ever would again.

"Thank you for your time and attention," she said, and walked away.

The practice of spiritualism might well be an affront to the will of God. To be entirely honest, Florence was less than sure in either direction. What she was sure of was that without spiritualism, her life would have been very small, and very lonely.

For a sixteen-year-old orphan, options were not thick on the ground. Perhaps if she'd been a sixteen-year-old boy, they would have been better, but that happy fate was not to be her own, and much as the children who came to play in the parlor of an afternoon would sometimes look at her lanky, lengthening limbs with envy, she suspected that she was seeing what she couldn't hope to have through clouded eyes, painting the flaws in pretty swirls of lace and roses, when things would have been just as difficult, if not more so.

She couldn't say that her gifts were in any way connected to her feminine nature, but she could say that most of the spiritualists she knew were young women, most a few years older than herself, some a few years younger, but not many—the august practice was, sadly, on the cusp of falling from fashion, and were she any younger, she would be concerned about her future prospects.

The dead weren't going anywhere simply because the living tired of their attentions. The dead had been present since the beginning of time, and they would be present when the keeping of clocks and calendars had become a quaintly outdated habit of the rich and indolent. But they might find themselves excluded from the process of decision making, if the people in positions of power decided they were tired of seeking the wisdom passed through young, unmarried girls.

So there was every chance that Florence would reach her majority and find herself without a means of supporting herself, and that would be a tragedy, if only on a small scale—there was no one else who would be terribly put out by the dissolution of her fortunes, not with her father being three years in the afterlife and not yet a moment in the grave. He had been an investor of some renown, working primarily with clients in New York and London via post and telegram, and had cultivated a reputation since his wife's death for seclusion and isolation. It had been no strange thing for his clients when he had sent out the neatly pinned letters in what appeared to be his own hand stating that the phone had been disconnected and would he only be supporting them in writing. As his investments had remained sound and his financial advice astute, they had been more than willing to stop incurring expensive long distance charges.

He might not move as quickly or nimbly as someone at a local investment firm, and indeed, Florence was sure that some of his clients were also seeing other advisors, but as she could allow him to possess her form long enough to craft a letter, but not to make a telephonic call, this had to remain their means of doing business.

So long as George Denver continued to manage the investments of his clients, continued to send his letters and make his presence known, there could be no question of his survival. The fact that the man had become somewhat of a recluse in the past three years was irrelevant. His young daughter was still seen out and about in the city, doing the shopping, taking her music lessons, even attending shows and parties, and always in the company of an excellent chaperone.

Florence had impeccable taste in paid companions. For all that she rotated them with acceptable frequency—to be seen too often in the company of a single spinster was to invite speculation of an affair on her father's part, or of some impropriety on hers—she had yet to hire anyone with a waggling tongue, or who thought it odd that she had never met the master of the house, even when receiving her wages.

Sadly, most of the other spiritualists of an appropriate age were too well-known to make good companions. Outside the home, they would attract attention, and inside the home, they ran the risk of being mistaken for a collaborator. That, too, would raise questions, and possibly lock her into a relationship with greater repercussions than she preferred.

No. It was best to keep the two sides of her life— the public and the professional—as distinct as possible. She walked briskly down the hall toward her room. Father insisted on her lessons, required that she attend them daily, regardless of how inconvenient they became, and had he not been willing to accept spectral teachers of good breeding and comportment, she would no doubt have found herself straining her masquerade through attendance at one of the local schools.

It was fortuitous that he had come from New York to San Francisco to make his fortune, and still viewed the wild West Coast with an easterner's natural suspicion for anything he believed untamed. And yet. Florence was quite sure the heart attack which carried him away from her would have done so back home in New York, where it would have been infinitely more difficult for her to pretend to be the daughter of a reclusive but still-living father than it was here.

No one *knew* them in San Francisco, not really. They had arrived scarce a year before her father's death, both still dressed in mourning for her dearly departed mother, Florence insisting, in her reedy twelve-year-old voice, that her mother might have died, but she hadn't gone anywhere, she hadn't left them, so how could calling her "dearly departed" make any sense at all? There had been time for them to begin the process of establishing themselves socially, and then her father had stopped breathing, and all the rules had changed.

In death, he was reunited with his beautiful Marian, who had been serving as Florence's spirit guide since her own demise, and who was more than happy to ease him into his new existence as a phantom. And together, they were in a fine position to watch over Florence and her interests. Half of her tutors had been hired by Marian, rather than by Florence herself, who was limited to lurking around schools listening for news that a teacher had recently passed away if she wanted to scout for a new instructor. Having a dead mother who could simply nip onto campus and hunt for available teachers was much more effective.

Florence supposed it was rather ghoulish of her to take deaths in the local community quite so gleefully, but as it allowed her to forward her education without being discovered or falling out of date, it was the best option of a bad lot. Pausing in front of the room her mother chose to make her primary haunt, Florence smoothed her hair with a quick, nervous gesture, stood a little straighter, and knocked three times. That was their key, and the number she asked her mother to invoke séance after séance, calling forth the spirits with numerological nonsense, claiming the "power of threes" and the "strength of perfect balance" would keep her credulous petitioners safe.

A long pause followed her final knock, long enough that Florence began to fidget, afraid that something had gone wrong. She was on the verge of breaking one of their sacred household rules and reaching for the doorknob without permission when it turned, seemingly of its own accord, and the door swung inward in invitation. Not far—only a few inches—but far enough to make it plain that she was invited into her parents' private chambers.

Florence took a deep breath, aware in that moment of the inherent irony of breathing deeply before she went to meet with the dead, and pushed the door open the rest of the way, stepping through.

Her mother was seated at the vanity, brushing her long curls with deep, slow strokes of a brush that ran furrows through her hair, but did not appear to Florence's still-living eyes. So it was with the dead. She could see their bodies, as solid as they had ever been in life, and the clothing they wore, but none of the things they interacted with, from hairbrushes and pens to weapons—and the weapons of the dead *could* do her harm, something her parents were quick to remind her of whenever she offered to venture too far from their home.

"How were your lessons, dear?" Marian asked.

"Miss Beecher had another riddle for our wall," said Florence. "She said 'half a minute's warning you will have, and if you're able, get yourself to safety in the shadow of the table.' Do you have any sense yet of what she's riddling at?"

"I've been asking the dead, but the ones who seem to see anything of what's ahead are just as vague as your tutor, and even less inclined to provide details." Marian resumed brushing her hair, eyes returning to the mirror. The more time passed, the less immediate interest she had in the comings and goings of her living, breathing daughter. Investment in the hot, swift world of the living was too much to ask of her. "Some of them offer half-truths and rumors. Most say that it's not their concern. We should have details soon, I hope. Are your little friends coming over again tonight?"

"Yes, Mama," said Florence. "We're hosting a séance for some of the richest men in San Francisco. Why, Kitty says there's a good chance we can find patrons among their number, and then—"

"Very good, dear," said her mother, opening her hand like she was dropping something onto the vanity. Nothing fell, but after a momentary pause, she rose, gliding frictionlessly across the room toward Florence. "Chin up. Let me look at you."

Florence stilled and quieted, lifting her chin for inspection. This, too, was a normal part of her day, as reliable as sunrise or her lessons, which happened every day now, even on the weekend, as her father began to lose touch with the calendar. His investments would start to falter soon, losing the acuity he had become famous for, and then the clients would go away, and the money would go with them. It was vital that Florence find a patron before that could happen, vital in ways her parents were no longer equipped to fully understand.

What use was it to have a ghost feeding you financial secrets if those secrets were slipping out of synch with the reality of the living? And what good could they do a teenage girl unable to play the financial markets to her own gain? This was the one area in which the assumed survival of her father did her no favors: concealing his death had allowed her a period of adjustment and relative freedom, constrained only by the somewhat laxer social rules of the golden coast, whereas revealing his demise would have seen her either destitute and defenseless, or loaded onto the first train back east and delivered into the hands of her maternal grandparents. The thought, even in passing, was enough to make her skin tighten.

Her maternal grandparents were religious people, pious to the point of pain, and would never have been willing to let her exercise her talents. While her gift for speaking with the dead was far from unique, she had always believed that to hoard a gift freely given and refuse to make use of it was the height of selfishness, and no doubt much more offensive in the eyes of their precious God than any dallying with the departed could possibly have been.

Plus the dead could tell when someone saw them, and she would find herself besieged by unquiet spirits if she stopped giving them their fair opportunities at address. No. A return to the east was not to be considered. That was the basis under which she had concealed her father's . . . condition . . . in the first place: to maintain her own fledgling place in San Francisco society, and in the greater society of spiritualists with which she found herself so willingly engaged.

Her mother's phantom hands skirted over her hair, barely stirring it, and stroked the skin of her cheeks, as insubstantial as a sigh. "Lovely," Marian finally said, drifting back. "Older today, I think, than you were yesterday. Your body's decay is a delight."

"Yes, mother." The dead were often fascinated by decay and growth, and found the ongoing aging of their living relations a true enchantment. When she conveyed messages of praise and admiration to the living from the dead, they were always entirely sincere. As long as you still drew breath, you were beautiful to them.

"I suppose you want to hurry off to your social engagements."

"That would be best," said Florence, trying not to shiver and betray how little she liked her mother's hands upon her, intangible and tickling like cobwebs. It was rude to shy away from one's own mother, even under such circumstances, but she found her attentions increasingly discomforting. "May I be excused?"

knock three times

"If you must."

Florence bobbed the quickest of curtseys before she turned and made for the door. She was almost there when her mother's voice said, like a whisper out of the darkness, "Flossy?"

Florence stopped, looking back. "Yes, Mama?"

"You're a good girl. You're going to live a long and glorious life. I promise you that much."

The dead were fond of making promises. Sadly, they were less fond—or perhaps, less skilled at the art—of keeping them.

Florence smiled at the shadows, her mother having disappeared once more.

"Yes, Mama," she said, and let herself out of the room.

The other girls envied Florence's freedom more than most of them cared to admit, seeing her ability to take her lessons in the home and set her own hours as marks of independence, and not marks that she took every meal alone, or that she only turned the light and heat on in those rooms of the house where she wished to be comfortable, leaving the rest of it to sink into sepulcher silence. She was never alone. She was always alone. The contradiction of her life was exhausting.

Still, she dressed to impress the rich men who were coming to tonight's parlor gathering, not too fine—too fine and they would think she had no need for their patronage—but not so shabby that they would assume her some sort of urchin, either, and ate a hurried sandwich in the kitchen before rushing to meet Kitty and Alexandra at the door. They arrived promptly at a quarter to the hour, as had been agreed, their own dresses of a style with hers, positioning all three of them as equally needing of support. Florence felt a pang of envy at the sight. For her, this was the only route that allowed her to avoid devastation, both financial and social. They were ostensibly playing on an equal field.

The field had never been equal in the least. Still, she smiled and preened for her companions, bidding them to accompany her to the parlor, where a small tray of sandwiches waited for them alongside the much larger tray prepared for the gentlemen. Those, too, had been constructed with a careful hand, balancing quality of ingredients with rustic assembly, to give the appearance that they had been thrown together with what was available and not cost half the grocery budget for the month.

The sandwiches for the girls were as much about quality control as they were making sure that everyone was fed. Kitty and Alexandra selected theirs, commenting on the artfully wilted lettuce and the slightly-too-scanty cuts of roast as they nibbled, and all three girls settled at the table to wait for their company.

The practice of spiritualism was falling out of fashion and, as with everything that fell from fashion, out of favor. Soon enough it would be the thing of children's games and party tricks, practiced by playground circles and not by serious occultists.

Sadly, Florence had to admit that girls like the ones she was now keeping company with—her friends— were part of the reason why. Their presence amplified her own power unquestionably, but on their own, neither of them would ever have amounted to much. Kitty could occasionally coax a spirit forth enough to thread a few strands of ectoplasm through the air or flicker the light of a candle; Alexandra was nothing more than a pretty faker, a hoax in pin curls and pinafore. Like many of the fakers, however, her continual cries to the dead had attracted enough of them to her side that she made things infinitely easier on her fellows.

If either of them caught the eyes of tonight's gentleman callers, it would be solely due to their better manners, refined by exposure to a wider portion of the world than Florence could import to her home, and not due to their abilities. Her friends were fakers. If forced to perform for experts, they would seem two more liars who had never been in contact with the other side.

But both of them had proven able to pierce the veil, providing Florence was there to guide them along their way. The fact that they couldn't perceive it on their own did not unravel their successes. She needed to remember that, and not allow envy to make her small, and hard. It was unkind. It was unfair.

It was unbecoming.

She sighed and nibbled at her own sandwich while her companions exchanged brightly vacant small talk, grateful to be among the living for however short a time, still worrying over Miss Beecher's riddle. Sitting up straighter, she turned to the others and said, abruptly, "Half a minute's warning you will have, and if you're able, get yourself to safety in the shadow of the table."

Kitty and Alexandra blinked at her.

"Does that mean anything to you?" asked Florence. "Anything at all?"

"No," said Kitty, in a dubious tone. "What are you trying to say?"

The bell rang, saving her from needing to answer. Florence rose, dusting her hands against her skirt. "Nothing," she said, and fled to let their chaperone for the evening in.

Miss Sellers was a nice woman, a true believer in the spiritualist's art, and a wide-eyed spectator whenever the girls came together to communicate with the other side. Kitty's father paid Miss Sellers a pittance to keep them company and safeguard their virtue, but she would have done it for half the pay—or, Florence suspected, for free—if the money had been unavailable. Simply being in the presence of such a working was sufficient to enthrall her.

She accepted the sandwich Florence offered politely, only asking once if all the ingredients had come from the living side of the veil. As if there were a market for ghost lettuces and phantom tomatoes! Once she was tucked safely into the corner where she would spend the evening, the girls busied themselves with lighting the curtains and arraying the tools of their trade across the table, crystal ball and divining spires, tuning fork and tangled pile of silver toothpicks.

And then, at half eight, the gentlemen arrived.

They approached Florence first, as the lady of the house; only right, with her mother once again feeling poorly and unable to attend on them. They all agreed that it was a great tragedy that such a famous beauty was denied to their society. How they had heard of Marian's looks, but not her death, was quite beyond

Florence. Her father hadn't been shy about his recent widowing when they arrived in San Francisco; quite a few of the society ladies had come to dance attendance upon him, trying to attract his eye. Somehow, it seemed, their brothers and nephews had quite failed to be informed.

It couldn't be helped. Florence saw them to the refreshments and her friends turned competition, giving them the space to present themselves for evaluation. That was her first step in this little dance completed. Turning back to the parlor door, she threw the lock, drew the curtains, and turned to the gathering, intoning darkly, "We are prepared to cross the border between the land of the living and the lands of the dead. Have you come prepared with your offerings and inquiries?"

"The departed must be addressed with respect and with clarity," said Kitty, unwilling to be left out of the fun. The candles flickered, as if caught in a spectral wind. Florence had to admire her for that. What the girl lacked in power, she made up for in showmanship.

"But they will attend us on this night, if we are patient, and if we approach them as petitioners, here to learn their wisdom," concluded Alexandra.

All three men nodded and murmured their assent. The girls smiled and led them to the table, where six seats had been arrayed for precisely this moment. One of the men kept hold of his sandwich, chewing untidily as he watched the scene with wide eyes. This was his fifth séance that Florence knew of, but he approached each one of them as if it were the first, not only in his experience, but in the entire world.

The seating order had been devised in part to

connect them all, and in part to avoid accusations of trickery. Each girl joined hands with the two men to either side of her, and each man joined hands with the two girls to either side of him, until the six of them had formed a perfect loop. The lights flickered overhead as Florence bowed her head.

"Come, spirits," she said, voice barely above a whisper. "Attend on us now."

It was all smoke and mirrors, of course. The spirits, if they were going to attend, would attend whether called in a whisper or a shout. And she had been priming the house all week for a spectral party. There were ghosts in plenty within calling range, all still invested enough in the motions of the living to be delighted by the opportunity to have a conversation with them.

Kitty was, as always, more theatrical. She flung her head back, eyes on the ceiling, and intoned, "We call you in the name of the living world to share your wisdom."

"Give us guidance," said Alexandra, in the most normal voice of the three.

A knock came from the wall next to the door, followed almost instantly by another from the far side of the room. Florence stiffened. This wasn't how it was supposed to go. The dead were supposed to wait until they were asked to knock, and then Kitty would trigger the beater on the bottom of the table with her knee. It lacked the power to pound on its own, but phantom hands could lift it just that little bit more.

"Three knocks means a presence is willing to speak with us," she said, hastily, as a third knock sounded from the ceiling directly overhead. One of the men gasped.

knock three times

Ceiling knocks were considered suspect, as they could mean someone was walking heavily overhead. Florence forced a smile, covering quickly. "Mama's rooms are on the other side of the house, and Father is with her," she said.

"The dead are here, they will speak with us," said Kitty, sounding ecstatic. She'd be ripping strips off of Florence for deviating from the plan after all this was over, but for the moment, she was playing along.

Florence cleared her throat, preparing for the next part of her routine, and paused as something stuck in her windpipe. She swallowed. It didn't go down. Then, to her shock and mortification, she began to choke, head jerking back and forth like a cat with a hairball. The men whose hands she was holding tried to pull away and found that they couldn't, as her fingers clamped down so tightly that there was no feasible escape.

Kitty began talking, very quickly now, trying to distract from Florence's distress. Florence kept choking, hoping to dislodge the lump, and was almost relieved when she finally felt it slip—only almost, because the sensation was immediately followed by her mouth filling with what felt like a thick fog that tasted, ever so faintly, of lime. She choked. She gagged. She opened her mouth and spewed vast streams of ectoplasm in the air, not vomiting it forth so much as providing it with a conduit to spill out into the space above the table, where it twisted and spun, resolving first into the form of her tutor.

"Half a minute's warning you shall have, and if you're able, get yourself to safety in the shadow of the table!" she howled, and vanished, replaced by the imposing figure of Florence's father.

"It races the sun," he said. "The sun will lose. When you go to bed tonight, be careful where you choose."

Then he, too, disappeared, and her mother coalesced out of the swirling gray. "Don't listen to them, my darling, and I'll hold you soon again," she cooed, and vanished, popping like a soap bubble. The ectoplasm dissipated a moment later, and Florence slumped in her chair, spent.

The two gentlemen finally pulled their hands away. "We came to speak to our own departed, not to witness some penny dreadful played out for our amusement," the first of them snapped at Alexandra, who blanched.

"There was no performance!" she said. "When the dead choose to speak, we can't control what they say."

Florence, sagging in her chair and panting lightly, said nothing.

Said nothing as the men rose, angry and afraid, and made for the door with Kitty and Alexandra following, spewing apologies, frantic to rescue their séance.

Said nothing as the youngest of the men, the wide-eyed wonderer, returned to her, crouched slightly, and offered her his patronage in a shaking voice. This was everything she had wanted, but she could not stir herself to accept it, could manage only the slightest of nods, which he accepted with a faint and unsteady smile before following his fellows out of the parlor.

Said nothing as Kitty and Alexandra came back from seeing their guests out to chide her, in loud and strident voices, about her selfishness and self-centered nature. Their chaperone slipped away, her own face wan and tight with too much knowledge; of all the people who had been there when Florence called forth the dead, only she seemed to have accepted the warning as it was given.

Said nothing as they all left her, alone with the dead, to sit in the darkening parlor as the night slipped away. And everything was still, and Florence cried.

Sleep, if it came for her at all, came fitfully in the hours to either side of midnight, and left her without even the memory of dreaming. She woke to an aching bladder and a freezing chill in the room, rose and took care of her body's demands, and returned to the table, where her chair at least held to the memory of heat. Shivering, she rubbed her arms and hunkered down.

The safety of the table. That was what she had to count on now. The safety of the table.

The sun was not yet up when the ground began to shake. It was fierce and startling, enough to snap Florence out of the light doze she had fallen into, and she wasted precious seconds blinking off her confused surprise.

Thirty seconds, if you're able . . . whispered the voice of her tutor.

She flung herself under the table, into its shadow, just as the shaking began in earnest.

The ground rolled under San Francisco, rolled like the city rested on the back of a great bear that had been disturbed in its slumber and now threatened to wake and rise. Above her, Florence heard objects splinter and fall, until it sounded like the entire house was coming down atop the sturdy oak table she used for her practice. She hunkered further down, whimpering, as the shaking continued for what felt like an age . . .

And finally stopped, air split by the sound of masonry collapsing, distant sirens, and what sounded like screams. By pushing aside the remains of what must have been a bookshelf, she was able to poke her head out.

The entire house had collapsed in on itself. A bubble of open space remained above the table, a fallen beam keeping the ceiling from crushing it entirely, but had she been anywhere else in the house, she would have died when the walls came down.

"Get yourself to safety in the shadow of the table," she murmured.

All around her, the city settled like bones tossed into a crypt, flames licking at the remains of businesses and homes, and the spirits of the newly dead rose to join the unsettled throngs, as Florence waited beneath the table for rescue to arrive while there was still time. The dead had given their warning; she had listened, and as the city burned around her, the patronage of wealthy men seemed suddenly irrelevant.

Florence breathed, and in the moment, that was enough.

the curious story of susan styles: a psychical romance

CATHERINE LORD

" *Susan Styles*," the name is not a romantic one, and yet it is associated in my mind with a curious series of incidents, which, were I a member of the Psychical (or ghost investigating) Society[1] I might have brought under the notice of that body.

I first heard of Susan Styles some two years ago.

My wife and I had just taken up our abode in a house in a country town, attracted there by the existence of a good and cheap Grammar School—a very sufficient inducement to the parents of five boys, whose education had to be provided for on a small income.

We had just settled ourselves in our new home, fresh with all the glories of new paint and paper, and were expecting calls from the neighbors. Hence I was

---

[1] The Society for Psychical Research was formed in 1882, 11 years before this story was written

rather annoyed to find the name which gives the title to my narrative scribbled on the spotless surface of our dining-room wainscot.

"My dear," I remarked to my wife, pointing to the offending inscription, "these boys must really learn to respect some room in the house. They have their private den in which to execute any mischief they desire, and I cannot have every wainscot in the house defaced by their scribble."

"I suppose it was poor Bobby," said his mother; "he always has a pencil in his hand. Dear little fellow, I often think he will be a great artist one day."

"I shall rejoice to see the results of Bobby's pencil on the walls of the Royal Academy, but I cannot admire them on my new paint," I answered sternly, for, with five sons one has to be firm on the question of willful damage to property, and I knew my wife to be a weak ally against the boys.

I carefully effaced the name and the subject dropped. But two days afterwards, "Susan Styles" was again scribbled on another part of the room, and this time I remonstrated more strongly.

"It is not the boys," retorted my wife; "you are always so ready to blame the poor fellows. I asked Bobby the other day and he said he did not know anything about the writing."

"I believe all my sons to be truthful lads as boys go; but does the most honest schoolboy readily plead guilty to an act of mischief? Besides, as Bobby is eternally scribbling everywhere, might he not be honestly oblivious of some acts of his vagrant pencil?"

"I dare say it was the new housemaid; she is a stupid sort of girl," added my wife.

"Had the name been John or Will Styles I could have better understood it," I remarked; "but a girl of that sort would hardly have the name of another woman so constantly in her thoughts that she was obliged to scribble it everywhere."

"Well, I am sure the poor boys had nothing to do with it," was my wife's Parthian shot, as I left the room.

"Look here, James," cried my helpmate a few hours later, "even you will allow the boys could hardly have written the name here," as she pointed triumphantly to a corner of the ceiling where, in the same faint, apparently penciled characters, was visible "Susan Styles" again. "Only a ladder could reach up there, and we have not such a thing in the house."

"I suppose it was done by one of the painters in love with a Susan Styles," I remarked; "but I wish he had chosen some other place for his inscriptions than our walls and ceiling. It is so odd, too, that I never observed the writing before."

"Ah, you always notice things when you are out of sorts," said my wife, with an air of conviction; "whenever you begin grumbling, I always know you are due for a fit of the gout."

The occurrence passed out of mind as the days went by, and though I occasionally noted the persistent "Susan Styles," scrawled faintly on some place on the wainscot, I contented myself with rubbing off the inscription, supposing that I had overlooked it before. We had moved into our house in the dark, cold days, and the spring sunshine doubtless showed every nook and corner more clearly.

Some months later I was obliged to go to London on business, and was glad to accept the friendly offer of a bed for a night or two from an old college chum, who had recently married a widow of considerable means, a trifle older than himself, but the soul of good nature, as fat and elderly folk so often are. I was but slightly acquainted with Mrs. Wilson, still she received me with the utmost cordiality.

"And we've a treat for you tonight, Mr. Harper," she added; "Miss Jones is coming to us." I endeavored to look properly elated at this intelligence, but as Miss Jones was a total stranger to me, the announcement conveyed little information. Wilson perceived my embarrassment, and proceeded to explain. Miss Jones was a great personage in what may be called "spiritualistic circles:" she was a professional medium, and like Owen Glendower, undertook to summon "spirits from the vasty deep," or anywhere else.

I found that my hostess was a sincere believer in table-turning, spirit-rapping, and the like, and that Wilson, for obvious reasons, found it best to abstain from open ridicule of her fancies. "Most women have some silly fad," he remarked to me after dinner, "and my wife's is a very harmless one, after all. It pleases her and doesn't annoy me."

When I remembered Wilson's very struggling existence before he married his wife, and glanced round me at the luxuriously furnished apartment, and sipped the choice old port, I felt that silence regarding the miracles of spiritualists was not, perhaps, an overwhelming price to pay for such comforts.

For myself, I may say that I have the profoundest disbelief in "mediums; " I have attended more than one "*séance*," at which the spirits of the great and talented of the earth have been supposed to rap out replies. I have noted on such occasions how sadly mental gifts deteriorate in another world. The shade of Lord Byron had been credited with balderdash which would disgrace a bell-man; while Scott and Addison appear to have forgotten, not only their graces of style, but even the humbler art of spelling their native language, to judge by the replies they dictated through their mediums.

Therefore I attended Miss Jones's "*séance*" with languid interest, more especially as I perceived that the lady in question much resembled others of her profession whom I had previously met, an example that the spirits were not particular regarding the rank and education of the persons they selected as messengers.

A crowd of devout believers had gathered in Mrs. Wilson's drawing-room, receiving ambiguously and somewhat ungrammatically worded messages with profound admiration. Wilson had slipped away, but I was obliged to remain out of politeness to my hostess.

"Now, Mr. Harper, you must ask a question," cried that lady. "I believe you are as bad as Richard, and think it is all imposture."

I felt a guilty thrill, for the accusation was all too true, and, to disguise my embarrassment, answered: "I should be most happy to do so, Mrs. Wilson, but I really don't know what to say."

"Oh! ask to communicate with some deceased friend or relative," said a young lady near me, who had just been en rapport with the spirit of her dead sister. I felt a sensation of disgust at the suggestion. I have lost loved ones, like other middle-aged people, but to profane their dear and sacred names by uttering them in an assemblage of strangers, to submit my most holy and cherished memories to the common gaze, never, never! Even were it true that that vulgar woman could bring me a message from the dead, would it not seem profaned by passing through such lips? I had even too much reverence for my favorite authors to pretend to call them up—and hesitated a moment.

"Oh! do say something," implored Mrs. Wilson. A name flashed upon me.

"Well, I said, "I should like to communicate with Susan Styles. Even the medium started at the loud and emphatic rap with which this lady proclaimed her presence and willingness to answer questions, and my own interest was suddenly awakened.

I do not expect anyone to believe the narrative that follows. I hardly think I believe it myself. Anyway, were it a coincidence or chance, the results were singular. It took time to arrive at the history of Susan Styles, as spelt out by means of knocks on the table, but I was now as eager a listener as the rest of the company. It was a very old story of sin and sorrow—an unwedded mother, a little life sacrificed to save the parent's reputation.

"No one ever knew that he was born, or that I killed him," said the guilty shade; "but I buried him under the drawing-room flooring."

That was all we could extract. The spirit reproachfully said she "had tried to communicate before."

Then came silence, and the medium announced that the "*séance*" was concluded for the evening.

the curious story of susan styles

I was now plied with eager questions. "Who was this Susan Styles? Had I known her? Had I ever seen her?"

I may remark that the spirit had been sparing in its communications, merely answering to its name, and stating its crime as explaining the reason of its desire to communicate with us. I had no mind to discuss the matter with Mrs. Wilson and her friends, so contented myself with replying that Susan Styles was a total stranger to me, but that the name had caught my memory, and I mentioned it as the first that came into my head.

When I next saw Wilson alone, however, I told him all the circumstances.

"It is curious, very curious," he remarked. "I think, in your place, I would have a look under the flooring."

This was exactly what I was longing that someone should suggest to me, though I was ashamed to propose it myself. Few of us like to acknowledge that we are setting out on a ghost hunt.

I felt so ashamed of my own credulity that I determined to wait for a week, when my wife and family would be away at the seaside, and to then prosecute my explorations secretly under the cover of the general house-cleaning. I had long promised my wife to erect a little conservatory outside the drawing-room window, and determined to make this pretense for engaging the services of a carpenter. All was quietly arranged. I made an excuse to slip back from the seaside "just to see how the workmen were getting on at home." and met Wilson, who was curious enough to come down from town to assist at my investigations. As we walked together from the station I began to think what a pair of fools we were. Talk of superstition and credulity, I should be ashamed to laugh at the nursery maid who believed in a dream-book.

I was thankful that I said nothing about my expedition even to my wife. The only thing that inclined me to prosecute further investigations was that I had discovered that Susan was, or had been, a real personage I had made cautious enquiries in the neighborhood and discovered that some years previously a young woman of that name had been in service with the family who had formerly occupied my house—that she had been left in charge of the premises during their absence for some six months and been dismissed on their return, after which she abruptly left the town. As regards her character, it was difficult to gain authentic information, but the baker's wife said she was "flighty" and a "giddy lass," and the butcher's wife remarked darkly, "Yes, she had known Susan once, but the girl got herself talked about latterly."

All this was somewhat corroborative evidence of the story told in Mrs. Wilson's drawing-room.

We found the house exactly as we had hoped—both servants out, a deaf old aunt of one of them strangely in charge of the premises, and our old carpenter languidly at work in the greenhouse.

The old woman readily admitted us (she would have done the same to a burglar), and the old carpenter was only too pleased to leave his work on any pretext.

I made up some story of doubtful drains and a desire to investigate under the flooring, and the carpenter readily undertook to remove the planks in the drawing-room. Wilson and I watched with an eagerness of which we were secretly ashamed, but, to our utter disgust and humiliation, nothing was discovered. Dust and emptiness—but no sign of a tiny form once hurried away to avoid detection of a crime.

"I always thought it was stuff," observed Wilson, very unjustly, for had he not believed enough to come a railway journey to investigate the matter?

Of course, we had not taken the carpenter into our confidence, and the man sat placidly on his heels, remarking that "he never thought as drains ran under this room, nor under the drawing-room neither, for that matter."

"This is the drawing-room," I said.

"Well, sir, I was a-speaking of the house as it used to be when I worked here in Captain Hardy's time. The room across the passage was the drawing-room then. They were a large family, and took this room, being bigger, for the dining room."

"You have just reversed the case," said Wilson. "Your dining-room was their drawing-room."

An idea struck me. Were we examining the wrong room? And I now remembered all the scribbling had been on the dining-room walls.

"Come in here; this is where the bad drains are," I said hurriedly to the work-man, and in a few minutes the dining-room planking was being taken up. And here, hidden in a corner of the room, under a plank that bore traces of having been disturbed, we found a little box.

I need not detail all that followed. The police were called in, and the remains of the infant discovered. Neither Wilson nor I saw fit to give the reasons for our examinations of the flooring, and the discovery of the box passes as an accidental occurrence in the search for defective pipes. But the investigation that followed clearly established a strong case of suspicion against Susan Styles as the mother and the murderess. She had had ample time in six months' sole occupation of the house to conceal the remains of her victim, and her dismissal on the return of her employers was chiefly owing to the unfavorable rumors they had received regarding her conduct.

No trace of her could be found. I, for my reasons, believed her to be dead. We never found any scribbling on our walls after, the poor little remains had been decently interred.

I told my wife the curious circumstance which induced me to make the discovery, but I grieve to say she only smiled at my supernatural explanation of them. The inscriptions on our walls were, in her judgment, clearly traceable to some former lover of the mysterious Susan Styles, on whom his thoughts had run while painting and white-washing.

As for the "*seance*" at Mrs. Wilson's, my wife believed the story to be a pure invention on the part of the medium, desirous of attracting interest by a sensational tale. The verification of the tale by the discovery was a mere chance coincidence. All this may be true, most likely it is; I am no believer in mediums or ghostly appearances. Still, the whole story is a curious one and might interest enquirers into spiritualistic communications.

Wilson and I have certainly kept the tale from reaching the ears of his wife. We feel that she would score it as a victory.

talitha cumi

CHESYA BURKE

"*Do miracles exist?* And if they do, do they prove there is a God?"

As soon as the age-worn photo flashed through the overhead projector, Talitha Cumi knew the sadness in the little girl's eyes, understood the forced smile on her face that was there to reassure the world, even when there was no hope for herself. She knew the girl as soon as she saw the image appear on the screen. She knew and understood.

"Who is this?" the professor asked.

Before Talitha knew it, she responded: "Saint Bernadette of Lourdes."

Professor White smiled. "Yes. That's absolutely right. Saint Bernadette of Lourdes," he repeated. "And what is she known for?"

"Pain." Everyone stopped to look at her. Talitha was Catholic. Not devout, like her mother. But she knew pain. The young woman sat up in her chair to the best of her ability, distinctly aware of the others watching her. She closed her eyes only for a moment, opened them, and sighed. "Saint Bernadette of Lourdes is the saint of the ill and poor. She was known to have seen The Mother, *Mary*, many times."

"Good. Good," Professor White encouraged. He was short and thin. She liked his class more than most—not that it mattered. She needed a degree and he taught a class that was required. The man went on "and how did . . . "

Before he could finish, Talitha Cumi interrupted him. "She lived in chronic pain and died really young. Many people never believed her. They thought she made up the pain and suffering." Talitha paused and thought for a long moment. "No one makes something like that up, they don't." The entire class was still staring at her when she finally finished.

There was silence before the professor responded, "Yes. Right. And Mary told her to dig into the ground until she found an underground water source that supposedly had healing powers to anyone who drank or bathed. While she suffered all her life from a debilitating pain, once she died, and was exhumed, her body was incorrupt—as you know, the Catholic term for preserved. Perfect. Is this evidence of miracles? Of God?"

"No!" Chad, the rich boy who studied religion just to argue. "This isn't evidence of miracles. I mean honestly, if the waters worked so well, why didn't she heal herself instead of dying young?"

"Saint Bernadette believed it was her business to be sick and in pain," Talitha said. "And Mary promised to make her happy in the afterlife." She stopped abruptly. She really *did* know too much about this hundred-year-old saint. Because of her mother.

Chad seemed offended. "Bernadette suffered because Catholicism conditioned her to believe suffering was pious. They used her pain against her. That's abuse, not righteousness."

A year ago Talitha would have argued with him. She had believed that God wants his children to suffer to prove they are worthy of a place beside him. She believed she was worthy of that place. She'd had faith. Now she didn't know anymore. She hated herself for losing her faith.

Talitha Cumi was stern, but soft spoken. "For a believer, that is enough. Everything is evidence when you think God favors you. For nonbelievers, there is never enough. Nothing you do, see or experience is evidence."

"Very good, Talitha."

"I don't accept that," Chad replied. "Don't you all think that's a copout?" He looked around the room for support. When no one responded, he kept the fight going on his own. "Saint Bernadette was a charlatan who preyed on people's faith. She's no better than so-called mediums."

But Talitha Cumi knew mediums and the harm they caused. The girl shook her head. "Spiritualists prey on the weak. They use people's faith to exploit them for money. Saint Bernadette never did that."

Professor White raised an eyebrow. "Perhaps your bias favors Christianity?"

No, she thought, *I see them both for exactly what they are.*

The professor continued, but she was lost in thought and didn't hear him or speak for the rest of the lecture.

After class, Noah walked up and stood over her as she was gathering her things. She hated when he did that. It always took her longer than other students, so he playfully rushed her. "Little girl, I say to you, get up!" Noah loved the literal translation of her name, Talitha Cumi. As a major, he was learning to speak Aramaic, the language of Christ. Like her name.

After her bag was packed, he steadied himself, leaned back, and used all his weight to pull her to her feet. During the time she had been in class, her knee had stiffened, causing pressure to expand in her joints. Putting weight on it was almost unbearable, but she didn't like to show overt expressions of pain to others. It is rude, she was always taught, to make people uncomfortable with personal problems. So, she never showed the unbearable pain she existed in.

As she stood, she shifted from one leg to the other, dragging the imperfect one behind her. Talitha Cumi never had to actively show people she was in pain, they could see it for themselves in her limp, in the broken stride that had marked her as different since she was a child. Her pain embarrassed them, and in turn, she never quite related to people the same as everyone else.

Outside the night had won its war against the day, and the brilliant white of the snow casted glares on the windows from the moonlight. Since the class was a seminar course, it was three hours long and it had gotten very dark while she was inside. Everyone else had long gone, their limbs not weighing them down like a burden of gravity. The snow fell harder than it had when she entered, and all tracks were almost completely covered.

"Are you headed home?" Noah asked. "I'm going that way."

"I'm going to hit to the library."

He looked disappointed, but evidently also didn't want to go out of his way. "Okay. See ya." She was thankful he didn't offer to walk her. She needed to be alone tonight.

Her heavy leg left an impression in the snow that was a telltale sign of her presence. There was no hiding for Talitha Cumi in a D.C. winter. But, of course, that wouldn't be any problem now that this was the last week of classes before Christmas break. Only she and a few other students would stick it out alone, hoping to catch up on that thesis which had taken over all their lives. The campus would be almost completely empty in a few days.

At the library, she went straight to the archives. There was an elevator in this building—a godsend—so she took it to the third floor. Clearly, she was one of the only people in the building, as the sound of nothingness surrounded her. The silence only a library can produce.

She walked straight to the text, pulling it from the shelf, as she had only a few days before. Since she worked for the library, she had access to this archive anytime she wanted. The book was a copy of *La Vietata*. In English, it simply meant "The Forbidden" and was an obscure text from the 14th century. Talitha had spent hours examining the book when she first found it, but it had scared her. There was definitely something "forbidden" about it, something old and absolute. It was completely nondescript—bound in old, worn leather that looked like any other used book. But it felt wrong, mentally heavy in a way that she did not understand. Of course she had no idea if that feeling was fostered by her over religious upbringing and aversion to anything dealing in magic, but a week of pain changes one's mind, making prohibited things seem less intimidating. If she did it right, this ritual would ease her pain and that was all she cared about.

She pulled out three prayer candles from her bag, each with vivid images of a white, blue-eyed Jesus. The fourth and fifth were of the Virgin. She lit them and arranged them in a circle on the floor between the aisle of dusty books shelves, opening *La Vietata* to the ritual. The ceremony would invoke "The One" to bring her protection from pain.

It would work. Now she had faith.

Bending her knee in agony, she knelt down, the pressure becoming excruciating. But pain was good. God could feel her suffering; know her conviction. Her classmate, Chad, was right; suffering is pious.

In this position she moved slower than she liked, but she lifted the book and began chanting, softly at first, then louder.

Something came over her and time stopped.

The snow outside the window froze in mid-air.

The wind was silent.

Nothing moved. She continued chanting.

At first she was afraid, so she stiffened up and closed her eyes. But Talitha Cumi had a mission, and faith and God were on her side. She did not doubt herself, and it was abomination to doubt God.

The room became dark, then light enough for her

eyes to adjust. Right before her, in the middle of the circle of candles, the floor fluttered. She strained to see in the darkness, her chants dying in her throat. It was like a ripple of water, fluttering in the floor tile.

Something slender emerged. Like a limber caterpillar.

A second appeared right beside it, and then a third and fourth, each shooting out, reaching upward, toward the ceiling. They were close to three feet long, as she realized they were fingers, attached to an arm.

The giant hand made its way through the shimmering tile, as a second set of four fingers appeared, arching its elbows to rest its fingers on the floor.

That's when Talitha saw the long black nails protracted from each finger. The thing—the angel—that she'd prayed to was wrong, all wrong. The sharp claws tapped slowly on the tile floor, as if to cement the point that this was not right. Menacing. Dangerous?

She was frightened, things weren't in her control anymore.

Her knee was locked, the pain so intense she almost passed out. But you see, as Bernadette had told the world many years before, Talitha Cumi was born to experience pain. So, she gathered all her strength and jumped to her feet, her good leg catching all her weight. As she backed away, the thing's two arms bent, resting on the edge of the hole, its neck crooked in an unnatural angle, still submerged within the depths. Its back arched.

Talitha ran.

Not like an ordinary person, but as fast as her abled

body could take her. She grabbed her bag but left the candles and book which had fallen in the abyss. She didn't stop until she was outside, in the snow. It was falling again, like normal, as if nothing had happened. Maybe nothing had. Maybe she had dozed off and imagined it. Maybe it was like before.

Framed by the moon, her shadow casted long projections in the snow. She stopped for a moment, looked back, and then at her shadow. It was wrong, like someone else was there with her. Feeling her shoulders, moving from side to side. The darkness followed her movements precisely, as if mocking her.

She looked around campus, but the solitude of the D.C. winter was absolute, no one else was around. As she turned back, the shadow seemed to reach out, trying to grab her. Falling back into the snow, she dropped on her bad leg. It stretched oddly behind her.

So, so much pain.

Behind her a tree's shadow waved in the snow twenty feet before her. She sighed and chuckled at herself because she was so spooked and needed to calm down. She could handle this. She had made a choice and now she had to live with the consequences and accept responsibility for her actions. Taking a breath, she started the work of pulling herself to a standing position and made her way home.

She was wet and tired and freezing when she reached her warm, safe dorm room. When she was young, she used to have weird visions sometimes when the pain got too bad. At one point in her childhood, Talitha had convinced herself that she'd seen St. Bernadette and that the woman had blessed her because of her pain. She knew now that the influence of her mother had caused these delusions. Perhaps this was what had happened tonight. Perhaps Talitha Cumi had seen things that weren't there because she'd wanted it so badly and because her pain had been so intense.

After a shower, she sat on the edge of her bed in the dark, and sighed. It had felt so real, too real. She whispered the prayer she had said as a kid: "Lord our Father, I saw visions again today. But thy are with me."

The darkness answered back: "But He is not."

Most people just don't understand pain. Not in the way that Talitha Cumi experienced it. All of the ways we relate to ourselves comes from our own understanding of our bodies. Talitha Cumi did not have that luxury. Her body was always in conflict with her mind. Every moment of every part of her life was agony. She had spent the last two years hobbling in and out of class and yet had never imagined what she would do with a Religious Studies degree. There had been no time to think that far ahead. As a child, she never even thought she would make it to adulthood. Her mother's obsession with her faith had ironically made her feel nothing but hopelessness—coupled with her constant pain, she had shut down completely.

Now Talitha sat in bed, waiting. She didn't know what had spoken to her. But she felt it, something in the room with her. A heavy presence that was mentally and physically overwhelming. She had strange thoughts that told her things, that played in her head like a record. She didn't want to fully access them because she knew that would make them real, urge her to do things, bad things. She realized now that the night before in the library had actually happened. She had done something horribly wrong. Horribly selfish. She'd just wanted to ease her pain.

Now that the sun had risen, things were physically brighter, but not better. Her room was still heavy and wrong. So much of what had happened since the night before was illogical and she didn't know how to process it.

She didn't move for a long time, not wanting to do the thing that she knew she had to. But it couldn't be avoided. Jumping out of the bed, the young woman dressed and left her tiny dorm room.

She couldn't be in this space any longer. It did not belong to her anymore.

As Talitha stepped out of the car outside her mother's house, she felt something watching her from the abandoned field across from the road.

She looked out into the distance and saw a young man standing in the center, staring at her.

The young man, she knew instantly, was dead. No, dead wasn't right. This thing had never actually been alive, not the way people were. It simply existed, lived within the place that people and space separated. She didn't know how she knew all of this, but she felt it. Like she had felt it with her all night in her dorm room.

It was him, that thing she had summoned the night before, whose spirit now stared at her from the other side, leaning against a tree trunk stump.

The sun was shining bright, shadowing the thing

in the field. But there was no protection from this creature in the light. And that went against everything she had ever learned from her faith. God's light was supposed to defeat the darkness, He was absolute, the Alpha and Omega. But here, in her hour of darkness, where was He now? Why could she feel the presence of this monster, and yet not know or sense the deity she had worshiped all her life?

Talitha pushed those thoughts away. She had been gone from her faith for too long, studying it as if she were an observer and not a devote follower. This was heresy and was exactly what had gotten her in this predicament in the first place. When she entered school two years ago, she had done so to affirm her faith. She never would have gotten on her knees to bow to anything other than her Father. But this school had corrupted her, and she had changed. She knew she was supposed to be ashamed of who she had become.

In the house, her mother made her a plate of chicken and dumplings, warm and thick—just how Talitha liked it. She felt uncomfortable being with her mother, eating and being normal. She hung her head, shoveling a spoon full of food into her mouth, still tasting the foul smell of the thing standing out in the field watching her. She forced a smile for her mother. "It's good."

Above her mother's home altar in the living room there was a picture of white Jesus, his hair straight, and eyes staring at anyone and everyone in the room. The table was covered by a white cloth that was blessed and vivid. There were six candles, flanking a giant gold cross. Next to Jesus, Saint Bernadette of Lourdes's image was just as sad, but accusatory in a way that

Jesus's never had been. There was no brightness around her, no happiness. The woman knew things, secrets that she never told, lies that others pretended didn't exist.

Her mother stood over her as she ate. "What's wrong?"

Talitha Cumi never came home if given the choice. It wasn't that she didn't love her mother. But once she had left for college, she had purposefully distanced herself from the woman's devout religious lifestyle, even if she couldn't completely free herself mentally.

Talitha had been blurting things out too much lately. But there was no point pretending nothing had happened. She was afraid. So she'd come home, where Jesus ruled. And told her mother everything.

The woman was speechless for the first time in her life. She had done everything in her power to try to keep her daughter from the evil in the world and now the girl had willingly brought it onto herself.

She felt ashamed but defensive. "I'm in pain, Momma. All the time. Pain."

The woman still did not speak.

"I wanted something other than hurt. Is that so bad?"

Silence.

The woman balled her hands into fists. "In all of the time that Bernadette of Lourdes suffered and still served our Lord, did she once ever summon a demon? Not once!"

"She died at 30, Momma. Do you want me to die at 30?"

Her mother gave her a straight face. "It would be better than this."

talitha cumi

The spiritualist arrived at the house several hours later. Talitha's mother was not happy about the woman coming, but she'd refused to call her own priest because that would mean admitting to weakness in her faith. It didn't matter that she had not done anything wrong in the eyes of God. It still looked bad on her for not having taught her daughter better. Appearances mattered.

The woman was heavy set, short and carried a lot of age in her face. Talitha had known about her for years. She had a reputation in the spiritualist community. The old woman opened the door and ushered the spiritualist in quickly, looking around to make sure none of the neighbors saw. Talitha didn't know if her mother was more embarrassed for having a medium in her house or a white woman before she's had time to clean properly.

Before speaking, the white woman looked at Talitha, closed her eyes and ran her hands back and forth over Talitha's body without physically touching her, as if a forcefield were blocking her from going any closer. She wore several energy gemstones, bracelets, and necklaces with symbols that Talitha didn't recognize. She certainly looked the part.

Her mother said nothing. There was nothing to say, she supposed.

When she finished, she looked around the room, focusing her attention to the prayer altar in the living room. "Why am I here?"

Talitha hesitated, not because she was ashamed, but because she had hoped the woman would know what the problem was without telling her. Obviously she had set her hope too high. She told the woman what had happened, just as she had told her mother hours earlier.

"What did it look like?"

"A monster."

The woman nodded. "Was it dark? Did it feel heavy? Were you afraid, and did you feel cold at the same time?"

"Yes, yes."

"He's a malevolent being who wants to feed from your pain and the hopelessness you feel. He wants you, Talitha Cumi."

Talitha didn't like the sound of this. She didn't like what this woman represented or being forced to call her and to use her this way. But if this woman could help, then she was going to let her.

"Incubi are hard to banish," the spiritualist continued, "because they bind themselves to the person quickly and feed on their sexual desires."

"I always told you that the desire for flesh is the way to the devil," her mother said, finally breaking her silence. "Why did you not listen to me? Why have you brought this thing into your life?"

The medium nodded in agreement.

"I told you what I was trying to do, Momma. I was not looking for an incubus. I didn't do that. That's not what this is." But by now no matter what she said her mother wouldn't believe her. She had lost the woman's trust and she didn't know if she could get it back.

The white woman looked to her. "I trust you have the fee I told you over the phone?"

Talitha Cumi walked over to her purse, pulled out

her wallet and pulled out many hundred-dollar bills. It was too much money. The last of her cash in her checking and much of her savings. But this woman was well known in the community, and she was not cheap. She handed the money over to the woman who balled it up, put it in her bra, and winked.

"Let's get started."

From her bag, the old woman pulled out several items: a hand-shaped figurine made of plaster, candles, and some bottles filled with mystery liquids. She took out a white tablecloth, similar to the one on her mother's altar, and covered the kitchen table. Then she placed all the items on the table in a circle and told Talitha to light each of the candles. They exploded as the flame hit them, as if there was energy within the room. More likely, Talitha Cumi realized, the woman wanted them to believe.

After she was finished, the white woman knelt in front of her self-created altar and said a silent pray. Her head peeked just above the face of the table. Talitha watched the woman but her mother took that opportunity to say a prayer of her own.

Then the woman stood and told them she had said the prayer to perform the spells that would cleanse the house and Talitha of any negative energy that may have attached itself to her.

"Please come close to me." The pair moved and stood next to the woman. "Now, clear your heads of all negative thoughts. Let it all go. Any pain and anger. Any negativity." Her voice was soft and soothing, a performance that fit the mood.

Talitha could not help imagining the woman standing in front of a mirror practicing to herself so that she could get her performance just right. Still, Talitha put the negative thoughts out of her head, as she had been told, and just trusted the process. She allowed her faith to take back over in a way that she had not in a long time.

The medium clasped her hands together and bowed her head, and the two followed her lead. Deep beneath the earth of the house, the ground rumbled. The woman's face showed concern. Talitha, however, smiled; maybe. Beside her, her mother didn't move. She couldn't be bothered to care right now about her mother's anger. She shouldn't be bothered to care about anything other than clearing her head for what would come next.

Standing over her items on the table, the spiritualist gripped one of the bottles and flung sprinkles of the contents at Talitha. The droplets sprayed her face. She chanted loudly, but Talitha didn't understand the words, having learned only a little Aramaic in college. The woman repeated her chant for the third time, stopping on the last word, making it reverberate throughout the room.

The blaze of the thick white candles flickered and dimmed to a tiny light, but did not extinguish.

She smiled. "This is a good sign."

Just then something broke within Talitha Cumi's head. Like the night before, she couldn't stop images from flashing in her mind, but this time, she simply could not get control of them. She was helpless as the creature controlled every part of her. Horrible images ran through her mind. She imagined grabbing her mother and slitting her throat with a knife from the kitchen. She was horrified that she found pleasure in seeing the woman gasp for air. She felt the soul fade from within her mother. She found pleasure in this woman's pain. She knew that for her entire life, the woman had allowed her to suffer, and that she had told her she was special because of it. That she, because of her pain, was like the saints that had come before and that she could be as great as them one day.

She could not exist this way anymore. There was no future for Talitha Cumi.

The psychic spoke, but Talitha would not listen. She could not risk coming out of this mental state because she needed to be in this place, with this creature she had summoned the night before. Like her mother, the spiritualist had been a plague on the community. She charged people money, giving nothing in return. Her bag of "powerful potions" was a sham, of oils and tap water. Many people had died coming to see this woman instead of seeking the medical attention they needed.

Her head was full of thoughts and memories and pain, which she realized was no different than any other day in her life.

The room finally grew quiet.

This silence was good, but like so much of her life, it was wrong.

The creature taunted her in her thoughts. It knew her, knew her life, her deepest fears and desires. It knew what she was when the lights went out.

It wanted her—not for sex as this charlatan had claimed—but to revel in the misery that her mother had created in her.

It wanted what everyone eventually wanted from her: to witness her suffering. It fed from the deception the people put into the world. She knew this because she had taken a lot of time to study it before calling it to her.

The creature searched within her head, bringing more pain. But this was nothing compared to what she endured daily, so she waited. For just the right moment.

"You're not stupid," the thing said inside her head. She responded without words. *"No."*

"What do you want?"

"Take the pain away."

"What do you offer in return?"

"Her." She pointed to the fake physic. The two women in the room could see her hand gestures but heard nothing.

The creature paused for a moment and seemed to consider her offer.

"She's not enough."

It did not take Talitha a second to respond. *"Then take the other one too."*

The thing laughed. *"Your own mother?"*

"You've read her soul. You want her."

"Yes."

"Then is it a deal?"

The reply came from silence. There was silence in her mind and silence in the house. She summoned the courage to open her eyes. Around her the room was dark, as the sun had set, but it was calm, still. Her mother and the white woman were no longer standing next to her. She was alone. She chuckled; pretty much as she always had been. As her mother had always

talitha cumi

required of her. No friends, no other family, just her mother and relentless pain.

But now she realized she felt no pain. None.

Talitha Cumi walked out of the house, painless, limpless.

Free.

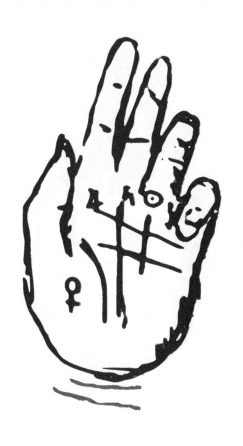

true love waits

Nadia Bulkin

Dale gave him the assignment because he wasn't a fan of Daniel Larsen—not out of any dislike, say, but because he generally found the extremely accomplished to be extremely untrue to the general shape of life—and because, unlike Dale, he had nothing better to do.

"Are you sure it's him?" he asked when he read the blind item: *Code violation! This tennis ace is leaving his wife for a 23-year-old hottie.* If he'd read that prompt cold, Larsen wouldn't have been his top guess.

"I know," Dale said, looking happier than he'd been when Ben Gleeson was busted for performance-enhancing drugs. "Isn't it crazy?"

In truth, it made Alex sad. It had nothing to do with Larsen. Such stories simply did not end well for anyone. Not the cheater, not the cheated-upon, certainly not the cheated-with. The very endurance of these stories affirmed to Alex that humans were apt to not only snag themselves on barbed wire fences, but to disembowel themselves while trying to escape.

A celebrity affair, even a marriage-ending one, wasn't crazy or interesting or even very notable except for the hypocrisy, he supposed, but even that assumed that athletes were honest in their press conferences, which they were not. Especially not Larsen, who had made diplomatic pablum his specialty. Talking about trying his best when he lost in embarrassing fashion. *So thankful for my wife* mixed perfectly into a sea of utterly meaningless noise.

"Why do you even pay attention to these people?" his roommate said when Alex mentioned the assignment. "They're all horrible."

"They're just like everyone else," Alex answered, which wasn't really an answer.

There was nothing in the news about Larsen's personal life, except a puff piece about the recent drowning death of his longtime coach, and the invisible toll this had taken on his psyche. Not *that* invisible—Larsen had not exactly been playing well. It was true that Larsen's wife had not been in his player box recently, but they also had small children. Larsen's camp was tight-lipped to the point of silence, and none of them would have talked to the press unless the jilted wife was seeking blood-soaked revenge—so Alex went to a rival camp instead.

When he called Niko Horvat's camp, Alex got referred to an anonymous trainer who had seen Larsen and a young woman who wasn't his wife sitting on a bench near the end of the Springwell Open, two months earlier. Larsen had lost early, and the trainer was confused, at first, to see him still hanging about without his entourage—but then he noticed that Larsen was speaking in hushed tones to this girl, and then it all made sense. The way she was grabbing his knee, dropping her mouth open just so. And then what? And then they got in a car—she was driving, he found that odd, but then realized so shitty of a car had to belong to the girl, not Larsen—and went on their way. "Obvious what was happening," the trainer told him. "Guess nobody's perfect after all."

This was something Alex himself might have said, so he wasn't sure why this acerbic statement crinkled his heart. He imagined Larsen in a fog of grief and shock, trying to find or destroy meaning in a chance tryst that had now spiraled out of control.

So this girl, Alex asked, did the trainer know who she was? Only that she was dressed like tournament staff. He offered a physical description instead. Writing "a 7 out of 10," even in quotation marks, made Alex want to climb to the roof and lean over the edge, to remind himself that if there was no more to life than these sour calculations of human value, he could always check out early.

He drove six hours north to the site of the Springwell Open, hoping to find someone who knew this mystery girl. Without a tournament the grounds were quiet, re-assimilating into the surrounding woods. He found a groundskeeper leaning against a chain-link fence, watching teenagers in posh athleisure hop around, shrieking, on an outer court. Did he know a girl who matched this description? Would have worked here during the Springwell Open? Drove a shitty car? Alex didn't mention the affair. Some chamber in his heart wanted to protect her.

"Sounds like Jenny," said the groundskeeper. "She was one of our volunteers."

Volunteer? Was she rich? No. She worked double-shifts at an ice cream store and had a thirty-minute commute in and out of town. She lived with her mother in some village farther north. Arcadia, that was the name. She was always tired. But Jenny was on a mission. What kind of mission? The groundskeeper made a derisive noise. A doomsday mission, he supposed.

"She seem particularly close to any of the players?"

"I heard something about her sneaking in and out of Daniel Larsen's locker room," he drawled, and finally turned his head to face Alex. "But I don't want to spread gossip."

And that was how he learned Jenny's name.

He found Jenny's mother by searching for "Jenny" and "Arcadia." The mother was a self-proclaimed medium, and mentioned her daughter on her website: *My daughter Jenny is my light.* A picture showed them hugging before a bright blue lake, Jenny a gawky teenager in a racing swimsuit, not a hottie homewrecker. She had her mother's world-greeting smile.

He wrote a softly-worded email to the mother, then started clicking through information about the town. Arcadia was an insect trapped in amber, it seemed—no mall or hospital or public transport, and certainly no tennis courts, but it did have a Town Hall and a Main Street and a single "church" that looked more like a gothic mansion. Its claim to fame was an annual summer spiritual "camp." Smiling people at picnic tables throughout the years. They looked too relaxed to be evangelicals. "Change Your Life at Camp Arcadia!" they bragged.

Maybe that's what I need, Alex thought. *A changed life.*

And then his phone buzzed, because the mother—Cora, short for Coraline—had replied. *Hello!* she said, with an enthusiasm that nearly made him smile. He asked if she could connect him with her daughter, but she demurred; Jenny was being cautious about people right now. But she'd be happy to answer what she could. When they actually got on video and he saw how small and overwhelmed she looked below her overflowing bookcases, he felt compelled to apologize for making her go to all this trouble.

It was no trouble, Cora said. She'd had to learn how to do video consultations with clients to keep up with the times, and she preferred it to phone calls anyway. She liked the eye contact. "Is there anything you'd like me to ask Spirit about on your behalf?" she asked.

"No thank you," Alex replied out of instinct; by the time he thought of his questionable job and missing sense of purpose and whether the pressure in his heart was something to worry about, it felt too late. "I don't want to upset you. But I wanted to ask about your daughter's relationship with Daniel Larsen."

"I figured as much," Cora replied, looking not at all upset. "Those of us who are in touch with Spirit, we feel a responsibility to pass on messages we receive, bring peace to both sides. Jenny happened to get a message from someone that Larsen man knew. His coach? Something like that. She found him and we spent a week in communion here in Arcadia—he was very worked up about the whole thing, had no idea about Spirit—and then he went home."

Alex cocked his head. "So she was more of a . . . spiritual advisor than a . . . "

"A what? A girlfriend?" Cora laughed aloud. "No. I know what you're thinking—how would a mother know? But Jenny told me everything. I knew all about her little crush. She asked if my guides had told me anything about their compatibility. Poor thing."

He had, in fact, been thinking *why would Jenny tell her mother*. "And what did you say?"

Over Cora's shoulder, a young woman peeked out from behind a wall, her feathery honey-colored hair tumbling over her shoulder. She had big baby doll eyes, deep and sunken like a '70s starlet. She was not smiling. She was more than a 7 out of 10. He cleared his throat, but Cora waved it off. "It's all right. I'm not telling you anything she doesn't already know. I told her what Spirit told me: that life was not meant for her," Cora said, and Jenny tossed her head dismissively and withdrew.

That night, Alex's phone rang at two a.m. He'd been dreaming about a burst water pipe that had flooded his dark motel room and a young woman who looked like Jenny sitting on the bed with her foot on his ankle, rooting him to the mattress. When he awoke the afterimage of her silhouette was still pulsing behind his eyes, and his ankle was still a nest of pins and needles.

On the phone, a girl's voice whispered, "What are you bothering my mother for?"

He immediately sat up and started fumbling for a light he could not find. "Is this Jenny?"

true love waits

"Yes." He glanced at the phone screen, but the number was unavailable. "Your turn."

There was bite in her words, but her voice was a low, silken invitation. He was suddenly wide awake. "I'm a reporter. I'm checking out a lead about you and Daniel Larsen, whether there's anything going on between you." He was embarrassed by the plastic emptiness of this statement; she ought to hang up on him, he thought. "But your mother says there isn't."

Jenny paused; Alex waited, holding his breath. Eventually she said, "He was my destiny." The sadness in her voice was so cold and pure he imagined it dropping like a marble into his hand. "My mother thinks I was wrong. But Spirit pointed him to me. Pointed me to him."

"The vision you had of his coach."

"Spirit sent his coach to me on Valentine's Day. I woke up in the middle of the night and he drifted into my room, all pale and bloated and choking. He was looking for Daniel."

For the first time, it occurred to Alex that this girl he was chasing might be insane. He pictured his headline dissolving, rearranging into an unreadable blur. And strangely, the thought of submitting a pixelated blur to Dale made him giddy. "That sounds frightening."

"No, not frightening. Just sad. Then Spirit really laid it on and started playing a song on my phone—you know that song by Radiohead, "True Love Waits?" That's something Spirit has said to me since I was little. The closer I got to Daniel, the more it started playing. That's how I knew: he was the love I'd been waiting for my whole life."

Alex turned this over in his head; it was backwards logic, he was sure. It wouldn't be the first time that a chance encounter with a celebrity had pushed a mentally fragile person over a precipice. She was at the right age for schizophrenia. He remembered the raw vulnerability he'd felt at twenty-three. He'd doubled up on alcohol and caffeine, and this depressant-stimulant cocktail hardened into a shell that had made his day-to-day feel survivable. Maybe Jenny had no such shell. Maybe she didn't want one. Maybe she liked what lay beyond the doors that her insane backwards world opened up.

He tried to keep her on the line. "But how did you know what Spirit meant?"

"Come to Arcadia." He imagined her smiling as her "ah" trailed off. "You'll see."

Truly, he did not need to go to Arcadia. He could, right now, dismiss Dale's blind item as a red herring planted by Horvat's camp—whether or not Jenny and Larsen had actually fucked seemed irrelevant at this point. But now there was a lightness in his ribcage, like curtains opening, that he didn't want to go away. It was want, he realized. He *wanted* to go to Arcadia. He *wanted* to say yes to Jenny.

So he did.

Jenny gave him a set of oddly abstract directions through Arcadia. Turn right after you pass the school. Take the left just before the very top of the hill. Keep straight until the very red maple tree.

When he pulled up in front of the house Jenny said was hers, he saw Cora outside in a lawn chair.

true love waits

"Hello, Alex," she said, pushing her sunglasses onto the crown of her head. "Had a feeling you'd be along today. How was traffic?"

"Not bad." He wasn't sure why he felt so nervous. "Jenny invited me. I've never been to this part of the state. It's . . . nice." He was thinking of the emerald-green foliage draped like fondant over the hills surrounding Arcadia, the merciful cloud cover that filtered all sunshine into thin golden rays. *Ladders to God*—he'd read that in a book somewhere.

"Yes, we like to reduce the amount of noise for Spirit to cut through," Cora said. "Jenny's not home right now, but you're welcome to wait with me if you like."

Alex checked the time. Jenny had just told him to arrive "whenever you feel like it," although he explicitly said he would try to be there around two.

"She does her own thing," Cora said, smiling. "Come on, Alex. I'll make chocolate milkshakes. Jenny's favorite."

The house was brighter than it had looked on the video call, with large bay windows overlooking a backyard with a trampoline and, beyond it, that sparkling blue lake. He didn't know what he'd been expecting—menacing black-and-white ghost photos on the walls? The smell of mildew? Maybe he'd just expected to feel less comfortable. While Cora busied herself with the blender, he sat down on a couch and had the sudden urge to burrow into the cushions and disappear. Let Jenny pull him to the waking world with a grin and a "wake up, sleepyhead."

He stood back up, trying to shake himself to life. "So when you say that you and Jenny were in communion with Daniel Larsen . . . " he started, but Cora corrected him with a wagging finger.

"In communion with Spirit. In this case, with his coach."

"Right. And I assume you got paid for . . . making this connection."

Cora gave him a slightly mischievous look that said all that needed to be said. "Everyone has to make a living. You circulate gossip about people who can throw balls, and we circulate messages from a higher realm of consciousness."

He couldn't resist laughing, and Cora smiled with him. "Well, that sounds fantastic."

"Hmm. Fantastic as in splendid, yes, fantastic as in fantasy, no. We firmly believe that science will vindicate us, eventually." Cora handed him a frothy chocolate milkshake in a glass. "Think of what you know about death. The heart stops, the brain stops, the body falls over. It's permanent, right? But *nothing* is permanent, that's the thing. All the smartest people, all the world over, have said that over and over. Matter transforms. It doesn't disappear."

Alex hadn't felt so comforted by an idea since he realized, at the age of eight, that he could take himself clean out of life if he really wanted to. It wasn't that he wanted the finality of death. It was that he wanted to exit the present.

"So why in the world would *life* just *end*? No. Consciousness goes on. Soul goes on."

Cora was holding his gaze very intently. He was relieved to break eye contact when he thought he heard something down the hall—maybe a window shutter rattling. He imagined Jenny climbing through the

true love waits

window just because she felt like it, swearing to herself as she stumbled. It reminded him of a youth he hadn't quite had. "Is that Jenny?"

Cora's gaze had become less certain, like she was debating whether or not to say something. He glanced down the hallway and saw Jenny at the other end, shimmering slightly as if she'd just gotten out of the lake. He blinked and she'd disappeared; she must have gone into her room.

But when he followed her down the hallway and into the pale blue sunlit bedroom leaking the scent of honeysuckle, she wasn't in there, either. Had she dived under her bed?

No. Nothing there but some old dishes and dried flowers. The windows were closed, the translucent drapes were still. She couldn't have possibly folded herself into those drawers. He spun around but only saw Cora, idling in the doorway.

"Alex," Cora said, "Jenny's already been released from her body. It makes her a bit tricky to follow, sometimes. Kind of goes where she wants to."

He didn't understand what she meant at first. Released from her body? He got hung up thinking about trap doors and even astral projection, until the thud of the truth finally hit him. At which point he suddenly became extremely nauseous.

"How did she . . . " He saw it now, Jenny's body hanging from a ceiling fan. An alien, pounding rage filled him; the terrifying certainty that he would kill Larsen if he'd driven her to this end. "Did she . . . ?"

Cora cut him off before he had to say it. "Oh, goodness, no. Nothing like that. She was shot. At a gas station. You remember the shooting in Coldhook? She and five others. Some mad man, who knows. The cops gunned him down."

He oh-so-vaguely remembered a mass shooting at a gas station—remembered photos of police tape roped around red-and-blue gas pumps, anyway.

But he did remember that it was last month.

And he did remember that he had spoken to Jenny *this week*.

"But I just talked to her. She called me. I just saw her! Right there!"

"I know, and I'm thrilled that she wants to communicate with you!" Cora gave his hand a squeeze that was near-painful with all the antique rings she wore. "We are truly fortunate that she's decided to stay so close to earth side. I guess she pities her poor lonely mother. And you! She must really like you. I suspect she thinks you're a kindred spirit. Pardon the expression."

What hurt the most was realizing that this was probably why he'd come to Arcadia; because some entombed and very lonely part of him had wanted to meet this Jenny whom Fate had quite randomly pulled into his path. And that part of him had been expecting, assuming, counting on—for reasons he was hesitant to admit—a girl who was alive.

"They sent me a letter. Larsen and his wife. It was very nice. Do you want to see it?"

He very badly did *not* want to see anything that defined Jenny as "dead," but Cora had already sailed off, singing to herself. She returned holding open a scrapbook as thick as her fist. He imagined the previous pages stuffed with memorabilia of a younger Jenny—swimming ribbons she'd earned, Mother's Day cards she'd made—and felt his stomach twist like a rag.

true love waits

"There," Cora said, setting it on his lap, "See?" He only managed to digest a few words near the bottom of the page—*if there is anything we can do please*—before bile crept up his throat and he slammed the scrapbook shut, barely managing to drop it on Jenny's bed instead of the floor. Cora looked startled. "Are you all right, dear?"

No. He was not all right. And in his distress, he blurted out the rudest thing he could think of: "You're telling me Spirit didn't give you any warning so you could save her life?"

Regret had already started to fill his throat before he finished the word "warning"; he'd tell himself later that maybe he wanted to give Cora someone to lash out at. Maybe he wanted placid Cora to show some anger on behalf of her dead child.

"Spirit did tell me," Cora said. She was trying to keep her voice steady, but her eyes were wet. "Spirit told me that life wasn't meant for her. I just didn't know what all Spirit meant."

He left Arcadia half an hour later. The only thing Cora said was "take care now" as he hurried out the front door. Her glazed eyes drifted, as if looking through him to some beautiful vista only she could see. From inside the pine-scented safety of his car, he saw a toothy grin on her face that he hadn't noticed before. Or maybe hadn't *allowed* himself to notice.

He stopped at a gas station before he left town. It was the end of May, and the Camp Arcadia seekers were starting to trickle in for the summer with their RVs and taped-up station wagons. *I want to believe!* one bumper sticker said, and it made him tremble.

He caught a stray whiff of sweet honeysuckle dancing above the stench of gasoline and thought of Jenny stopping for gas in Coldhook on her way home, checking her phone to see if Larsen had texted her to say he'd changed his mind, hearing someone yell "what do you think you're doing?" and turning her head to meet her fate. He inhaled sharply. The fresh air stung his teeth.

"It was nothing," he told Dale when he got back to the city. "It's a non-story."

Dale was incredulous—*what the hell have you been doing all this time if it's a non-story?*—but Dale's self-important anger bounced off his soul like a pebble skimming water. Poor Dale, he thought, had no sense of the world's truth. Alex would have quit on the spot if it didn't seem like such a massive expenditure of energy for a thing of such little consequence.

His roommate asked him how he knew that Cora wasn't lying. Maybe mother and daughter were pulling an elaborate prank; wouldn't it have come up in his search if Jenny had died in a shooting? But he'd never looked at Coldhook and a mosquito-like whisper in his ear reminded him that Jenny was sometimes short for Eugenia, and when he altered his search parameters, she came right up. Her smiling death.

"Then you probably weren't really talking to her," his roommate said, as if it was obvious. "It was probably her mom, doing a voice. It was probably some other girl walking through the house. Do you seriously think you were on the phone with a ghost?"

He didn't *think* that. He *knew* that. Just as sure as he *knew* that Jenny was the one shutting off his alarm clock in the morning, turning off his television after he fell asleep. He'd been afraid at first. But then he realized that she was only trying to express her care for him, delicately pulling a thread between his earthly plane and wherever she was now. It had to take effort on her part. He was flattered.

"Jenny?" he started asking anytime he was alone, and whenever he got any sign of her enduring presence—a gust of wind, a tipped cup, a lull in his tinnitus—his heart would swell, and he would start searching for his next opportunity to be alone. When the city was silent, a hole would open from his heart to his stomach that he couldn't cauterize.

In early July, Jenny stopped making contact. Alex wondered if maybe she was across the sea, watching Daniel Larsen. So he drank chocolate milkshakes and tuned into tournaments, telling Dale that he was "reporting" on matches, but taking no notes. He only watched Larsen, and he wasn't watching Larsen so much as waiting for his opponent's racket to come unstrung, for a ball to mysteriously change direction in mid-air.

None of that happened, so he preoccupied himself instead with watching Larsen's wife. She was in the front row, resting her chin on her bejeweled hand, clapping and yelling and biting her nails to the beat of her husband's footsteps. The distance between the couple seemed at once so great and so small. Shared scowls and fist pumps and squints at the umpire, throwing their heads back in simultaneous righteous exasperation when he made mistakes.

In press, Larsen said he was reaching a state of peace regarding his dead coach. "It's been helpful to speak with family and friends," he said, and then shivered a bit and put on his track jacket. "Without my wife," Larsen went on, "I'm nothing." And Alex believed him, this time.

Because he was nothing without Jenny.

Every night before he slept, he'd set out his phone on the pillow beside him and invite Jenny to play a song. "Whenever you're ready," he said. It became a meditative habit, his first-ever exercise in faith.

And she did return at the end of the month, playing "True Love Waits" at two a.m. and anointing the room with honeysuckle. In her presence, the world finally felt real.

And yet to everyone else, she was invisible. The empty space he kept staring at. The preoccupation fraying his thoughts. "Alex's lost it," he overheard his roommate saying, but surely he could only feel *loss* if he'd *had* something in the first place.

Alex was used to being invisible. He was used to slipping between the cracks of existence, an unmemorable guest, an anonymous byline. It had never really bothered him—he had nothing to offer the world and the world had nothing to offer him, and it was only fair for he and the world to slip past each other without impact. But invisibility seemed terribly unfair to Jenny, who even in death carried more vim, more commitment to her personal vision, than anyone else he knew. She was all impact. A most beautiful bruise.

He returned to Arcadia in August, just in time for the end of summer camp. Campers and residents were hugging and crying in driveways next to packed-up cars. When he turned off the radio and rolled the window down, he could hear singing through the cherry trees.

Alex pulled up in front of Cora's house and she was already out on the front stoop, waiting for him. He had no idea how he could explain his presence, but as he suspected, he didn't need to. "It's all right," she said, patting his back as she embraced him. "No one dies in Arcadia."

Until she said this, he had no grasp of the true measure of his sadness. He felt a brief sense of crystalline joy at this sudden revelation, followed by a longer, deeper panic. His knees buckled into Cora's body. A howl briefly escaped his mouth before he managed to stifle it biting into his fist.

Cora took him to the church he'd first seen online, the gothic mansion now called the Renewed Spiritualist Church of Arcadia. The renewal had evidently not been physical—a bucket stood in the foyer collecting drips, the damask wallpaper had faded to a dusty gray—but a sense of open possibility did saturate the dark. Excited whispers carried hope. Everyone they passed had this look in their eyes—a giddiness, a *relief*. These poor souls thought they had run up against the brick end of the world only to feel those bricks magically give way to a vast and limitless universe.

"She gets clearer with time," Cora said as they sat in what used to be a sitting room, now filled with rows of mismatched folding chairs facing a table with a lectern. "She gets oriented, you know, in the Spirit realm. She gets better at gathering energy, at composing herself the way she wants to be seen. On the day she went, she was just a willow wisp. *I could feel her, because I know my girl, but she was nothing like she is now. Ah! There!*" He could hear her pride as she pointed. "Can you see her?"

He squinted in the direction of her finger, toward the sheer navy curtains on their right; in his head, in his heart, he was straining, terrified that he wouldn't see Jenny.

But he did. A missile of light that broke off from the sunshine and pushed against the curtains, billowing them out in a girl-like shape, and everything else in Alex's life that he'd ever perceived to be important receded, as if being left on a distant shore. "Yes," he whispered. He had the urge to run to the curtain and pull it aside, but he steeled himself; space and materiality were not as straightforward as he'd always been led to believe. "I can."

That night after a potluck dinner, he sat on the damp sand behind Cora's house, listening to the gentle ripple of dark waves and wondering how long he would need to wait to be reunited with Jenny. The way Cora talked, the way she calmly spooned mash potatoes onto plates and laughed at her neighbors' jokes, she and the other people of Arcadia were adequately comforted by the fleeting incorporeal presence of their loved ones, the shape of a hand against the curtain, the whisper on the phone.

But Alex wasn't. The ache that Jenny had opened up inside him—no, the ache that she had salved, and then torn open, and then stitched over again, because he'd always had this sense of loss, hadn't he, this heavy anchor of absence that he hadn't been able to identify until he lost her—was no longer alleviated by half-measures. "True love waits," Jenny said, but he had spent his whole life waiting, floating on the surface tension of the world.

So when he heard a splash and looked up to see a shimmering bundle of light refract out from beneath the surface of the lake—*my light*, Cora called her—he got to his feet, and started wading in.

the shape of her soul

MICHELLE BELANGER

*T*he new clients contacted Valerie by email. The chiming notification startled her while she repotted an ivy. A handful of loamy soil cascaded to the floor, and Aunt Bea, hovering as usual, tsked.

"I told you, duckie, you shouldn't be doing that over the nice carpet," she fussed. "Now how will you clean that up?"

"With a vacuum, Aunt Bea," Valerie said. She snuggled the ivy into its roomier home, then set down the brightly-colored clay pot. The ivy rested amid a regiment of others, glossy alocasias and fat succulents, a riotous basil and a pendulous spider plant. This room with its creaking floor had once been a wide back porch where the previous owners could rock and converse in the slanting afternoon sun. That same sun now gilded all the windows, making a perfect home for her plant-friends.

Sixty seconds later, the notification repeated, a jangling intrusion in her weekend calm. When she'd chosen that tone, she'd found the chimes soothing. No longer. Still, if she didn't have notifications on, she'd never get around to answering her messages.

Ignoring emails was a good way to lose clients. Most people didn't like waiting once they'd reached out for help about their haunting. It took too much effort to admit the haunting existed in the first place. Valerie understood. The reality of the paranormal was daunting. It had taken her many years to embrace her ability with spirits as a gift, not a curse.

Aunt Bea pressed closer, a tremor of excitement passing like contagion from her to Valerie. The elderly woman had been in a mood all day, restless for something to do. Earlier in the kitchen, she'd knocked over the teapot. She hadn't meant to break it, of course. She never meant to break anything. But she'd gotten it into her head to make tea while Valerie finished up breakfast, and Aunt Bea's hands didn't work the way they used to. She never seemed to learn.

"Is that a phone call?" the older woman asked. "We never get phone calls anymore. I miss talking to people."

"I'm not people?" Valerie laughed. She wiped her hands on her sweatpants then picked up the device, silencing the notification.

"Oh, duckie, you know what I mean," Aunt Bea said. "*Other* people. We had a partyline, you know. After supper, my friends and I would talk for hours. We didn't gossip, just traded stories about everyone in the town." Little difference, but Valerie didn't feel like upsetting Aunt Bea by pointing it out. "Those were the days."

Valerie moved from the sunny former porch to

what was once a front parlor. Drifts of papers and partly-read books cluttered her desk. A second-hand computer, close to a decade out of date, lurked under the mess. Haunting investigations paid the bills, but just barely. Valerie excavated the keyboard as Aunt Bea trailed after her.

Nothing loaded quickly on this machine anymore, and Valerie was tempted to read and reply to the email on her phone. But the tedium of using a keyboard smaller than a business card dissuaded her. Instead, she waited, idly sorting through files of past cases. A decade of work crammed this room, stacked on the desk and tacked to the walls. Valerie had never set out to become a ghost investigator, but her psychic gifts created such a synergy with her training in therapy that it felt as much a calling as an occupation.

Aunt Bea fluttered and fussed, pressed against her back like a tattery grey bird. The long-skirted woman didn't really understand the computer, but she knew this space was important to Valerie, and Valerie was her only real connection to the world anymore. Valerie tolerated Aunt Bea's gentle assault. She loved the old woman in ways she had never cared for own blood family. But Aunt Bea's agitation, well-intentioned as it was, began to spread to the other residents of the house. Heavy footfalls in the rooms upstairs meant Ivan was up. And if Ivan was active, Griselle would soon follow.

Griselle was always a handful.

Valerie sighed. She'd been looking forward to a calm, *quiet* Sunday afternoon, maybe finishing one of the books that lay perpetually half started.

"Aunt Bea," Valerie said. "Maybe you should go check on Tommy in the yard."

"Tommy?" the elderly woman echoed.

"Yes, Tommy. In the yard. He's still trying to catch that frog and you know he can't swim."

Valerie hated herself a little for bringing it up. But when Aunt Bea got like this, Tommy was the only way to get her to refocus. In a rustle of skirts, she'd march into the yard and look for the boy, and then she'd come back, and remember what year it was.

They'd been through the cycle more times than Valerie cared to count.

"Tommy," Aunt Bea pronounced, as if waking from a dream. Then she called for the boy, her voice ringing through the back hall, already fading.

Tommy was fine, of course. He would always be fine now, though the frog perpetually eluded capture. Aunt Bea was simply too caught up in the past to hold that knowledge for long.

"All right," Valerie muttered, clicking her browser. "Let's see what this is about."

The email started like so many others. The sender—a woman with the unlikely name of Mrs. Hattie Pendergast—apologized through several iterations of, "this is probably going to sound crazy" and "I don't expect you to believe me," before working up enough courage to share the actual details of her haunting. She related a tale of paranormal activity escalating in her house over the last six months, witnessed by both herself and her husband, Mike: footsteps, a persistent voice, something agitating the family dog—all fairly textbook experiences. Nevertheless, Hattie insisted on calling the spirit a demon, a term that made Valerie cringe.

the shape of her soul

The detail about being dragged from her bed was interesting. Hattie included several blurry photos of the bed itself. One photo included an image of the family dog, an unbearably cute designer breed that looked like a miniature husky. She wasn't sure what she was supposed to make of the blurry bedroom photos, but the dog looked sweet.

Normally, the instant Valerie saw a client describe their spirit as a demon, the case was a hard pass—not because Valerie feared such beings, but because of the inevitable struggle with the clients' own beliefs. She had no illusions about how thoroughly most people misinterpreted their experiences with the spirit world, and once religious convictions got tangled in the equation, it was hard to steer them toward a compassionate approach to their ghostly residents.

Confrontation with the living was exhausting.

And yet something warranted a further look. Not Hattie's turgid descriptions of her supposed spirit, certainly, but all the details left unsaid: what the spirit looked like on the occasions Hattie "saw a figure;" precisely how the spirit was "tormenting" Gus, the adorable Pomsky; the sound of the spirit's voice as it called obsessively in the night—and, more importantly—what it said.

Maybe Hattie omitted these details intentionally, maybe she was simply trying to pack too much emotion into one email and got overwhelmed. But Valerie sensed there was more to the story.

An initial interview in a safe, open space couldn't hurt. And she needed to get out for groceries.

A string of vehicles snaked through the Starbright's parking lot, winding from the drive-thru almost to the street. People loved their coffee, especially when it came with a birthday cake's worth of sugar and flavorings.

Aunt Bea, had she been able to bring herself to leave the house, would definitely have opinions.

Valerie sat awkwardly at one of the outside tables, twisting a bit of napkin in her hands as she waited for the Pendergasts to arrive. A vintage silk peony, its petals the palest of pink, bloomed from a velvet choker at the throat. A sunny floral mask covered the lower half of her face. Some had abandoned their masks as soon as they were able, but Valerie took comfort in the sheltering cloth. She liked what it protected as well as what it obscured.

This many people made her nervous—had done so long before all the variants of the airborne virus had changed the world. Some customers, cautious as Valerie, still went about masked, although for many of these, the masks were more an excuse to wear their favorite edgy design. The new band T-shirts courtesy of COVID-19. Again, she imagined what Aunt Bea would say had she been able to come along. The elderly auntie no doubt would have expounded on the endless tribulations of the influenza epidemic, *tut-tutting* at how cavalier so many of these people were about breathing everyone else's air.

If they could see what Valerie saw, maybe they wouldn't even leave the house. The silent dead, wan and confused, drifted in the wake of what Valerie presumed were family members, maybe friends. Most of them hadn't worked out that they were dead yet, so they locked into patterns familiar and ingrained. One or two bore a dawning expression of self-awareness, and their resultant pain and frustration crashed against Valerie's carefully maintained mental defenses—defenses it had taken her years to hone.

She hated being out like this, but what was the alternative? She didn't know the Pendergasts well enough to meet with them at their house. And she certainly had no intention of inviting clients into her own home. That was her family's sanctuary, never to be disturbed.

So she waited. And she bunkered her senses. And she tore three more napkins to tiny shreds before her clients arrived.

Mike Pendergast found her before she spotted him. "Hey. I bet you're the psychic," he said, as he grinned and sucked his teeth. Was it an intentional sound? He used it like punctuation. "That blue hair's gotta be a pain to keep up."

Before she could react, he dropped into the seat beside her, braced his elbows on the little bistro table, and leaned in close. Reflexively, Valerie pulled her hands away from his. Bits of shredded napkin scattered everywhere, skirling across the table. He smelled of cigarettes and beard oil and sweat. A thin sheen of it beaded beneath the bill of his baseball cap. A black and white American flag adorned both cap and T-shirt, each flag bearing a solitary line of blue.

Valerie's stomach clenched. This was a bad idea. The demon claim should have been warning enough.

"I don't really call myself psychic," she said. The metal legs of her chair grated across the patio's cement as she put some space between them.

Mike grunted, neither an assent nor an objection.

"Honey, please," Hattie called out, hurrying from the doors of the Starbright's, an iced confection in one hand.

Mrs. Pendergast was not at all what Valerie expected, especially after her unceremonious introduction to Mike. Where her husband was sweaty, dressed in battered jeans and muddy boots, Mrs. Pendergast was pristine. Her hair was black and glossy, neatly dressed in stylish waves. Her deep brown skin drank the sun and gleamed with answering warmth—a sharp contrast to the dour man still pressing into Valerie's personal space.

"Nope," Valerie said, for no one's benefit but her own. She got up, then hesitated.

The wife crossed the distance from the coffee shop's doors to Valerie's far table. As she drew closer, Valerie spied a nest of lines around her eyes. Sleepless smudges bruised the flesh beneath her lower lids. In her strappy shoes and sunny clothes, Hattie smiled at the world, but it was a fight.

Stay, a voice whispered.

"Ivan?" Valerie hissed. The thinnest presence of his familiar energy shifted near her back. Only Mike was close enough to hear, but if he caught the exchange, he didn't react. Even so, she shifted to thoughts. *When did you come along?*

Felt you could use the backup. A soldier in life, at

least for some of it, Ivan often fretted when she left the house. Of all her gathered family, he remained the most protective.

I don't know about this, Valerie thought, knowing Ivan could still hear. Mike Pendergast turned fully to his harried wife, his pasty grin a lop-sided pretense of apology.

"I'm just trying to see what we're paying for," he said. He leaned back in his chair.

Stay, Ivan repeated. *I think there's someone who needs you.*

Valerie stood taut as a harp string, the rapid thud of her pulse trembling through the petals of the silk flower. She didn't want to be here. Mike was everything she struggled to avoid, and nothing about the supposed demon seemed worth the cost of subjecting herself to his snide behavior.

"Mike, honey," Hattie said. "Why don't you go wait in the truck." It wasn't a question.

One hand fisted on her hip, Hattie towered over her seated husband. Mike scrunched his face—he wanted to argue, felt it deep as a biological need. But Hattie quelled him with a look. She hooked a thumb in the direction of a black Ford F150 squeezed into one of the spots reserved for takeaway guests.

"You still got that fertilizer to pick up," she persisted. "You been talking about it for a week. Go on over to the hardware store. That should give us ladies plenty of time to talk."

He grunted and stood so fast he nearly upended his chair. But he left. Valerie relaxed as Ivan pressed invisibly to her back.

Mrs. Pendergast set her iced coffee on the table,

absently brushing away the remaining tatters of Valerie's ruined napkins. She looked over to where Valerie stood tense with indecision. Mrs. Pendergast cranked her smile to full wattage.

"You have to forgive my husband," she said. "The past few months have been rough."

Reluctantly, Valerie approached the table, still not fully committing to the space. "This is just an initial interview," she cautioned. "I can't guarantee I'll take your case. I have a lot of questions."

Hattie took a long swallow from her drink. She gazed past Valerie, seeming to focus on the traffic along the busy road. She didn't say anything right away, but all the skin on her arms pricked up despite the summer heat. "I'll understand if you can't help me," she said. "But we're desperate. We've tried everything."

Valerie dragged out her chair and sat down. She took out her phone and set it to record. "This is for my notes," she explained. "I need to hear a little more than what you told me in the email before I commit. Have you noticed any triggers to the activity? Have there been significant changes in your lives or in your house over the past six months? Are there specific messages or behaviors you associate with the ghost?"

"It's a demon," Hattie corrected. The down-turned scoring at the corners of her mouth deepened, aging her a dozen years. Valerie had initially placed her in her early forties, but now fifty seemed more reasonable. "You have to understand what we're dealing with." She took another sip from her cup. Lines of condensation dripped from her hand. "You're not the first person we've called about this. Mike is over it.

the shape of her soul

He thinks we should just move. But I like our house. We raised our baby in that house." Her voice broke.

Valerie always worked hard to avoid eye contact. It was too intimate a connection, heightening everything she normally sensed from other people. The only thing more invasive was physical touch, which is why she held her hands so stiffly clasped against uninvited contact. But in the brief moment she met Hattie's eyes, the other woman's emotions tsunamied through her. The external world faded—the oppressive heat, the endless murmur of customers and cars, the uncomfortable rigidity of the patio chair.

Everything except a deep and relentless anxiety. Desperation. Fear. And such a burden of grief that an instant echo of tears welled at the back of Valerie's throat.

Peace, Ivan whispered.

She closed her eyes and focused on her breathing until she became a rock anchored in the torrenting stream. Hattie's feelings still raged around her, wild and undeniable, but she kept them outside. There, she could observe and learn.

The grief, especially, was interesting.

"All right," Valerie sighed. "We can come back to why you think it's a demon later. But I need to establish a timeline." She continued to breathe with focused rhythm as she rode the surface of Hattie's emotions. "When did the activity begin? You said six months in the email, but I got the feeling that was an estimate. Do you recall a specific day?"

Hattie shook her head. "It was late last fall. It crept up on us, you know. Little things. Gus barking when no one was there. The sound of footsteps in the hall. And the whispers." She was back to looking at anything except Valerie—the cars behind her, the little pool of water sweating from her cup, the tiny arc of rhinestones glittering from one thick acrylic nail. "The whispers were when I knew something bad was in the house."

"Why? What did the whispers say?"

"They played tricks," Hattie said. She kept the tremor from her voice but it was there in her suddenly exhaled breath. "They sound like a little girl crying. There's no little girl in that house. Never has been. That's how I know it's a demon. The whispers lie."

Valerie swallowed her urge for explanation, how spirits weren't beholden to haunt the spaces where they died. They could travel, and often did. Especially once they themselves realized most of what the living believed of spirits was untrue.

"It says my name," Hattie groaned. "It calls me mommy." Again, that distant stare fixed to places beyond the cheery coffeeshop and busy street. "*Mommy, mommy.* I hear it from the bed at night. And Gus barks, and the door slams, and something grabs my arm. Yanking me."

She swept back tears. Valerie rode the emotional waves—insult; indignation; a steely, wounded rage—and all that above the abiding well of grief.

Hattie sniffled and fumbled in her handbag for a tissue. Mascara smeared around her eyes.

"This next question—I don't mean to imply anything you just told me is unreal. Believe that," Valerie assured. "But I need to understand the full extent of the situation."

Cautiously, Hattie nodded.

the shape of her soul

"The things you described . . . The footsteps, the whispers, the door slamming. How much has your husband experienced?"

Hattie blew her nose, then meticulously folded the used tissue onto itself so none of the damp showed. "Mike denied it for months. He's like that. Ignores things and hopes they fix themselves. You can guess how well that works." The smile she showed was all bitterness. "But I knew. I knew for a fact he heard it. It woke him up same as me. And when I got grabbed—and let me be clear, this thing nearly pulled me straight out of the bed—Mike first thing called up our minister."

Valerie felt the sharp uptick of her brows. Tried to suppress it. Failed.

"When I said this thing's a demon, I did not exaggerate," Hattie declared. "We've had a deliverance and two exorcisms. Two. One of them was this Catholic bishop. Some kind of demonologist. That was Mike's idea," she added. "And let me tell you, that man tossed buckets of holy water through the entire house. None of it worked. If anything, it made things worse."

Valerie puffed her cheeks, carefully choosing her words. "So . . . all the clergy you employed previously were in agreement? The spirit is a demon?"

"Two Christians and a Catholic agree," Hattie replied. "It's a demon."

That's three Christians, Valerie thought. *All of those are Christians*. But she knew it wouldn't help anything to say it out loud.

She could always walk away. This was an interview, not a promise. "No" was the most powerful tool in her arsenal. But Ivan had a point. There was something more here, and the less Hattie's story added up, the more she wanted to see the haunting for herself.

"Why me?" she asked finally. "I'm not clergy. I don't do exorcisms. I don't even send spirits into the light. It says so right on my website."

Hattie seemed genuinely perplexed. "I never laid eyes on your website."

"How'd you even find me then?"

Hattie reached again to her handbag, this time withdrawing a neatly folded note. The paper was the soft taupe of faux parchment bearing a whimsical border of butterflies and flowers drawn in colored ink. As Hattie passed it across, Valerie caught an oddly familiar scent. Her thoughts raced as she struggled to place it.

"I'm an RN, but my side hustle is home health care," Hattie explained. "There's this elderly lady I care for. Margaret. Normally, I don't talk about my own business when I work, but the woman's got a sharp eye. When she asked what was up, I told her. Worse she could do was ask for another caregiver, right?" Bitterly, Hattie laughed. "Well, Margaret believed me. Every word. And she had her own story."

Margaret. That perfume. The design on the paper.

Behind her mask, Valerie's mouth dropped open in a perfect, soundless O. Ivan's presence surged against her neck as the scent filled her head.

"Maggie. That's her artwork," Valerie managed.

"Sure is," Hattie replied. "Eighty-three years old, but she's still sharp. Draws every single day."

With numb fingers, Valerie unfolded the note. A familiar cursive, looping and large, waited for her on the page.

the shape of her soul

—Tell Ivan I'm almost ready.—

"She said to give you that when I asked for your help. Said you'd know. I didn't mention it in the email because it seemed like the kind of thing you have to see to understand."

Valerie closed the note in her hand.

Ivan's widow did not play fair.

In the parking lot, Valerie blasted the air conditioning on its highest setting. Her hands fisted round the steering wheel as she fought to steady the thunder of her heart. Her mask sat discarded on the passenger seat alongside the note from Margaret, which Hattie let her keep.

"Did you know?" she demanded of Ivan.

The dead soldier had practically crawled up her back through the last few minutes of the interview with Hattie Pendergast. But now he was conspicuously absent.

"Goddammit, Ivan," she snapped, and immediately felt bad about it. She tapped a purposeful rhythm on the hard curve of the steering wheel, breathing in a seven-count. "I'm sorry," she said. "I don't want to be harsh with you. But I need an answer. Mike really freaks me out. I don't trust all the demon talk. And I would probably walk right off this case if not for that note from your wife."

Another moment of hesitation, then the air inside the car quivered. The damp, slightly musty scent of the air conditioning faded, replaced by Ivan's familiar combination of cherry pipe tobacco and Old Spice.

I haven't been to see her, he said meekly.

"You can go anywhere," Valerie reminded. "Literally anywhere. You just have to think it."

He continued to hover incorporeally around her, wafts of tobacco and cologne the only signs of his presence. *I know.*

"But why stay away? You've been doing so good, and I know you miss her. You two were married nearly sixty years." She believed him, of course. Despite all the media portrayals of spirit trickery, lying was incredibly difficult for them. Emotions were more than half of what a spirit was, the indelible imprint of joy and trauma and lived experience.

A long silence hung in the Kia. Finally, a tremor on the air: Ivan's spirit-equivalent of a sigh.

I'm not ready, he said.

Valerie nodded, trusting the spirit to perceive her intent if not the physical action itself. "That's valid."

The tension between them eased. As it did, Ivan settled into a more palpable manifestation, flickering in and out like cloud shadows scudding across the sun. He appeared in the passenger seat, mask and note still visible through the remembered crispness of his naval uniform.

"I'm sorry I yelled at you," she said.

Apology accepted.

She tapped her fingers, finally beginning to feel settled after the shock of the note. "Here's the thing. If you didn't set this up, then we've got some serious synchronicity going on. It's been nearly seven years since I met you through Maggie. And after I did the job, she was so upset to learn it was you. I didn't think we'd ever hear from her again."

the shape of her soul

I hate how having me around scared her so badly, Ivan sighed. The phantom's shoulders slumped and the idealized visage of his youth faded seamlessly into the lined and weathered face he'd worn closer to his death. *I never meant any harm, you know.*

"I know. Of course I know," Valerie assured him. "You were new. You wanted to let her know you were still around. It happens. Adjusting is hard, Ivan."

He lifted the memory of his big-knuckled hand and placed it gently atop her own. The contact tingled, faint and electric.

Thank you for taking me in, he said.

They sat together, the living and the dead, in the easy silence of chosen family.

You taking this case or what? Ivan finally asked.

"Only if you have my back," Valerie responded.

For as long as you need.

That Friday, Valerie packed up her satchel of supplies as Ivan stoically observed. Aunt Bea fussed and even Griselle came down from upstairs to see what was up. As a ghost investigator, Valerie traveled light. She wasn't a fan of the latest gadgets (and usually sucked at using them anyway). She had a pendulum and dowsing rods, though they were mostly for show. Her most valuable tool was something she could never leave behind even if she wanted to—that special quirk of her mind that enabled her to perceive spirits as easily as the plants in her parlor or the birds in her yard.

She did add her incense, spirit dagger, and blessed water just in case there actually was something to the demon claim. It was never demons though, even when the clients insisted. But there was a first time for everything, and it didn't hurt to be prepared.

"Ready to go?" she asked Ivan. He was in full dress blues today, his memory of the precise appearance of the uniform imperfect, so the insignias shifted and smeared like words in a dream. He nodded, slipping a cap over his crew cut the instant they were out the door.

The Pendergasts lived on the other side of town, and the drive to their sub-division took Valerie through a twisting maze of back roads and cul-de-sacs. With Ivan so present in the car, the map function on her phone kept glitching, delaying her by nearly fifteen minutes.

After a full restart, she managed to get back on track, wending her way through an upscale neighborhood of flawless yards and pretentious houses. The flags and political signs that proliferated across those aggressively green lawns made her heart skip.

What's the matter? Ivan asked. Emotions were not a thing one hid from a spirit, even if trying—and Valerie hadn't been trying.

"Just . . . confused why Hattie would stay in a place like this, especially if moving out were an option." She gestured to one household where a regiment of flags hung over the porch—Thin Blue Line, Don't Tread on Me, the Confederate Stars and Bars, and a fourth with a Viking rune of interlocking triangles that she knew had once been innocent. "I wouldn't feel safe walking these streets."

Ivan, whose service to his country had played out

the shape of her soul

several wars ago but still informed the core of his identity, regarded the place through the lens of Valerie's perception. *Wrapped in a flag and carrying a Bible,* he grumbled. *They warned us. I never believed 'em. Makes me happy I'm out of the world.*

"Some of us still have to live here," Valerie said bleakly.

The Pendergast home was a bare two streets away from this, nestled at the end of a tree-lined cul-de-sac. A two-storey modern structure with a brown brick facade, it overlooked a yard as meticulously kept as all the others. That yard sported its own collection of flags and signs, all in keeping with the T-shirt and ballcap Mike had worn at the Starbright's. Perhaps Hattie believed it all, too. The family's pickup dominated the middle of the driveway, freshly washed and shiny as a beetle's carapace. Beyond the truck, the garage stood open, tools and a riding mower visible from the street. Valerie parked halfway down the cul-de-sac, angling her aging Kia close to the curb.

You think it's really a demon? Ivan asked.

"There are people who would have said you were a demon, Ivan." She adjusted the silk peony at her throat. "People are the real demons. Every single time."

She slipped the loops of her mask over her ears and got out. Movement drew her attention to the open garage and she spied Mike wrestling bags of mulch into a sturdy metal wheelbarrow. He didn't look up and she didn't draw attention, not even for a perfunctory wave.

Hattie answered the door as she walked up. Her bright yellow sundress and whimsical earrings made her look like the goddess of summer picnics. She smiled to match the outfit, but weariness still claimed her eyes.

"Valerie," she said, stepping back from the threshold. "Come in. You want some seltzer water? Lemonade? Coffee, maybe?" The entryway had a high ceiling from which hung an enormous pendant lamp. The light refracted through geometric panels of glass. From somewhere upstairs, a dog gave one excited yip then fell silent.

"I'm fine, thanks," Valerie said reflexively. She hefted the old leather doctor's bag she repurposed for investigations. "I'd rather just start."

"You can take off your mask while you're inside, you know," Hattie urged. "We're all healthy here."

"It helps with my allergies," she replied.

"Okay." Hattie rubbed her hands on her thighs, maybe smoothing imaginary wrinkles, perhaps only soothing herself. "Okay," she repeated. "So . . . what do you need from me?"

Valerie took a moment to study the house. She kept her senses flung open, expecting to feel something as she entered, if not a dark presence, at least the familiar heaviness that accompanied the manifestation of a spirit. But the Pendergast home felt . . . empty.

A living room opened to her right from the entrance. Two big leather couches orbited a flat-screen TV mounted on the far wall. To the left, slightly behind where Mrs. Pendergast stood, carpeted stairs led to the second floor. A door on the left stood partly open. This seemed to lead to a laundry room, although an overburdened coat tree obscured most of her view. Straight back from the stairs, a short hall led to a

the shape of her soul

kitchen of crisp white cabinetry and sleek stone counters. Everything was impeccably decorated, but all the art had a soulless, corporate feel, as if someone had studied a concept board showing how an upper middle-class suburban home was supposed to look and then bought it all.

Except one piece.

On a wall in the living room, showcased within a heavy gilt frame, a gorgeous woman posed in resplendent dress. The style held shades of Erté, but through an African lens. Golden light limned her deep brown skin. Elaborate jewelry spangled her throat, her ears, the sweeping coils of her hair. Valerie went straight to it, noting the defiant lift to the woman's strong chin, the easy confidence in her gold-rimmed eyes. This was a custom piece. Hand-painted. The brushstrokes bold and unmistakable.

"Wow," Valerie said.

Hattie joined a few steps behind.

"My son's work," she explained. "He painted that for Mother's Day in his senior year of high school."

Beyond the laundry room, a door opened and closed with a *thud*. The dog roused again to give one quick huffing bark, like it knew the sound but couldn't bear to let it pass unnoticed. Valerie paid little attention, captivated by the vibrant tones and intricate details of the painting.

"This is magnificent," she breathed. "Please tell me he went to art school."

From the laundry room, Mike snorted. "Not my kid." He kicked off boots heavy with mud. "Art degrees don't pay the bills."

Valerie recoiled as much from his presence as his

261

callous words. Hattie moved to intercept, soothing Mike in a conciliatory pattern so familiar to Valerie she felt dizzy with memories of her childhood. The tension on Mike's face suggested things might escalate but any further conflict was interrupted by the staccato barking of the little dog. This time it wasn't a solitary sound but a rapid series of high-pitched yips. Somewhere upstairs, a door slammed. The barking changed in timbre but didn't stop.

"Gus!" Hattie cried.

"That damned dog," Mike complained.

"You know it's not just Gus," Hattie snapped, already racing up the steps. "Gus! Stop it!"

Amidst the chaos, almost eclipsed by Hattie's sharp response, Valerie felt the first tingling signs of a presence.

Upstairs, Ivan said.

She nodded, striding after Hattie to leave Mike scowling near the hulk of the coat tree.

Upstairs, Hattie knelt at the end of the hall before a closed door. Gus barked endlessly from the other side. She scrabbled at the space beneath in a panic. Valerie wasn't really a dog person, but the little Pomsky didn't sound like an animal in distress.

"Gus, come out of there!"

As Valerie drew closer, she passed a bathroom, then what had to be a bedroom. A quick glance through the partly open door showed a familiar four-poster bed topped with a patterned comforter. A dog crate angled beside a dresser matching the bed. The door to the crate swung gently on its hinges.

That didn't seem right.

"Gus!" Hattie continued. She stood and frantically

worked the handle, pressing the whole side of her body against the door. It opened inward like all the others on this floor. As Valerie watched, the door gave a little under Hattie's weight—just enough to see a slice of brightness from the room beyond.

Then, a shadow swooped across that sliver of light.

A moment later, the door shoved back, violently. Hattie stumbled away with a cry. From the other side, Gus continued to bark, the yips of a puppy eager to play.

One thing struck Valerie as she watched: there were locks on this door. Three, in fact, all screwed haphazardly into the frame from the outside. Each was a type of security latch—something a person would have to lift and twist in order to open. Currently all hung loose, but Valerie suspected that wasn't ordinarily the case.

"Don't just stand there," Hattie cried. "Help me get this door open. Gus isn't supposed to be in that room."

Valerie stepped closer, uncertain what she could physically do to assist if Hattie couldn't shove the door open. She called on her other skills instead. Eyes fluttering, she sought the shadow on the other side. What was there? And why did that room warrant such an aggressive set of locks?

As the dog continued to bark, Valerie made contact with . . . *something*. At her touch, the being recoiled. In the same instant, the door swung open, nearly carrying Hattie off her feet. Gus—a black and white bundle of fluff no bigger than a cat—hopped and pranced delightedly around Hattie's ankles. With a rush of admonishments, she scooped him up, cradling him against her shoulder like a Husky-shaped infant. He wiggled and licked her face.

"This wouldn't keep happening if you just got rid of the dog." Mike stood at the top of the stairs. He remained at the far end of the hallway as if unwilling to come closer to the offending room.

"It's not Gus's fault and you know it," Hattie said. "Poor Gus. Let's get you back in your little house."

Valerie stepped aside to let Hattie pass, then edged toward the door with all the latches. In the room beyond, something shifted as she drew closer. It fluttered like a veil across the light of the south-facing window, a figure of shadow and film. Then it was gone, and the room was only a room. There was a bed and a desk and a bookshelf, all neatly kept.

But the walls were covered with women. Not the glossy pin-up posters some boys hung in their sanctuaries. This was art. Hand-drawn and beautifully rendered, each was identical in style to the magnificent oil painting framed in the living room. From every picture, the same figure peered out, her dark hair scintillating with artful jewels. She was tall, her lean, muscled arms provocatively bare. Every dress was a fully realized experience—color, pattern, texture all vibrantly brought into being through a variety of mediums. Hattie's son wasn't merely an artist. The pictures demonstrated an eye for fashion that belonged on a runway.

A single name appeared on every image. Valerie leaned closer to make it out. *Angelou.* Artist's signature or the name of the character, she couldn't be sure.

Abruptly, Hattie swept past and seized the handle to the door. She shooed Valerie back into the hallway and pulled it shut.

the shape of her soul

"We keep this room closed," she said. "It belongs to my son." With the rhythm of habit, she worked each latch in swift succession. Mike watched from the other end of the hall.

Again, that subtle, trembling sense of movement in the room. Valerie listened hard with her inner ear and could just make out the rustle of fabric beyond the locked door. Some things were beginning to make a painful kind of sense, and she suppressed a flash of annoyance that Hattie had withheld such an important detail.

Very carefully, she asked, "Where is your son?"

Hattie flinched as if slapped. That was answer enough, but Valerie needed to hear it out loud.

Two things she had learned in the years of doing this work—no demon was ever really a demon, and every family lied.

When the lies weren't insultingly blatant, they were lies of omission.

Those were often worse.

Valerie hefted her old doctor's bag, the worn handles creaking with the weight of supplies. "If you aren't willing to open up," she said, "there's nothing I can do for you."

Michael broke the silence. "Our son is dead," he said. He turned to stomp back down the stairs. "Should've cleaned all the garbage out of that room months ago."

"I can't!" Hattie cried. "I won't." The naked sound of her grief got the dog barking again. Tears lustered in her eyes as she turned back to Valerie. "It's how the demon torments me. I can't bear to clear that room, so the demon always messes with it. Pulls things down.

Slams the door. Locks poor Gus in there every chance it gets."

That doesn't sound like a demon, Ivan observed.

Valerie couldn't have agreed more, but now was not the time to throw it in Hattie's face.

"Maybe we should sit down," Valerie prompted. She glanced pointedly to the sealed door. "Somewhere away from the focus of activity."

Hattie nodded, sniffled, then dashed past her to the bathroom as a string of snot threaded to her upper lip. "I'm sorry," she called, noisily blowing her nose. "I'm so sorry. I shouldn't let it get to me." The water ran. "I know better. These things eat human emotion. We are all a feast. That's what that bishop said. We're just a meal of suffering." Her voice echoed hollow among the tiles. When Hattie stepped back into the hall, moisture beaded her face.

Valerie gently herded Hattie toward the stairs.

"Those exorcisms failed 'cause I can't be strong." She paused and teetered at the top of the staircase. A wretched keening wracked her. "But how can I be strong when my baby's in the ground?"

She wailed her grief and the little dog howled from his cage in her room.

Valerie swept forward, ready to catch Hattie before she could tumble down the stairs. But instead of pitching forward, the woman simply sank like an elegant skyscraper brought down with charges. She buried her face in her hands and sobbed on the topmost step. Valerie, who regularly navigated grief for both the living and the dead, stepped softly back.

As she waited for the storm to pass, another voice joined with Hattie and Gus. Muffled through the door of the locked room behind them, it called, "Momma. Oh, Momma. I'm so sorry." It was unmistakably the voice of a woman. And she, too, wept disconsolately.

Valerie's stomach dropped at the sound.

She understood what was going on.

She understood, and it hurt.

With a little coaxing, Valerie finally got Hattie down to the living room. They perched across from one another on the creaky leather couches, a low glass table between them. Hattie clutched half a dozen wadded-up tissues, still intermittently scrubbing her nose. To Valerie's utmost surprise, Mike wordlessly fetched his wife a mug of strong coffee. As soon as the cup was in her hands, he retreated back to the laundry room to silently lean against the doorjamb. A taciturn specter, he remained half in and half out of the space, every tense line of his posture telegraphing that he would rather flee to the sanctuary of the yard. But he stayed.

It didn't make Valerie like him any better, but it earned a sliver of respect.

Valerie dug a thumb into her palm, fighting back so many useless words. Behind Hattie, the regal woman painted into being by her talented child presided over the room. Now that she understood what she was looking at, the resemblance to Hattie was impossible to miss. Mike's jawline was there, too.

Finally, Valerie said, "I'm going to ask you some questions. They're not going to be easy."

Hattie sniffled. "Whatever you need to free me from this hell."

That was not a promising start. Valerie nudged up

her mask as it dragged against her nose, striving to formulate the best and most compassionate approach. If she only had Hattie and Mike to consider, the answer would be simple. Drive out the spirit and be done. But the dead had as much right to kindness as the living, and Valerie refused to ignore such obvious agony as she'd witnessed upstairs.

"My first question, and I apologize if it dredges things up, but . . . " Her elbows dug into her knees as she leaned forward. "When did your son pass away?"

Hattie caught her breath and from the spike of emotion, Valerie fully expected her to begin keening again. Instead, she pressed the wad of tissue against her mouth, rocking forward as she squeezed her eyes shut.

"Last fall," Mike said. He shifted against the doorjamb but made no attempt to approach.

"Right before Thanksgiving." Hattie's thready voice emerged muffled by tissues. "He was supposed to come home. For the holidays."

Valerie puffed out a breath, imagining herself as that immovable rock as Hattie began sobbing again. At her back, Ivan paced his agitation, and she was relieved that only she could hear the plodding rhythm of his heavy boots.

Doesn't she know already? he demanded. *How can't they know?*

"Shh," Valerie managed, addressing both Mrs. Pendergast and her companion spirit. It mollified neither. "This next question—I know I'm not the first investigator here. Not even the third. But I have my own way of doing things, and I need to rule this out, okay?"

the shape of her soul

Eyes still squeezed shut, Hattie nodded.

Valerie gathered all her courage and asked as evenly as she could, "What makes you believe this spirit is *not* your son?"

"What a stupid question," Mike roared. He pushed off the doorframe, hands fisted as he stalked toward them. Valerie tensed, but he stopped just inside the room. "You heard that thing up there. Did that sound like a man to you?"

"My son is dead," Hattie pronounced. An icy calm settled over her. Valerie felt it snap into place with all the ponderous gravity of a blast door. "I pray to God that he's in Heaven. But my boy is dead."

She met Valerie's eyes and dared a contradiction. Mike positively vibrated with threat. And above them all, the painted queen gazed down, her form and features a conscious, prefect echo of both parents.

"All right," Valerie conceded. She sat back against the couch, hugging herself to suppress a chill. It wasn't cold in the house, quite the opposite. The air in the room had grown oppressive. But she couldn't bulwark herself against the parents' icy denial. Knew that rejection so personally, she almost fled.

But there was the spirit to consider.

With a deep breath, Valerie collected her antique doctor's bag from the floor beside her. She placed it on the coffee table, flipped the rusty latch, and began removing one item after another. She did so in measured silence, soothing herself as much with the activity as redirecting the agitated Pendergasts. All of it was theater. A silver ritual blade. A pungent bundle of incense. An amber vial of anointing oil. A small flask of blessed water. One after another, she pulled the items out, turned them over in her hands, then arranged them on the glass surface.

They were the tools of spiritual warfare. They spoke a language the Pendergasts recognized: violence to drive out what they could not understand.

"Here's the deal," Valerie said and her voice shook only a little. "I can get rid of your demon, but you have to leave me alone in your house. I'll understand if you don't trust me enough to do that, but that's the only way this is going to work."

Husband and wife exchanged glances. There was an awful moment where Valerie became convinced their answer would be no. Mike spoke first.

"We have a complete list of every valuable here," he warned. Then he turned on his heel and stomped away. The door to the garage slammed behind him. Gathering her flotilla of used tissues, Hattie hurried to join him.

Behind her, Ivan got worked up enough the heavy frame of the painting rattled ominously. *You know there's no demon*, he growled.

"This is not about them," Valerie soothed. She lit some incense and set it to burn so the house would smell different when the family returned. "Let's go see if she'll talk to us."

Upstairs, Gus whined from his crate. Valerie released the little dog and he went straight to the sealed door. The eager Pomsky pawed at the frame, adding fresh marks to the ragged scoring along the wood. Tentatively, Valerie extended her senses to the room beyond. No presence reached back, no shadow moved across the thin seam of light. Gus yipped once then sneezed at the door.

"It's a good thing none of these locks needs a key," Valerie observed, undoing them. Gus shoved his way inside as soon as she turned the handle. Barking a greeting, he hopped onto the bed and bounced in delighted circles.

Valerie stepped softly into the room, closing her eyes for a moment to better focus on the feel of the space. When she settled onto the edge of the bed, she reached a hand out to the dog, but Gus showed no interest. He maintained his endless rotation, pausing only to bark in the direction of the desk.

Ivan hovered near the entrance of the room in a struggle with his own complex emotions. Valerie gave him space for his thoughts.

"I know you're in here," she called to the open air. "I haven't come to bother you or ask you how you died. But you are dead. Everything gets easier once you realize that."

With a sense rooted deeper than her physical ears, she closed her eyes again and listened. All her tools still lay on the coffee table downstairs, the faint scent of incense wafting through the home. She didn't need them. "You don't have to talk to me if you don't want to," she said. "But I thought you'd appreciate some time with Gus."

For a long while, nothing happened—just the dog catching his nails in the comforter, now and then yipping at something only he perceived.

Then, all at once, the hairs along her arms rose to attention. At the window, the light convulsed and something passed between her and the glass.

Perfume, warm and sweet, flooded the room. A dark-skinned face briefly reflected in the dresser mirror. Then an explosion of force. All the books on the bedside table scattered. Gus yelped and fled.

"GET OUT!"

Valerie jumped despite herself, but didn't budge.

The voice rose again, this time a wordless howl. More books cascaded from a nearby shelf, a few torn pages drifting like autumn leaves. The artwork fluttered in a phantom gale but remained tacked to the walls. Valerie steeled herself amidst the onslaught. Ivan swooped to her side, fully in soldier mode and ready to defend. With a thought she soothed him. *Wait, wait.*

"I'm not going to hurt you," she said out loud.

"LIAR!" the spirit cried. Like a hurricane of whispers and grieving, she raged through the room.

"I know they brought in people to cast you out," Valerie said. She shielded her face from a torrent of papers blown from the desk. "That must have felt terrible. Your own parents treating you like that."

"SHUT UP!" the spirit wailed. The bed beneath Valerie shook so violently, the headboard dented the wall. Tiny chips of paint and drywall scattered across the pillows. She could almost see her now, coalescing from a disturbance of light. Bangled limbs and swirling fabric emerged with a face that echoed every gorgeous drawing in the room.

"And you only want them to see you," she continued. "To love you for who you are." A small, dense object—statue or bottle of cologne, she couldn't tell—launched from the dresser. It whizzed by her face, so close the wind of its passage lifted a few strands of her hair.

the shape of her soul

"No!" the spirit howled. She manifested fully, a towering figure of elegant limbs. Thick locs whipped around her head in a wind of her own creation.

"No, they didn't see you or no, this isn't who you are?" Valerie persisted. She rose from the bed, undaunted by the furious vision before her. The spirit's extremity of emotion protracted her features. Impossible light glittered from the depths of her eyes. In this state, it was easy to see how some could mistake her for a demon, but the distortion was nothing but trauma.

Such a deep and wounded prison of pain. Valerie understood it all too well.

Moving with slow purpose, she stepped past the looming spirit to stand before the largest of the drawings. "It can't have been easy growing up here," she said. "Your mom seems like she means well, but she's so busy trying to manage your father, how would she even know?" With one finger, she traced the arc of a broad cheekbone, the stern angle of the jaw. The intention was so obvious. Behind her, the gusting wind abated. "Did they think you were drawing her for pleasure? Because this was someone you wanted to meet?"

"Stop touching that," the spirit said.

Before complying, she placed her fingers against the stylized word at the bottom. Angelou. There was a poet with that name. As choices went, it was a good one. Strong and powerful. Worthy of a queen.

Valerie gazed up at the spirit, noting how her face slowly shifted to something more natural, although her locs still undulated as if caught in a storm. "It's terrible when the people closest to you can't see what's right in front of them," she continued. "But I see. Every time you drew her, you were showing them the shape of your soul." She took a long, unsteady breath, prepared for another violent outburst. When they were like this, so raw and new, spirits' reactions could be extreme. "I see you, Angelou."

At the sound of her chosen name, the spirit collapsed into a heap of vibrant garments on the floor. A low and desolate keening—distinctly reminiscent of Hattie Pendergast—reverberated through the room. Gus yipped querulously from where he'd retreated, then decided it was safe to emerge. The little dog ran whining in circles where the spirit now huddled, trying to nudge her with his snout. He got progressively more agitated when he couldn't.

A boney hand reached out to pet the dog but passed ineffectually through his ears. He yelped and jumped back. Angelou cried even harder. "I'm sorry. I'm sorry," she wailed over and over.

Poor thing, Ivan said, still holding back.

Valerie knelt down on the floor beside her. "Hey. It's okay. Your anger's okay. All this pain is okay. Don't feel bad for feeling any of it," she soothed. "Grief isn't easy to get over, especially when we're grieving ourselves."

"Get away from me." The hand snaked out again but Valerie steeled herself and the phantom fingers passed with as little impact through her flesh as through the dog. "What could you possibly know?"

"I know you," Valerie said. "I *was* you—suffocated by narrow family, desperate for their approval, wounding myself day and night with the hope they could just see me for who I always was." As the words poured from her, her mask slipped. She had nothing to hide in this room, not from Angelou, certainly not from Ivan. She swallowed against the taut velvet of her peony choker, keenly aware in that moment of the shape of her voice box and how it would always feel wrong.

Angelou stirred from the huddled heap on the floor. She didn't lift her head, but scrabbled for Valerie, reaching for any comfort or contact.

"I just want them to know," she wailed miserably. "I didn't mean to scare her. I know she knows it's me. Why is this so hard?"

"They're not ready yet," Valerie said. She hovered a hand over Angelou's, touching but not as energy passed between them. "They might never be ready."

"But your parents are supposed to love you," the spirit sobbed. "I want to hate them. I want to. But I can't!"

Ivan moved closer to offer his support and Gus hopped unselfconsciously into Valerie's lap. Before she could react, the dog shoved his face into hers and licked away her tears. Valerie laughed in spite of everything, burying her nose in his warm fur.

Sometimes we have to move out before we can move on, Ivan said.

Valerie felt speechless in the wake of his words. For a span of many heartbeats, none of them spoke. Even Gus held still in Valerie's arms.

"I left my blood family years ago," Valerie finally said. "Walked away and never looked back." Her hand strayed to the silk peony at her throat, a relic of her great-grandmother and one of the few mementos she had been unwilling to abandon. "It was the hardest thing I ever did. But also the best. Once I started to build a life on my own terms, I realized I'd been living like a ghost all those years—a presence everyone resented, and no one wanted to see or hear."

Angelou sat up. The two women faced one another knee to knee upon the dull grey carpet. In another life, they could have been girls trading secrets at a sleepover.

"Wasn't it lonely?" Angelou asked.

"Yeah," Valerie responded. "It sucked. Then I moved into my house and I made a friend. I called her Aunt Bea because she'd been dead so long she didn't clearly remember what her name originally was."

She's a hoot, Ivan observed. His presence wrapped around both of them in something that felt exactly like a hug.

Angelou leaned into the soldier's stalwart presence. "She's from that long ago? And she accepts you?" she whispered.

"What's not to accept?" Valerie asked. "Look at yourself. You are exactly as you feel yourself to be. I've worked with spirits for years, and that's one thing I know to be true. We are our feelings, our memories, our dreams. That is all a spirit sees."

An invitation passed wordlessly between Ivan and Valerie.

Of course. Of course, she agreed.

We got a whole family of misfits, Ivan added. *C'mon, kid. You'll fit right in.*

american remake of a japanese ghost story

LAIRD BARRON

There's a curse in folklore known as a geas. That's when a witch, or a fairy, or the supernatural entity of your choice, compels a hapless mortal to undertake duties on the creature's behalf. Woe betides the mortal who shirks the quest; increasingly worse calamities befall them until they relent or die.

Somebody, somewhere, laid one on me.

A much younger, blissfully ignorant, Jessica Mace would've glibly asserted that fairytales are bullshit hoodoo made up by gullible peasants. Problem is, when I neglect to investigate the various mysteries in my path, I get epic migraines and nightmares. The more I rebel, the more intense my misery until it becomes debilitating. "Debilitating" sounds dry—I suffer projectile vomiting induced by the sense fire ants are hollowing my skull. Exactly as the legends describe, right? Call it a form of madness or a kind of placebo-effect. Odds are Hamlet told Horatio the truth about the denizens of his undreamt philosophy. Whatever, whichever, however: the world shows you its dark side, you take notice. That fucking needle starts skipping, you're a true believer.

Beasley, a boon comrade and sometime lover, once questioned my motives. We were dumping the corpse of a serial killer down a mineshaft in eastern Montana. The killer, a Richard Ramirez lookalike, had picked me up at a roadside tavern. RR Jr. chauffeured me to his favorite dump site while I batted my lashes and stroked his thigh. Thank whichever patron saint is in charge of such details that I'd managed to open the passenger door and light the cab for Beasley to take his shot. I'd only been half-strangled before the bullet came through the windshield. As the late, great Al Davis would say, *just win, baby.*

In the aftermath, we recovered with a bottle. Beasley said, *Jessica, you're a bright woman. You got an education. Why schlep all over the USA looking for horrors to battle? Why live your life as bait in a trap?*

I recall pouring another healthy dose of whiskey into our glasses and lighting a cigarette. I drank the booze and smoked most of the cigarette before coming up with a succinct answer. *If I don't, the horrors tend to come looking for me.* Bless him, he caught my drift.

Ever consider the possibility you're cursed?

Halfway into the bag, it was probably a throwaway comment. I had, in fact, never entertained the notion. A pit opened in my mind. A pit with all manner of darksome surprises at the bottom.

american remake of a japanese ghost story

Shortly after wrapping the horror mockumentary, *Torn Between Two Phantom Lovers,* which was based on archival footage of a tragedy in Japan's Sea of Trees circa 1977, director Gil Finlay and his wife Rikki bought a defunct farm near the Catskills. The way I heard it, the previous owners, a retired couple, passed away unexpectedly and their lawyer unloaded the deed for a song. A big American Gothic structure updated to resemble something Argento might've used as a set in the heyday of vinyl and exploitation cinema. Gil invited a few of us to the housewarming. I rode along with a sound tech and a gaffer. Cold and starry, but not quite winter. Basically my mood writ large.

The creepy part was when we pulled into the yard and the place perfectly resembled my recent bad dreams right down to the peaked roof, nearby shed, and fields and woods. The dreams themselves were vague and disjointed as dreams are wont to be. I recalled wandering fields by moonlight, then an endless maze of dim hallways. Occasionally, someone or something on my periphery plucked at my hair . . .

"Jessica, baby!" Rikki hugged me on sight. Almost didn't recognize her in a cocktail dress, her hair done up and face put together. Bowie-level glam. She usually dwelt in the background, organizing Gil's life and dousing fires as his unofficial publicist. She was a genius at it, too. Otherwise, I sincerely doubt he would've remembered which direction his pants went on in the morning.

She apologized for the mess. Renovations were behind schedule—carpenters had knocked down a wall here and there, drop cloths covered half the furniture, and a crew of electricians hadn't finished rewiring the house. Lamps shone in the main areas while outlying rooms were either strung with plastic bulbs or left utterly dark. "A housewarming isn't a party, it's a get-together, right?" she said. "Like casual Friday, but for a house."

I advised her not to worry—as long as she kept the booze flowing and nobody fell into an open pit, guests would let the decor slide. She nodded gratefully, then dashed off to holler at Gil who'd tramped in from the muddy backyard (in reality, a pasture) while still wearing a pair of clodhoppers. Plenty of his homies had made the scene, including assorted C-listers and a couple of LA suits. The suits in particular seemed bemused by the rustic location.

It promised to be a long grind of an evening. I lurked on the stairs, not far from the front door, weighing the pros and cons of abandoning my mission and doing a French leave even if it meant trudging down the dirt road that led here. This dude in a starched shirt handed me a can of beer and said running wouldn't do any good—he'd tried it once or twice. I introduced myself and waited for him to recognize me; either from my striking features or the jagged scar on my throat. His expression remained neutral. Apparently, enough years had passed people didn't recognize me on sight. Twenty-four-hour news cycle was erasing our collective memory like California shoreline. I popped the top (ensuring the seal hadn't been violated) and drank to the continued decline of civilization and my own celebrity.

"I'm Lee," Starched Shirt said. "How are you associated with Mr. Big Shot Film Director?"

Instead of a wiseass response like *Where do ya*

think he gets his blow? or *I'm the entertainment, bitch!* I played it straight. "PA for *Phantom Lovers.*" Not a lowkey brag so much as a confession. Production assistant was a polite showbiz definition of lackey. Fetch doughnuts, tote equipment, hold a character actor's hair back when she puked after a bender; whatever old job came along. "You?"

"We've been through the wars."

"Which wars?"

"I scouted locations for Gil on *Bleeding Mansion* and *The Ornithologist.*"

"*The Ornithologist*, huh? Nasty."

"You screened the whole thing? Impressive."

"Between my fingers."

"The critics did too," he said. "An eight-minute scene of a dying naturalist getting his asshole pecked out by vultures is a bridge too far for normies. Great writing, nonetheless."

"Okay, my burning question: was *The Ornithologist* an homage to Hitchcock or snide commentary?"

"Snide homage. Getting even on behalf of Tippi Hedron, maybe. Should ask him yourself. Or Rikki. Saw her squeezing the literal shit out of you earlier."

"She's a sixteenth grizzly bear." Another swallow of cheap, warm beer and then I slipped it in. "Somebody said the old owners died. That true?"

He nodded with sagacity borne of incipient drunkenness. "Gil says the husband dropped dead in the yard. Brain aneurism? Heart attack? I don't know. Wife clicked her heels and went back to wherever. Gil and Rikki were looking for a country retreat . . . "

"That explains the frantic renovations."

"Rikki needs to make it her own—"

"She *needs* to exorcise the ghosts."

"Well, again, the guy died in the yard . . . Does that count toward a haunting?"

"If you're the kind to put stock in hauntings, then yep. It counts."

He nodded the way one does when one doesn't mean it. Then he stiffened with his mouth quirked oddly. "Weird, I wanted to say something. It's gone." He shook himself and his eyes unglazed. "Maybe it'll hit me in a minute."

"Five minutes after you get home," I said. "That's how it always happens."

Lee nodded another polite nod and raised his beer and sipped. His eyes darted with an animal's dismay.

We stood there as the silence grew awkward. Because I was suffering a combo of boredom and edginess, I said, perhaps a trifle stridently, "My opinion about *The Ornithologist*? Gil's subconscious was broadcasting a public service message: leave Mother Nature the hell alone. Fuck them loggers. Fuck them tourists and farmers. Fuck them Richard Attenborough types, too. She didn't ask for any of it."

"Okay, then," he said, glancing toward the other guests as if one might beeline over to rescue him.

Meanwhile, I'd already drifted miles away, scoping the layout once more and reassessing avenues of escape. Yeah, pulling stakes for town was tempting. I wouldn't do that; not while afflicted with a geas, or my compulsion, or call it what you will. What were my options? The aforementioned stairs at my back, climbing into the unknown. Front door and farmland. Brightly lit kitchen through an archway where the hardcore extroverts instinctively gathered. Dark passage on my left, a cluster of green bulbs glowing at the far end.

"Adios. Gotta powder my nose." I handed Lee my mostly empty and left him mildly befuddled with longing. Beasley could've, would've, commiserated.

Something was wrong. My plastic divining ball had decreed it so.

Divining ball, you ask? Best way to describe it would be as an off-brand Magic 8 Ball, way smaller than the original. I could palm it, easy. Several years ago, a circus strongperson named Mary stuck it into my pocket; a parting gift at the conclusion of a harrowing adventure. She'd inherited it from a fortuneteller who'd met an unforeseen demise. Mary warned me to restrict myself to a couple of questions per week. *You fight the forces of darkness with forces of darkness. Beware, kiddo. This is a portal to the void.* Previously I'd relied upon chance to guide my quixotic journeys as a professional final girl. These days, the mini-oracle and my innate gifts combined to ensure I never missed the chance to become embroiled in the most bizarre and dangerous circumstances.

To that point: upon receiving the housewarming invitation (and subsequent nightmares), I'd casually rattled the ball and said, *Dear Oracle, is anything fucked up happening at Gil's house, and if so, should I be concerned?* Which, I presume, is how the petitioners at Delphi phrased their entreaties regarding love, life, and invading Spartan armies. The pocket oracle generally responded with yes, no, or maybe. Occasionally, it escalated to cryptic phrases and symbols. This time, its little window flickered and red-limned letters coalesced to spell SHE WAITS. A bit disquieted, I pressed my luck and asked if people were in danger. Upon shaking the ball, a skull bobbed to the surface.

Damn. I should've asked if *I* personally was endangered. It probably went without saying.

After ditching Lee, I ducked outside and smoked a cigarette. The stars were still twitching; the moon had made some progress. Their supreme indifference to the insignificant horrors of human drama was pleasant, emotionally stabilizing. Back indoors, I began my tour of the premises by skirting the living room. None of the clustered guests struck me as a round character much less a serial killer. I've an unerring sense regarding these matters. Two girls were bumping and grinding to classic era Depeche Mode. I recognized them from craft services; they'd dutifully arranged sandwiches and refilled carafes day and night, rain or shine. Illumination was funny here; it made bands across their eyes. Straight out of a giallo flick.

I left them, too.

Prickling neck hairs and the queasiness in the pit of my gut acted as faulty Geiger counters—the physical manifestation of hyperactive intuition. Lacking clues, besides a vague, but escalating sense of danger, all I could do was bumble around waiting for one or more of my alarms to trip. Dowsing for evil, more or less. I moseyed along the hall toward the rear of the house, projecting myself into shadow. Part of the weirdness was a natural consequence of transition—white patches on the walls where old photos once hung, not yet covered by the new. To walk through an abandoned home is to traverse the confines of an open grave. The floor lamp beckoned me with its wan light. I ignored doors on either side. This was a mundane adult party, which meant unlike the barn burners we had in high school and college, people hadn't gathered to do keg stands, nor paired off to fuck on piles of coats.

Swim to me, swim to my shoal, the lamp said. A metal door let onto the back porch. Half-bath on the right—I peeked inside. A bearded guy camped on the toilet, pants around his ankles, chin cupped a la *The Thinker.* Candles burned on the sink. He nodded. I reversed with a quickness. Another door, on the left, ajar. A chain of plastic bulbs twisted in descent, nominally illuminating old, grooved steps that had weathered the drag and scrape of many feet.

Down, down into a brick and beam cellar because what goes up, and so on. Three women sat on the floor near the furnace, each haloed in crawling green light. They hunched over a homemade Ouija board. Which figured. Two men perched on a matched washer-dryer set, sharing a joint. Looked like bros to me.

"Shh! It's a séance," Dryer Bro shushed before I could even get my loud mouth in gear.

I don't know why some people assume raised voices are antithetical to communing with spirits while others are full speed ahead with hymns and hosannas. "Oh, that's stupid." I lit a cigarette. "You don't screw around in a house where somebody recently kicked."

"I thought you didn't screw with the *infinite,*" Dryer Bro said.

Washer Bro apparently hadn't heard the news. He almost dropped the joint. "Somebody died here? Totally uncool. Hey, Shelley. Maybe you should ixnay—"

The brunette leading the "séance" was probably three or four years past her high school goth peak. She opened her smokey eyes and shot daggers at Washer Lad. "Maybe you should cram it, Ashton."

"Hey, Shelley," I said. "Your boy here is on the money. Ixnay."

"Who the hell are you?" Smokey Eye Chick said.

"Last of the red-hot Samaritans. I'm curious. Where'd you call?"

"Huh?"

"Activate a witchboard, you're making a call to a random payphone across the veil. Could be a bad neighborhood. Anybody can pick up. Scary part is, whoever's on the other end has deluxe caller ID." I tapped my head. "Mr. Ghost of a Psycho Killer's got your name, number, and home address." True as far as it went, although I might've overstated the danger a wee bit.

"There's a psycho in here, for sure." Her smirk reminded me of every foe I'd dreamed of socking in high school and a couple I'd actually punched.

"See? This shit is already going sideways, kid." My heart wasn't really into yanking her chain. Didn't have to consult the oracle to confirm I'd hit a dead end. The sense of dread had faded to a dim background thrum. "Your funeral," I said with as much menace as possible while exiting the basement.

Back in the living room, somebody lowered the stereo volume and cued *Bleeding Mansion*, Gil's debut feature film, on a wall screen. As the title credits rolled over a still of the eponymous giallo mansion, I realized it was a ringer for this very house. Gil's mansion possessed slightly different angles, yet the spirit of it unnerved me. The house in my nightmare was a composite of both; I didn't like that, either.

Bam! Dread restored to one-hundred percent. An impression spiked into my brain, a vision, if you will, of a slack-faced man being pulled by his hair up through a hole in the ceiling. I leaned against the wall, playing it casual as a wave of dizziness receded. This kind of destabilizing, traumatic sense of collocation rarely occurred, but when it did, boy, howdy. The image faded like a pop flash, imprint wavering, wavering, gone. The room I'd glimpsed was small and lighted by afternoon sun. Second floor bedroom or office? Only way to know was to poke around, even though I really, truly, abso-fucking-lutely wanted to do anything but.

"Yo, lady."

I pivoted, left hand resting on the knife under my jacket. A formidable blade; slim and easy to conceal. Smokey Eye Chick had apparated out of the shadows on my six. She stared an owlish, luminous stare as if trying to drink my soul.

"Lady," she said again with a flat affect. "I was supposed to tell you something. You should go upstairs now." Her lips kept moving after she finished. She regarded the ceiling, turned, and walked off; neck craned so far backward her head flopped as if the vertebrae had come undone. Our inverted gazes locked as she wobbled down the hall.

Frankly, I was at a loss. The million-dollar

question: how much did I care for the fate of Gil and Rikki? Followed by: will you wind up wearing adult diapers if you defy the curse and bail? The answers were, a lot, and, probably even worse.

We, the cynical audience, hunker in seats of a darkened theater and mock the heroine who fumbles around, shining a feeble light into corners while meekly calling, *Who's there?* Where's that cynical movie-going wisdom for those who reenact variations of that scene in scores of homes every evening? Yeah, we scoff at heroines and then stumble into our own fates at the first point of crisis. It's because we've trained ourselves to ignore the little warning voice that says, *Don't investigate the noise that woke you. Don't cross the empty parking lot after hours. Don't be a fool.*

Speaking of fools. The second floor was dark. Party echoes were muffled; a warning that I'd drifted from shore into deep waters. I tried a wall switch to no avail. Then, before I resorted to my penlight, fifteen or twenty feet directly ahead, a floor lamp (cousin to the one downstairs) snapped on. Off. On. Off. On. Faster and faster until it strobed. I approached and crossed into a small office—desk, file cabinet, bookshelf, couch. Another wall switch, also dead. The strobing lamp eroded my composure. I glanced up and saw the inevitable ceiling panel partially ajar. An invitation.

I pushed a footstool beneath the gap and, penlight clenched in my teeth, levered myself into the attic. Warm and musty. Cobwebs, exposed rafters, and fiberglass insulation. Stacks of cardboard boxes and bundles of magazines and newspapers. Home for mice. Home for termites. Home for something else, too.

My feeble penlight probed edges, traced contours of a larger, obscured geography; a midnight continent waited for its latest pilgrim to venture a step too far. Among the detritus, a wooden placard lay propped against boxes. I gleaned just enough kanji to deduce someone had smuggled it from Jōren Waterfall in Japan. Jōren Falls, famous for its natural beauty, was also the origin of the legend of a beautiful spider demon who, in bygone days, lured travelers to their doom. Occasionally, the gods dispense with omens and hand you an actual fucking sign.

A millisecond after I shined my light on that placard, metaphorically speaking, the piano music ceased mid-note. Someone sighed, followed by a sound like cartilage separating. A shape developed like a photographic negative among the rafters—broad, softly angular. Bulky, but nimble. She. Nothing else to call her except she. Her pale visage glimmered against the black frame of her hair, the black of her body. Her eyes were enormous like those of Smokey Eye Chick last I glimpsed her in the hall.

"What do you want?" I said. As if I didn't have a good guess. As if I wasn't stalling, hunting for a crucifix, some magic words of protection. Could I take her on with a knife? Could I take on a bear with a knife? May as well ask, could I leap off a cliff and survive?

"Final . . . girl," she said. "My dream." Her voice was mine by way of a child's mimicry. "Dream . . . "

"Same. You summoned me. Why?" I sensed the only thing keeping me alive was our shared uncertainty. Some power, perhaps the one that cursed me to unravel mysteries, had brought us together. On this occasion, perhaps she craved an answer as much as she craved other forms of sustenance.

Her long, segmented arm that was not an arm unfolded. She brushed my cheek, once, then withdrew. "Sad," she said. "Hungry."

I froze. Everything in my bladder wanted to escape. The flesh of my cheek felt abraded and raw. And yet. Years before, I'd seen news footage of a man in a hot, dusty village, extending his water bottle to a cobra dying of thirst. A gesture of humanity in a moment of tremendous peril. I clung to that notion of compassion now. I clung to the notion that even in this impersonal, inscrutable universe, there exists a purpose. "You're lonely."

"Alone." A correction or confirmation. Her bloodless expression gave nothing back. Pitiful, tiny me reflected in her eyes.

"Is this really where you belong?" I said as an idea bloomed. "Hidden away in an attic?"

"Waterfall," she said and gave me another jab with her psychic stinger.

A falling curtain of water misted me; it boomed against stone. I glimpsed the silhouette of a lovely woman enfolding weary passersby to her bosom. Men, usually. Faithless, straying men.

"We could find a new fall. Would that make you happier?"

She leaned forward. Roofbeams creaked and sagged. "Happier."

The face of the killer back west floated in my mind's eye, attached to a mobile of a bunch of other creeps cut from the same bolt of cloth. Men who'd tried to do for me and failed. Stranglers. Shooters. Slashers. She regarded my thoughts and saw them too.

I raised my arm a bit. This took more resolve than I can properly convey. Instinct more than courage, honestly. "So you know, I meet a lot of assholes in my travels."

Didn't take long for her to decide. She crawled across the beam, contracting, diminishing from colossus to a speck, from an imminent hazard to a threat, and alighted on my palm. I gently nestled her into my coat pocket. She curled around the oracle.

Trembling, I clicked off the penlight and stood in the heart of the void. "Are you a force of darkness?" I asked my new friend.

"Darkness," she said, almost a whisper.

"It was a rhetorical question." I smiled with the euphoric dregs of terror and lowered myself down into the light.

the end

Not if you want to dive into more of Crystal Lake Publishing's Tales from the Darkest Depths!

Check out our amazing website and online store (https://www.crystallakepub.com)

We always have great new projects and content on the website to dive into, as well as a newsletter, behind the scenes options, social media platforms, and our own dark fiction shared-world series and our very own store. If you use the IGotMyCLPBook! coupon code in the store (at the checkout), you'll get a one-time-only 50% discount on your first eBook purchase!

Our webstore even has categories specifically for KU books, non-fiction, anthologies, and of course more novels and novellas.

about the contributors

Gemma Files
Formerly a film critic, journalist, screenwriter and teacher, Gemma Files has been an award-winning horror author since 1999. She has published two collections of short work, two chap-books of speculative poetry, a Weird Western trilogy, a story-cycle and a stand-alone novel (*Experimental Film*, which won the 2016 Shirley Jackson Award for Best Novel and the 2016 Sunburst award for Best Adult Novel). She has two new story collections from Trepidatio (*Spectral Evidence* and *Drawn Up From Deep Places*), one upcoming from Trepidatio (*Dark Is Better*), and a new poetry collection from Aqueduct Press (*Invocabulary*).

Helen Marshall
Dr Helen Marshall is a Senior Lecturer of Creative Writing at the University of Queensland. She has won the World Fantasy Award, the British Fantasy Award and the Shirley Jackson Award for her two collections of short stories. Her debut novel *The Migration* argued for the need to remain hopeful, even in the worst circumstances. It was one of *The Guardian*'s top science fiction books of the year. She tweets @manuscriptgal.

Kathe Koja

Kathe Koja writes short fiction and novels—including *The Cipher, Skin, Talk, Under the Poppy*, and *Dark Factory* upcoming in 2022—and creates and produces immersive events. She's based in Detroit and thinks globally. Find her on Facebook and Twitter @KatheKoja and at https://kathekoja.com/ and https://www.patreon.com/kathekoja

Lee Murray

Lee Murray is a multi-award-winning author-editor from Aotearoa-New Zealand (Sir Julius Vogel, Australian Shadows), and a two-time Bram Stoker Award®-winner. Her work includes military thrillers, the *Taine McKenna Adventures*, supernatural crime-noir series *The Path of Ra* (with Dan Rabarts), and debut collection *Grotesque: Monster Stories*. She is proud to have edited seventeen volumes of speculative fiction, including Bram Stoker Award®-winning title *Black Cranes: Tales of Unquiet Women* co-edited with Geneve Flynn. Her latest work is non-fiction title *Mark My Words: Read the Submission Guidelines and Other Self-editing Tips* co-authored with Angela Yuriko Smith. She is co-founder of Young NZ Writers and of the Wright-Murray Residency for Speculative Fiction Writers, HWA Mentor of the Year for 2019, NZSA Honorary Literary Fellow, and Grimshaw Sargeson Fellow for 2021 for her poetry collection *Fox Spirit on a Distant Cloud*. Read more at leemurray.info

David Demchuk

David Demchuk has been writing for print, stage, digital and other media for 40 years. His debut novel

The Bone Mother was longlisted for the Scotiabank Giller Prize, shortlisted for the Amazon.ca First Novel Award and the Shirley Jackson Award among others, and received the Sunburst Award for excellence in Canadian speculative fiction. His new novel *RED X* will be published by Strange Light in Fall 2021. Born and raised in Winnipeg, he lives in Toronto.

Lisa Morton

Lisa Morton is a screenwriter, author of non-fiction books, and prose writer whose work was described by the American Library Association's Readers' Advisory Guide to Horror as "consistently dark, unsettling, and frightening." She is a six-time winner of the Bram Stoker Award®, the author of four novels and over 150 short stories, and a world-class Halloween expert. Her recent releases include *Weird Women: Classic Supernatural Fiction from Groundbreaking Female Writers 1852-1923* (co-edited with Leslie S. Klinger) and *Calling the Spirits: A History of Seances*; her latest short stories appeared in *Best American Mystery Stories 2020, Final Cuts: New Tales of Hollywood Horror and Other Spectacles*, and *In League with Sherlock Holmes*. Her collection *Night Terrors & Other Tales* was released in 2021. Lisa lives in Los Angeles and online at www.lisamorton.com.

Gwendolyn Kiste

Gwendolyn Kiste is the Bram Stoker Award-winning author of *The Rust Maidens, Boneset & Feathers, And Her Smile Will Untether the Universe, Pretty Marys All in a Row*, and *The Invention of Ghosts*. Her short fiction and nonfiction have appeared in *Nightmare Magazine, Best American Science Fiction and*

Fantasy, Vastarien, Tor's Nightfire, Black Static, The Dark, Daily Science Fiction, Interzone, and *LampLight,* among others. Her work has been translated into Spanish, French, and Russian, and she's been nominated for the Ignotus Award and the Kelvin Award in Spain. Originally from Ohio, she now resides on an abandoned horse farm outside of Pittsburgh with her husband, two cats, and not nearly enough ghosts. Find her online at gwendolynkiste.com as well as on Twitter (@gwendolynkiste) and Facebook (https://www.facebook.com/gwendolynkiste/).

S.P. Miskowski

S.P. Miskowski has received two National Endowment for the Arts Fellowships. Her second novel, *I Wish I Was Like You,* was named This Is Horror Novel of the Year, received a Charles Dexter Award *from Strange Aeons Magazine,* and was a finalist for a Bram Stoker Award. Three of her books (*Knock Knock, Delphine Dodd,* and *Muscadines*) have been nominated for a Shirley Jackson Award.

Her stories have been published in *Nightmare Magazine, Supernatural Tales, Black Static, Identity Theory, Strange Aeons, Other Voices,* and *Eyedolon,* and in numerous anthologies including *The Best Horror of the Year Volume Ten, Haunted Nights, The Madness of Dr. Caligari, Nox Pareidolia, October Dreams 2,* and *Darker Companions: Celebrating 50 Years of Ramsey Campbell.*

https://spmiskowski.wordpress.com

Seanan McGuire

Seanan McGuire writes things. It is more than usually difficult to make her stop. Some of the things she has written have won awards, so people don't usually try too hard. This story is one of the things she has written. Keep up with her at www.seananmcguire.com, or on Twitter as @seananmcguire.

Catherine Lord
Catherine Lord was born in Poona, East Indies in 1845 to British parents. After the death of her father when she was five years old, Catherine moved to England with her mother under the care of her grandfather Sir Thomas Joshua Platt (1788-1862). Catherine started writing under the pen name 'Lucy Hardy' in 1892 and her stories were published in *Argosy, Belgravia and The Sketch*. She died within a decade of becoming a professional writer and died in 1901 of exhaustion. Her short stories were never collected in her lifetime and she vanished into obscurity until Johnny Mains discovered her work in 2017 and published her first collection of short stories, *Our Lady of Hate* (Noose & Gibbet, 2020).

Chesya Burke
Chesya Burke is an Asst. Professor of English and U.S. Literatures at Stetson University. She has written and published nearly a hundred fiction works and articles within the genres of science fiction, fantasy, noir and horror. Her story collection, *Let's Play White*, is being taught in universities around the country. Poet Nikki Giovanni compared her writing to that of Octavia Butler and Toni Morrison and Samuel Delany called her "a formidable new master of the macabre." Visit Chesya on her website: thechesyaburke.com or Twitter: @ChesyaBurkePhD

Nadia Bulkin

Nadia Bulkin is the author of the short story collection *She Said Destroy* (Word Horde, 2017). She has been nominated for the Shirley Jackson Award five times. She grew up in Jakarta, Indonesia with her Javanese father and American mother, before relocating to Lincoln, Nebraska. She has two political science degrees and lives in Washington, D.C.

Social: twitter.com/nadiabulkin; nadiabulkin.com

Michelle Belanger

When not writing books, Michelle Belanger talks to dead people on television shows like Jack Osbourne's "Portals to Hell" and the hit "Paranormal State." A singer/songwriter with Nox Arcana and URN, Belanger resides in NE Ohio and owns a haunted B&B called Inspiration House. More at michellebelanger.com.

Laird Barron

Laird Barron spent his early years in Alaska. He is the author of several books, including *The Beautiful Thing That Awaits Us All, Swift to Chase,* and *Worse Angels.* His work has also appeared in many magazines and anthologies. Barron currently resides in the Rondout Valley writing stories about the evil that men do.

editors

Jess Landry

From the day she was born, Bram Stoker Award-winner Jessica Landry has always been attracted to the darker things in life. Since then, Jessica's fiction has appeared in many anthologies, including *Tales of the Lost, Twice-Told: A Collection of Doubles, Monsters* of Any Kind, Where Nightmares Come From, Lost Highways: Dark Fictions from the Road, and Fantastic Tales of Terror, among others. Her debut collection, The Mother Wound, is out now from Independent Legions Publishing, which includes her Bram Stoker Award-winning short story, "Mutter," and her Shirley Jackson Award-nominated novelette, "I Will Find You, Even in the Dark."

As a screenwriter, she has various projects in development, including her directorial debut, My Only Sunshine (with Eagle Vision); Anomaly (Buffalo Gal Pictures); as well as several Movies of the Week. Find her online at jesslandry.com.

Aaron J. French

Aaron J. French has a long track-record as a successful editor, with many years of experience working with NY Times bestselling authors and well-known figures in the film and art worlds. He is best known for editing several popular anthologies, including The Gods of H.P. Lovecraft, The Demons of King Solomon, Songs of the Satyrs, and the Monk Punk & Shadow of the Unknown Omnibus. He is also a scholar of religions and esotericism working in Germany.

Thank you to the wonderful backers who supported THERE IS NO DEATH, THERE ARE NO DEAD through the Indiegogo campaign!

Turtletrio, Bruce Baugh, richard.sheehan, Julie Sevens, baryon, Krysteen Damon, Adrien Robertson, Carrier, Patrick Malka, vexdragmire, Matthew O'Driscoll, Gareth Baddley, Tony Ciak, Brendan Detzner, Amy Sturgis, Wesley Teal, Yvonne Valentine, GMark Cole, edward yeatman, Adam LaFrance, Vashelle Nino, Natalie Carrere, ubuzach, Mara Businelli, Paul Sheldon, Chris McLaren, Denver Grenell, Theodore Weiter, Gareth Penn, faith dincolo, Scarlett R. Algee, Erin Couvillion, Luigi Minopoli, Kristina Spritely, valenzuelaje, Laura Elizabeth M, Matthew Henshaw, Ashley Risk, Susan Jessen, Shelby Gamble, sonoye murphy, Geoff Haney, Brittany Champion, Stuart White, Andrew Cook, Jessica Peterson, Jim Clark, Susan Vandergriff, Eric J. Guignard, Arina Cote, Sydney Dunstan, Seth Stauffer, William Jones, Sirensongs, David Thivierge, Gina Collia, Tom Fenton, Tony Ciak, Henry D Weisenborn, Janelle Janson, Tobias Carroll, Richard Leis, Kevin Wadlow, hannah burke, Candace Nola, Scifigreg, Stillsoulcake, haole0831, Caroline Couture, Richelle Gentry, Duane and Jen Watson, Amy Sturgis, Ryan McWilliams, Colbgreg, Adam Petrash, Jennifer McCarthy, Wil Dalton, Inna Effress, Villimey Kristin Mist Sigurbjornsdottir, Taylor Rhodes, melissa polk, Michael S Sturgis, Paula Foscarini, Nickscorza, Maria Cristina Phillips, Premee, Emma Gibbon, laura.e.schreiner, Carol Baker, Ruthann Jagge, R.C. Hausen, Jonathan, AJ Franks, Beverly Bambury, Miss

Charlotte J Platt, Kyle Dippery, Justin Lewis, Alex Ebenstein, Megan Hafdahl, Kenneth Skaldeb, Nicholas Diak, Lianne Riddell, Theresa Derwin, Amanda Headlee, Verity Holloway, Michael Harris, Shelley Nash, ryankj.murphy, Karmen Wells, Sky Reed, Rena Mason, Matthew Tarplee, Leonard George, Marcel Landry, Jasper Bark, Gregory Bloomfield, Ryan DeMoss, Eugene Johnson, Hailey Piper, Philip Liebel, karin.jeffery, willzo, Ron Crabtree, Alan Velazquez, Grant Longstaff, Aj, Steve Pattee, Lydia Peever, Christi Nogle, David Myers, Polly Schattel, Gina Cruz, Robert Bose, Richard Wood, David Chamberlain, Paula Limbaugh, daisydoom26, Leslie Rieth, Kfwilson, Michael Georgilis, Mackenzie Kincaid, Nancy Holzner, Andrew B Bockhorst, James Aquilone, and Tracey Thompson.

Special thank you to those who helped shape the Indiegogo campaign and the anthology with their generous support:

Sofia Ajram—Sofia Zakia Jewelry—sofiazakia.com

Kristi DeMeester—Scent From Hell candles—etsy.com/shop/ScentFromHell

Jana Heidersdorf—janaheidersdorf.com

Johnny Mains

Joe Mynhardt and the team at Crystal Lake Publishing

Readers . . .

It makes our day to know you reached the end of our book. Thank you so much. This is why we do what we do every single day.

Whether you found the book good or great, we'd love to hear what you thought. Please take a moment to leave a short review on Amazon, Goodreads, etc. No need to write an in-depth discussion. Even a single sentence will be greatly appreciated. Reviews go a long way to helping a book sell, and is great for an author's career. It'll also help us to continue publishing quality books. You can also share a photo of yourself holding this book with the hashtag #IGotMyCLPBook!

Thank you again for taking the time to journey with Crystal Lake Publishing.

Visit our Linktree page for a list of our social media platforms. https://linktr.ee/CrystalLakePublishing

Our Mission Statement:

Since its founding in August 2012, Crystal Lake Publishing has quickly become one of the world's leading publishers of Dark Fiction and Horror books in print, eBook, and audio formats.

While we strive to present only the highest quality fiction and entertainment, we also endeavour to support authors along their writing journey. We offer our time and experience in non-fiction projects, as well as author mentoring and services, at competitive prices.

With several Bram Stoker Award wins and many

other wins and nominations (including the HWA's Specialty Press Award), Crystal Lake Publishing puts integrity, honor, and respect at the forefront of our publishing operations.

We strive for each book and outreach program we spearhead to not only entertain and touch or comment on issues that affect our readers, but also to strengthen and support the Dark Fiction field and its authors.

Not only do we find and publish authors we believe are destined for greatness, but we strive to work with men and woman who endeavour to be decent human beings who care more for others than themselves, while still being hard working, driven, and passionate artists and storytellers.

Crystal Lake Publishing is and will always be a beacon of what passion and dedication, combined with overwhelming teamwork and respect, can accomplish. We endeavour to know each and every one of our readers, while building personal relationships with our authors, reviewers, bloggers, podcasters, bookstores, and libraries.

We will be as trustworthy, forthright, and transparent as any business can be, while also keeping most of the headaches away from our authors, since it's our job to solve the problems so they can stay in a creative mind. Which of course also means paying our authors.

We do not just publish books, we present to you worlds within your world, doors within your mind, from talented authors who sacrifice so much for a moment of your time.

There are some amazing small presses out there, and through collaboration and open forums we will continue to support other presses in the goal of helping authors and showing the world what quality small presses are capable of accomplishing. No one wins when a small press goes down, so we will always be there to support hardworking, legitimate presses and their authors. We don't see Crystal Lake as the best press out there, but we will always strive to be the best, strive to be the most interactive and grateful, and even blessed press around. No matter what happens over time, we will also take our mission very seriously while appreciating where we are and enjoying the journey.

What do we offer our authors that they can't do for themselves through self-publishing?

We are big supporters of self-publishing (especially hybrid publishing), if done with care, patience, and planning. However, not every author has the time or inclination to do market research, advertise, and set up book launch strategies. Although a lot of authors are successful in doing it all, strong small presses will always be there for the authors who just want to do what they do best: write.

What we offer is experience, industry knowledge, contacts and trust built up over years. And due to our strong brand and trusting fanbase, every Crystal Lake Publishing book comes with weight of respect. In time our fans begin to trust our judgment and will try a new author purely based on our support of said author.

With each launch we strive to fine-tune our approach, learn from our mistakes, and increase our reach. We continue to assure our authors that we're here for them and that we'll carry the weight of the launch and dealing with third parties while they focus on their strengths—be it writing, interviews, blogs, signings, etc.

We also offer several mentoring packages to authors that include knowledge and skills they can use in both traditional and self-publishing endeavours.

We look forward to launching many new careers. This is what we believe in. What we stand for. This will be our legacy.

**Welcome to Crystal Lake Publishing—
Tales from the Darkest Depths.**

Made in the USA
Monee, IL
04 April 2024

56368345R00177